Penduli Station

I0662872

Tyra Burton
and
Sherrie Fillion

Dunnhead Publishing

Acworth, Georgia

Tyra Burton and Sherrie Fillion/Dunnhead Publishing
PO Box 2719
Acworth, Georgia/USA 30102
www.larundalegacy.com

Publisher's Note: This is a work of fiction. Names, characters, places, and incidents are a product of the author's imagination. Locales and public names are sometimes used for atmospheric purposes. Any resemblance to actual people, living or dead, or to businesses, companies, events, institutions, or locales is completely coincidental.

Book Layout © 2017 BookDesignTemplates.com

Penduli Station - Larunda Legacy Series/ Tyra Burton and Sherrie Fillion. -- 1st ed.
ISBN 978-1-949256-04-8

To Shane who ensures the Tiki Bar
is always open.
- Tyra

To my brother Ron whose books drew me into
the world of Science Fiction & Fantasy
- Sherrie

Contents

Chapter One 7

Chapter Two...23

Chapter Three 39

Chapter Four 53

Chapter Five 75

Chapter Six 90

Chapter Seven 107

Chapter Eight..121

Chapter Nine 137

Chapter Ten...153

Chapter Eleven 173

Chapter Twelve 191

Chapter Thirteen 205

Chapter Fourteen 219

Chapter Fifteen 235

Chapter Sixteen...247

Chapter Seventeen..263

Chapter Eighteen..279

Chapter Nineteen 291

Chapter Twenty......................................307

Chapter Twenty-one 319

Chapter Twenty-two 333

Chapter Twenty-three......................................341

Chapter Twenty-four......................................355

Chapter Twenty-five......................................367

Chapter Twenty-six 381

Chapter Twenty-seven 403

Chapter Twenty-eight 413

Chapter Twenty-nine......................................425

Chapter Thirty 437

ACKNOWLEDGEMENTS 453

Special acknowledgements from Sherrie: ...455

Special acknowledgements from Tyra:........456

Chapter One

"**D**ocking at Penduli Station is commencing. Please, make sure your seat straps are locked and you're..."

Bang!

Annwyn gasped as she collided with the seat in front of her and landed hard on the floor. Burning pain radiated down her leg. Metal scraping on metal screeched around her as the lunar passenger ship dipped from side to side like a directional flag loose in space.

That doesn't sound good.

The ship lurched forward, sending unlocked tablets, baggage, and passengers into the aisles.

Annwyn leaned over a nearby seat and peered out the aft window, then winced at the awkward angle of the landing clamps.

The sound system crackled, and the audio garbled as the ship collided again with the space station.

Something is very wrong. Blades.

Screams and shouting erupted through the ship. Annwyn glanced up to see a large Scargilian male, his arms flailing, trying to maintain his balance set on a collision course for her. She scurried out of the aisle as he crashed to the floor where she was seconds before. Blood splattered and gushed from the gash along his forehead.

Annwyn closed her eyes and concentrated on her breathing. Her pulse raced and her hip screamed at the constant banging against the metal seat legs as the ship rocked. She must control her faculties, or she'd be useless. She took a deep breath.

In one, two, three, four.
Hold two, three, four, five, six, seven, eight.
Out two, three, four.

The tension in her shoulders eased, and the pain in her hip dulled to a small throb. She opened her eyes and started cataloging the cacophony of activity around her. The passengers scrambled while one voice shouted for the travelers to remain seated.

Really? Most of us are sprawled on the floor.

The ship dropped suddenly, and a loud clicking sound caused silence in the cabin.

"Docked!" someone yelled from the front of the ship.

The acrid smell of electronic components on fire wafted through the cabin, burning Annwyn's nostrils. First things first, the man's head needed tending to. She found a med kit tucked under the seats, removed the cover, turned it out on the floor and searched through the items needed. Tearing open several packages, she layered absorbing cloth, and pressed them to the man's wound. Byrne, the emissary from Aketi blinked.

"Can you hold this on your own?" She asked. After he nodded, she searched for additional injured travelers.

"I can't get the airlock open!" a Mycan female screamed as she pressed buttons and then banged her fist on the display.

Annwyn maneuvered her way over to the panel and caught the Mycan's fist before she could pound on it again. "Emissary Riaver? Let me try," she said calmly. "Why don't you see if Emissary Byrne is okay? His head is bleeding."

The woman stared for a moment, nodded, and relinquished her place in front of the door.

Annwyn removed the top panel of the display from the door and frowned at the fused wires. She pulled the hairpin from her tightly woven hair, releasing her long curls from their constraint. After creating a hook from the pin, she tugged the smoking wires from inside the console to where she could examine them. Basic wiring for a transport ship.

"Everyone should return to their seats while we determine the situation. Ma'am, take your seat. We have control of the situation," a deep male voice spoke from behind her.

"Seriously?" She turned toward the annoying voice, only to stare at the middle of a very muscular chest wrapped under a tight dark grey uniform.

"Do as you're told and let us handle the situation," he ordered.

Her gaze moved upward, taking in the vast expanse of the male in front of her until she reached pale blue eyes. She blew a lock of her rampant black hair from her face. *Great*. The Larunda Force guard joined them on the flight. Glancing down, she noted his furry grey companion stood directly behind him, as though linked by an invisible thread. He must be from the nomadic Oya's of Krizlar. She returned her gaze to the towering male and lifted her chin.

"I'm Annwyn Silk, the emissary from Haevis, and I am not a child." She pointed to two men trying to pull the airlock doors apart. "They will not be able to open them, no matter how much they pull. I need something to strip the wires, so I can get a clean…" She noticed a knife from one of the food service trays on the floor. "That will do."

Annwyn bent over, and her vision blurred when her injured hip sent a jolt of pain shooting toward her back. She sucked in a breath, and her head swam, causing her to lose balance.

The condescending guard wrapped one arm around her, gripping her waist, saving her from landing on the floor again. He picked up the knife with his other.

"My apologies, Emissary. Please, proceed. You won't mind if we keep trying to open it ourselves?"

"It won't work. It is a failsafe system." She turned her back to the man in uniform and started pulling wires, cutting, and stripping them. "They are designed so if a malfunction happens, you won't have random airlock doors opening since this model does not have a two-compartment system like the military ships do."

"Do you have any idea what the naiba you're doing?"

"We're about to find out." She touched the wires together.

The doors opened, filling the lunar ship with the sound of wailing sirens. An explosion rocked the ship. Paws landed on her chest and pushed her and the security guard to the ground.

Must keep safe.

The words reverberated in Damius's mind as a familiar canine tongue licked his face.

"Wren, I'm okay," he said as he opened his lids to see a pair of blue eyes that matched his own. "Thanks."

Wren emitted a short howl, then licked the face of the black-haired female emissary sprawled on top of him.

"What..." Emissary Annwyn Silk flailed her hands, trying to beat away the creature licking her.

Wren howled in response, then bounded off the tangled pair to sit next to his master.

The petite woman tried to stand, but fell back on top of him, knocking the air out of his lungs.

Her hand pressed into his chest and pinned him as she tried again. The ship pitched as a second explosion detonated.

"Stop," Damius demanded, grabbing her hands in his. He maneuvered her into his arms and quickly stood, cradling her. As he shifted to set her on her feet, Wren let out a piercing howl. He could feel his animal companion's panic in the pit of his stomach.

He threw Annwyn over his shoulder. "Move. Everyone off this ship now," he ordered. He nodded to the security detail, and they rushed inside to help the other passengers. "Move it. Go, go, go!"

Bolts of panic emanated from the passengers, nearly suffocating him. He tapped a quick finger on Wren, grounding himself with Wren's presence and blocking the emotions pounding at him. Wren's howl punctuated Damius's orders.

"Lt. Balder," he shouted at the last departing security detail, "make sure she gets to safety." He moved Annwyn from his shoulder to Balder's. "I'll clear the crew."

"Set me down right this instant. I can walk." Annwyn beat Balder's back with her fist.

"She's hurt. Don't listen to her. Go, and make sure the platform's cleared."

Damius looked around, confirming the main cabin was empty. Wren took off in front of him toward the cockpit.

A security crew approached the airlock and called after him, "We need to close this door."

"Let me get the pilots."

"You've got sixty ticks, then the airlock is shut. Can't risk another bomb going off."

Bomb?

Damius spun around and ran after his wolf. Tensions among The Directorate had been building, but bombs? Was this why he was assigned to bring a guard division here?

Wren was scratching at the closed cockpit door. Damius pulled at the knob, but it wouldn't open.

"I don't have time for this," Damius muttered as he pulled his blaster and shot the knob off. He opened the door to find the pilot and copilot slumped in their seats, blood splattered throughout the room. He quickly felt for a pulse on both and found none for the pilot. The copilot's pulse beat slow, but steady. Alive.

"Twenty!" the officer yelled.

Wren nuzzled the copilot.

"Out now, Wren," he yelled, slinging the copilot over his shoulder. Blood dripped down his clothes as he ran for the airlock. He and Wren dashed for the door as the officer counted down the ticks.

They jumped over the threshold as the door whooshed closed behind them. A medloc team took the copilot from his arms and started inspecting him. As they headed inside, one medical turned toward Damius and held out a recorder.

"I'm fine."

"You're bleeding," the medical argued.

"This isn't my blood."

Another loud explosion rocked the platform. This time Wren wasn't fast enough, and Damius slammed into the bulkhead of the space station central room.

"The ship broke free," one of the police crew muttered, staring out the window.

Damius stepped over and watched as the ship exploded.

ψ ψ ψ

"My scans indicate you only have bruising. I would suggest some ice therapy."

Annwyn tapped her finger against her side, trying not to be curt with the medical who read her bios. She'd confirmed the injury was only severe bruising minutes ago, but she'd waited patiently for the medical's equipment to tell her the same thing.

"Thank you. Are we done?"

"Yes." The medical closed her bag and headed out of the glass conference room enclosure.

After fleeing their ship, she and the other emissaries were hustled into the central command room for medical treatment and debriefing. Through the glass walls, she noted the video feeds monitoring various areas of the station. Several of them showed the destruction from the explosions. The replay of her lunar transport ship's demise played in a loop on one of them.

Was it cold to be thankful her belongings were shipped ahead of her, so she could move right into her quarters? Her loss was minimal, but she doubted the same was true for most of her fellow passengers. Tugging out her small tablet, she punched in the word that male had used during their escape. Naiba. She scanned the translation and sucked in a quick breath. That was one particular profanity she'd never use.

The door to the command room swung open, and a woman with several eight-pointed stars on her uniform collar walked in, followed by what Annwyn believed were lower ranking members of the command team.

"Lead Emissary Moiran," she said with a low-pitched voice. The ones who entered with her moved to stand near the portal opening.

"Admiral Carmichael." The Lead Emissary from Orias floated along the floor toward Carmichael and bowed at the waist. They made eye contact, and he nodded, yielding the floor to her.

Annwyn was still familiarizing herself with the intricacies of inter-planet communication. The Larunda Directorate had compromised on a slight bow being the universal greeting between planetary representatives. It was posturing and an unnecessary waste of time. But, if all the representatives thought it necessary, she wouldn't argue. Couldn't argue since they made all the rules for planet to planet behaviors. She studied Moiran in his long blue robes with silver weave along the hems. One day, she'd figure out how those Oriasins appeared to float when they moved.

"It saddens me to report your ship was destroyed. No lives were lost thanks to the quick action of Major Elkwood." Carmichael announced with a quick scan of the room.

"The medical said the pilot was on board when it disengaged," Emissary Leader Moiran said.

"Yes, but Major Elkwood determined she was dead before he got the copilot to safety. The copilot is still in critical condition."

"What were the explosions?" Annwyn asked, not able to contain her curiosity.

The Admiral turned toward her and bowed, remaining in the position until she returned the gesture.

Uh-oh. She recognizes me.

"You are Emissary Annwyn Silk, I believe?"

"Yes."

"Ah." The Admiral glanced back at Moiran before continuing. "We had three bombs detonate. Suspected acts of terrorism."

Dismissal at its finest, yet enough interest to cause curiosity among the others, based on the sly glances sent her way. *Blades*. Annwyn bit her lip.

The door opened again, but this time she recognized the person entering. Her pulse skipped and increased its pace. *Interesting*.

"Major Damius Elkwood reporting for duty, Admiral." He bowed in greeting, his wolf stopping beside him. "I apologize for the delay. I needed a change of uniform."

"It appears you have arrived in time, Major Elkwood. I understand you will lead the investigation of the station bombings. Do you have an alchemist in your ranks?"

"No, Admiral. I was unaware we would need one when I assembled my team."

Annwyn allowed herself to appreciate Damius this time. While she was sprawled on top of him during the confusion, she had noticed his sturdy body but didn't have time to truly catalog his assets. He towered over her by almost two feet. His short blond hair was the opposite of her long black locks. His light grey wolf loped over to her, nudging her palm until she laid it on his head.

She enjoyed feline animals when she was home, but this canine seemed special. She scratched him behind his ear, then squatted next to him so she could reach both ears at the same time. In return, he licked her again and nuzzled the side of her face. His contact calmed her racing pulse.

"Wren." Damius's admonishment to his companion brought a slight growl, then Wren nudged her hand again for more petting.

"Emissary Silk, I believe you have a background in alchemy," the Admiral said as all the attention in the room went to her and the wolf's love fest.

She stood, trying to ignore the wolf, but he licked her hand until she petted him again. The corners of her lips lifted, and she raised one brow at the Admiral. Finally, someone who recognized her abilities.

"Yes, I do. I'm quite well versed in both alchemical and chemical reactions and matter."

"Good. It looks like the wolf has settled the matter," Admiral Carmichael said.

"Excuse me, Admiral?" Damius said.

"Emissary Silk will work with you on the investigation. Unless for some reason you or she feels she should not."

Wren chose that moment to howl and sit right next to Annwyn as if to say it was a done deal.

"No, of course not," Damius said as he walked over to where she and Wren were. "I'm going to collect my team. Please, let the Admiral's aide know what you need to test the bomb deposits. We can share our findings later."

Damius took Wren by the collar to lead him out. Annwyn swore she heard him mutter to the wolf, "Traitor."

Chapter Two

"**W**e have the situation under control, but I ask that you go directly to your quarters and remain there until we sound the all clear." She paused a moment, then continued. "It is a long tone sent over the intercoms to announce it is safe to proceed with your duties. I have assigned a crew member to watch over each of you." The Admiral looked over the delegation and bowed toward Emissary Moiran.

"Let Larunda light your path," Moiran said to the Admiral.

"Yours as well." The Admiral turned and strode out of the meeting room.

Annwyn performed the required farewells as, one by one, each person left the room, except for Moiran. He floated across the floor to stand before her.

Moiran's golden eyes stared at her. "You do realize the gravity of the situation, Emissary Annwyn?"

"I do," she replied. No one wanted to jeopardize lives. If her father found out, she'd be sent back home, investigation or not. *Blades*. She bounced on her feet, then clasped her hands together. "If I may ask…" She swallowed past the lump in her throat. "Will my assisting in this investigation affect my position with the emissary team for new contact at Paramita Five?"

He stroked his long white beard with thin fingers. "If they cannot allow any ships to leave this space station, I doubt anyone will be heading to Paramita Five anytime soon. It's not as though we've made contact yet. That particular unexplored galaxy must wait."

Annwyn nodded. "I understand, sir."

"Good luck and keep me posted personally," he requested in a low voice, dropping his arm and bowing.

"Certainly, sir." She bowed.

How odd. She frowned as he departed, leaving her in the room alone. She tapped her fingertips together. Explosions, investigations, possible delay to Paramita Five, and personal reports. Very odd.

As she left the room, a crew member wearing a dark red wool uniform approached her. "Emissary Silk, I am Security Officer Cress. I will escort you to your quarters. The admiral has indicated you will need to visit our labs."

She followed behind Cress, trying to map the space station in her mind. The station felt like a maze, with each turn resembling the previous. She would need a map to orient herself. As they continued through another hallway, which looked the same as the last, she grinned as the image of the large, snuggly canine came to mind. What a sweet one. Too bad his master failed to be as sweet. Then again, that might not be a bad thing.

Damius's pale skin enhanced his blue eyes. She'd met Krizlars before, but none affected her like he did.

No time for dalliances. Another time...another place, perhaps. But not this time and not this place. Solve the attack mystery, then get back on course for new contact.

Cress stopped outside a portal, number three sixteen according to the placard beside it. "These are your quarters. Your servant and possessions were delivered earlier. I will remain here in case you need to visit the lab."

The sliding doors whooshed as she approached them, and she glanced around. Where was Gront? She opened her mouth to call her servant when he rushed out of the secondary room.

"Gront, I need my alchemy and chemistry reference tablets," she said.

"Yes, Princess."

"Don't call me that here. I am Emissary Silk. There is no need for them to know my stature on our home world. Where are my sleeping quarters?"

"To the left, Emissary. I have a room to the right."

Only two more life-seasons, then he'd be free. Would he stay if she asked? She shrugged, then entered her sleeping room. In contrast to the monotone, drab hallways, her sleeping quarters were decorated in the colors of her planet. Vibrant shades of green and turquoise eased the tightness in her shoulders. She laid her hand on the print recognizer and unlocked her clothing stow. Digging through the folding garments, she located her lab vest, slipped it on and returned to the main area.

Gront handed her the tablets she'd requested.

"I must go to the lab. Stay here. I believe the station is on lockdown. I may or may not return for dinner."

The door to her quarters swooshed closed behind her as she exited, and she turned toward Cress.

"They have a lab set up for me." Annwyn walked to stand in front of the hall dirosphere. "Can you tell me where it is?"

"Emissary, it is on level four.

Annwyn spun around and strode toward the labs.

"Emissary. That is not the most efficient route. Plus, I must accompany you since we are on lockdown."

Annwyn sighed as she turned around. *Relax. Cress isn't responsible for the situation.* She waved her hand before her.

"Lead on."

🕱 🕱 🕱

Damius strode into the control room to face his squad. They were going to complain about having a civilian working with them. Why wouldn't they? The last time they worked with a civilian, one of his men got hurt. He frowned as he headed to the front display console.

Civilians. All they did was cause trouble, and this one...this tiny little green-skinned breath stealer...this grey-eyed beauty whose curves sent every one of his senses on alert, spelled multi-atom trouble if she affected his men like she affected him. He clenched his jaw. Multi-atom trouble in spades.

Each member jumped to attention when he entered. He nodded, and they took their seats among the various portodesks and waited.

He cleared his throat and drummed his fingers against his thigh when he spoke. "Men, we're assigned to investigate the explosion. My contacts in the Aeron System informed me this is the second incident."

"Second?" one man asked.

Damius nodded. "Second." He tapped the console buttons and brought up a hologram of the ship approaching Penduli Station's landing dock prior to explosion. "This is a recap of the explosion." He tapped a second button, which showed the ship in motion with blue lines indicating its landing path. Within ticks, a loud pop echoed in the room, and the side of the ship tilted as it came within range of the landing clamps. Another pop occurred after it secured its position.

"Twenty-two on board with four crew." He glanced around at his men and waved them closer. They circled the console and scrutinized the animation of the accident. "Soul count confirmed with itinerary. All but one soul saved."

"Looks like an accident if it was an isolated incident, Major," his second-in-command, Nicheo, noted.

"Attack since it's the second," his logistics officer, Mirbeck, noted in a slow drawl." Anyone here know about the first one?"

Damius shook his head. "Only us and the Aeron System squad."

"No one has reported it to Command?" Mirbeck asked.

"No."

The men began all talking at once, and Damius raised his hand. Silence descended.

"It wasn't reported as it was a small supply ship with only two crew on board, and no one was hurt. The cargo wasn't even lost. The ship suffered minor damage." He punched three buttons simultaneously, and the current image faded and a different one replaced it.

All watched the reenactment of the first attack. The small cargo ship docked and locked on the platform. It shook twice before a black plume of smoke appeared near the back.

"Could be a practice run of some sort," Mirbeck suggested.

"So, who's behind these attacks and why?" Nicheo asked.

"No clue…yet," Damius responded. "Since the damage was so minor, no alchemist or chemist got asked to do an examination. I've called in a favor, and some of the debris evidence is being brought over on the next supply run."

"Major, I hate to point out the obvious, but we didn't get Dr. Nonyx in the squad for this run. Didn't think we'd need him," Cudala, the lone female Nushaoian on his team, said.

"I know. Admiral Carmichael recruited an alchemist for us," Damius announced.

The team groaned and mumbled various swear words.

Damius raised his hand once again. "Listen up. We needed one and we got one. Yes, I know civilians are a pain in the ass. But it is what it is. Suck it up and let's get this done." He shut down the animation and scanned his squad. "Lucky for us"—he smirked—"Emissary Silk is an alchemist and will join us later towards setting. Play nice, men."

"The Hunee?" one of his men asked.

Damius nodded, eliciting whistles from a few of his crew.

"At least this time the civie will be better to look at than old man Trudgeon."

"And softer," Sergeant Cudala cooed. Her pink luminescent skin sparkled reflecting against the bright blue of her hair.

The image of Annwyn's soft curves pressed in his arms came to mind, and Damius's stomach clenched. He pushed away the images of her before they could distract him.

"Enough. No distractions. And that includes you, Cudala." Damius shook his head, then continued.

"Nicheo, talk to Balder, get two of his men, and go scout for information. See what the word is around the station and who may or may not have had an issue with the ship's crew or passengers. Cudala, start looking at the political structure on Chalar, let's try to see who is running the show." He turned to his logistics officer Mirbeck. "I want to know who all had access to the flight plans and the ship prior to departure. We need to know where they were and their next stops."

Mirbeck shifted in his seat and avoided eye contact. "Um, I already did some digging, and there's something you should know." He tugged on his collar, staring at the table.

Damius stilled when the man's anxiety blasted his face. Wren growled, jumped up from his position near the console, and leaned against Damius's legs. Damius blinked, rubbed Wren's head, and waited.

"Of all the passengers, only one had no baggage with them," Mirbeck said.

Damius felt his heart pound against his ribs. No. "Who?"

Mirbeck flicked a glance up then down again. "Annwyn Silk, our new 'team member' with an alchemy and chemistry background. She rode without a single item." His brows rose. "Made me wonder why."

Everyone turned and stared.

Damius's stomach burned while his neck stiffened. "*Naiba*. Then she goes on the list to investigate." He glanced around at his team. "I'll take care of that one."

Snickers followed his announcement.

"She's a pretty little thing, if you go for green-tinged skin. But I hear those Hunee's know how to—"

"Stop," Damius ordered. "It's not that. She's on the team, like it or not, so this portion of the investigation is going to remain between us only. No one say anything about it. Understood?"

"Understood," they all said in unison.

"Then let's get to work," Damius said and stomped out of the room.

Dear Larunda. That's all he needed. Why didn't she have bags, carriers, anything? Why hadn't he noticed it before? All the passengers, except her, ran out with something in their hands. She didn't. Too many whys. . .

ψ ψ ψ

Annwyn slipped the small piece of metal debris into the extrapolator, set the timer, and stood back. She glanced at her tablet and reviewed her notes. Mercury fulminate had been outlawed on several planets a long time ago. Where had it come from?

The door swooshed open, and Damius and Wren stood there staring at her. She raised one eyebrow and said nothing. His move.

He strode in and glanced at the extrapolator before standing near her. *Why did he need to be so close?* Warmth radiated from his body. Her eyelids drifted closed as she inhaled his scent.

"What?" she asked.

"What do you have so far?"

"I thought we'd each be doing our own investigations and then collaborate." She grinned. "Giving in already?"

"Giving in?" Damius frowned. "I'm not giving in. This isn't a game. One soul has been lost, and more could have been."

Annwyn frowned and stepped back a bit. Wren followed her. "I'm aware a soul was lost."

"We work together whether we want to or not. The admiral ordered it." He shifted and walked away to stare out the port window. "This is the second such incident. The first event took place shortly after departure from Aeron Station."

She gasped.

"Portions of that ship's hull are being brought to us for examination. We'll need to see if the explosions are linked."

Annwyn stepped forward automatically, then checked herself and stopped. "A second attack. How bad was the first?"

"Where were you before you arrived here?"

"What?" Her pulse picked up its pace.

"Where were you before coming here? I assume Larunda Directorate's lead emissary chose you for the new contact assignment at Paramita Five?"

"How… Never mind." She waved her hand. "Yes. However, that assignment has been delayed by this investigation." She sighed. "Everything has been delayed by this investigation."

Why such personal questions? She studied his body. Wide, muscled back tapering to a slim waist with thick legs. A thousand catlums danced in her belly.

He turned and faced her. "Where were you assigned prior to coming here?"

"Why do you want to know?" His frown caused her pulse to pick up its pace. What was going on here? "What does this have to do with the attack? It is an attack of some sort, correct?"

"Yes, but that doesn't answer the question. The reason behind my questions are for the investigation and must be answered and stated in the reports. Nothing left to doubt."

"Doubt? You're thinking I had something to do with this attack?" How dare he assume she'd have anything to do with the loss of a soul. She planted her hands on her hips and stepped up to touch his toes with hers. Her lips tightened as she glared at him. "I was training on Aketa in the Isha System for the last solar phase." She bounced on her toes and poked a finger in his chest. "I have not had contact with anyone but Emissary Moiran since the moment before I boarded for the trip here. How dare you."

"And why were you without any baggage?"

Annwyn blew out a breath and spun away from Damius. The sudden movement loosened her hair knot, and tendrils of her long hair whipped about her shoulders as she stomped away from him. After pausing a moment, she whipped around and returned to face him, crossing her arms. "I had all my belongings sent ahead with my...with Gront." She glared at him. "He arrived three transports before mine."

"Who—*Where* is he?"

"He's in my quarters, and you can question him tomorrow. He's been ill and has needed to rest."

He strode to stand within a foot of her and dipped his head lower. She could feel his breath hot on her face as his scent wafted around her. Her heart beat against her chest when she met his dark gaze.

"Who is he?" Damius demanded.

Chapter Three

Damius's stomach hardened as his muscles bunched and stiffened. He sucked in a deep breath to ease the tightness in his chest. It didn't calm his racing pulse. A scent of lavender and musk wrapped around him. It was her. His eyes drifted out of focus as her energy glowed around her. Its green tinged gold coloring danced liked the frenetic energy he'd received from her in the conference room earlier.

He balled his hands into fists, battling against touching her. "Who is he?" he growled as he inhaled her scent more.

"Gront is a lawbreaker."

"Excuse me?" Damius stepped back.

"He is serving out his sentence for his crime by being my servant."

"His sentence? What crime did he commit?"

"He stole some papers from my lab," Annwyn responded avoiding his gaze.

"And now he is your servant?"

"Yes. On Haevis, the sentence for your crimes is paid via indentured servitude to the people offended. He broke into my lab, and now he serves me."

"For how long? Did he have a record before this? I will need his full name and file number. We'll need to run a background check on him."

Annwyn bounced on her tiptoes.

She's uncomfortable. Good.

"He is my servant for three life-seasons." She explained.

One life-season equaled three solar phases. "Do you pay him while he is serving out his sentence with you?"

"No, of course not. I provide him with food and a reasonable place to sleep."

"And he must do what you command," he snapped.

"Yes." Annwyn broke eye contact with him.

Damius took another step back. He'd known of her culture's laws, but had never met anyone with it enforced, until now, a criminal serving their sentence. His stomach churned as Annwyn's once enticing glow dimmed.

"Where I come from, the punishment fits the crime. A person may even be cast out of their tribe, but no one is ever made another's slave." Damius pinched the bridge of his nose.

"I see. Well," she continued, "as a member of the Larunda's interplanetary security, you are aware of various laws held by each planet."

"I am. Though, I'm not expected to memorize every nuance for all seven planets. Was this his first offense?"

"Yes, but it doesn't matter, and you know as much. Why are you pressing this?"

Damius stared at Annwyn until she returned his gaze and stopped bouncing. "I am sometimes amazed the treaties between our worlds hold with such differences between us." He turned and walked toward the lab door. *What did Gront try to steal from the Emissary?* He stopped, pausing before turning back to face Annwyn. "I will need to speak to your slave alone tomorrow...at star rise."

"His name is Gront. Star rise is too early. You may question him after our rising meal."

Damius laughed and stalked back to stand in front of Annwyn, making her back up to the wall behind her. "I am in charge of this investigation. I will interview him, or anyone I deem necessary, when I deem it time, for I am no one's slave. It would be best you remembered as much, Emissary."

Her eyes widened at first, then she scowled at him. He'd scared her, which made her angry, a dangerous combination. Good. Turnabouts were fair play.

"The first bomb fragments from the other explosion will arrive at star rise. I would suggest you get some sleep, but of course, you are free to do as you will." He smiled menacingly at her and turned back to walk toward the lab door again, this time exiting without stopping.

What an infuriating woman.

It was a good thing he left Wren in their quarters to rest. His companion had an unnatural attraction for the Emissary. Usually, Wren was a better judge of character.

Damius snorted.

"Major." Nicheo ran toward him.

"What is it?" Maybe focusing on the problem at hand would help him put the Emissary out of his mind. She was hiding something. She riled him, but she wasn't evil. He didn't have to like the way her people lived to work with her.

"Word in the station is there has been some unrest since it was selected as the jump point for new contact. There's been a few protests both here and on Chalar. Some of their religious leaders believe it is not in our best interest to make new contact this soon after discovery of its existence."

"The Directorate rarely takes such things into consideration."

"Major, they are concerned with profit. Bottom line is always what drives The Directorate. We all know that."

"Be careful what you say, Nicheo. We serve at The Directorate's whim."

"Yes, sir."

"Do you think we need to send a team to the surface?"

"I'm not sure it's warranted yet. The primary religious group, Silvergrass Circle, appears to be the only one with extensive political influence. Cudala is taking a shuttle to meet with Raine, the Circle's leader. Cudala has a way of getting people to talk."

"Thankfully, the leader doesn't know her real leanings."

"Oh, I'm sure *Madame* Raine will be pleasantly surprised. It is an all-female membership. I was deemed unclean when I asked to speak to them."

"Well, they didn't get that wrong, did they? We'll reconvene in the command center at star set." Damius dropped his protective wall momentarily, allowing Nicheo's emotions to wash over him.

Nicheo reminded him of when he was a child and his father would sneak him candy behind his mother's back. Nicheo was sneaky, but his heart was good and his loyalty unquestionable. So why had he checked?

Damius grimaced. He shouldn't have doubted Nicheo's ability or loyalty. Why did he fall back on using his forsaken talent? He was a hunter. And he needed to hunt. The bomber would be his quarry, but soon he would have to visit his tribe. He'd avoided it for too long.

ꙮ ꙮ ꙮ

The door swooshed closed, and Annwyn rested her head against the bulkhead wall, taking long breaths. She clenched her hands. How dare he attempt to provoke her? Who on Haevis did he think he was? Her father had warned her others didn't agree with their planet's system of punishment. He'd encouraged her to leave Gront under his care too. But he wouldn't have treated Gront fairly. Servants, slaves—they were all the same to him. Besides, Gront's alchemical knowledge rivaled everyone she knew but her own most times.

She straightened her clothes and tucked an errant strand of hair behind her ear. Damius's tall mass of muscles tempted her fantasies, until he opened his mouth. His ignorance at how her civilized society worked would be laughable, if he wasn't so imposing.

Her stomach rumbled. She'd been so focused on her work earlier, she forgot to eat. Usually, Gront would remind her or bring her food, but she hadn't brought him with her, wanting the lab to herself.

She punched up a floor plan of the space station on her terminal and located the dining facilities tracing her finger from the lab to its location. "Two turns left, one right, and down a floor."

She grabbed her tablet and uploaded her findings to take with her along with plans of the ship. Maybe a meal would help her understand the bombing puzzle more.

Annwyn expected the Cress to be waiting for her outside the lab, but the security officer wasn't there. She paused, scanning down one hall, then the other. Where did she go?

Does anyone do their job around here?

She sighed. She had told Cress she would be several hours. Apparently, the officer had chosen to take off. No matter, she could find her own way.

Annwyn's stomach rumbled again, this time loud enough to echo in the hall. Thankfully, she seemed to be the only one roaming the station at this hour. Some stations were twenty-four-hour hubs, but Penduli Station chose to follow the time-cycle of the planet it hovered over. Since Chalar believed in shutting down commerce at star setting, she had a short time to locate sustenance.

She turned the corner again and paused. Blades, where was she? *One should always know where they are going,* her father had drilled into her. Then she saw it—a virosphere with a blinking light which seemed like a beacon to her.

You are here the red dot on the virosphere indicated.

How did she end up near the cargo hold instead of the dining hall?

She could find her way around any lab easily, but otherwise she needed help, it appeared, especially on space stations with long halls. She took a snapshot with her tablet of the virosphere. Maybe now she could find her way to some food, or her quarters.

She kept her gaze down at her tablet and walked toward her destination. *It should be just around this bend.* Hushed voices reached her from the next corner. She hurried toward them. *Finally, someone to help her.* She opened her mouth to call out as she neared the turn, only to freeze when she recognized the speakers. She scooted to the edge of the wall and pressed flat, straining to hear them.

"Were you followed?" Moiran asked.

"No, I'm sure she is still in her lab. She said it would be several hours," Cress responded.

Why is my security escort talking to Moiran?

"Good. Were you able to install the listening devices in the lab?"

"Yes, she is still analyzing the bomb residue. But Major Elkwood did drop by to talk to her. It appears she was on the 'to be questioned' list for her belongings not being on the ship," Cress reported.

"I'm sure she enjoyed that. Anything else?" Moiran pressed.

"Yes, it appears they know about the other outpost. A bomb fragment is arriving tomorrow for her to analyze."

"I see. Seems I underestimated the Major's intelligence."

Annwyn peeked around in time to watch the Emissary leader reach into his pocket, pull out a few slips of the standard currency, and hand it to the officer.

"Officer Cress, you will keep me informed?"

"Of course. I can give you the receiving code, if you'd like, sir."

"No. I don't have time to watch her like you do. Keep doing as I ask, and I'll be sure you're compensated well."

Cress nodded and turned to leave. Annwyn scanned the wall and found a door. Quickly pulling the handle, she discovered a small closet. She crawled inside, shut the door, and peered through the vent in time to see Cress passing.

Her heart beat against her ribs. *Why is Moiran spying on me?*

There was no way she could return to the lab before Cress got there. She checked the photo of the virosphere, and realized she was directly below the dining facilities. Now, if she could find a port. She waited until she heard Moiran pass by, then silently crawled out of her hiding spot.

She retraced her steps to the virosphere. The port doors stood right beside it. Some smart Hunee she was, missing the port like that.

A bit later, Annwyn chewed on her first bite of the sandwich the chef had insisted on making her when Cress came running into the dining hall.

"Emissary, you are not to walk around the station without me," she chastised.

Annwyn deliberately set the sandwich down on her plate. If there was one thing her time as royalty taught her, it was the precise way to put someone beneath her in their place. She'd learned that at the hand of her father, who considered it a game to see who he could bend to his will. Obviously, Cress needed instruction. *This will be as easy as bending wood.*

She continued to move deliberately, wiping her mouth with her napkin, setting it beside her plate, before placing both her hands on the table and slowly rising from her seat. Her gaze moved from Cress's black shoes up to her face and directly into her eyes.

"Cress, you will refrain from telling me what to do. That is not a request."

"You are—"

"Stop. As I have already said, you are not to tell me what I can and cannot do. You were provided for my security, yet you were not at your post when I became hungry and had to seek food on my own." Annwyn paused, willing herself to remain perfectly still. "Where were you? I fear I will have to report you to your superiors for not performing your job. You did leave me unattended after all, and I had to find my way here alone...in unsecured halls...able to be accosted by anyone walking around."

"I had to..."

Annwyn studied Cress's facial expressions as they changed slightly. Cress was trying to think of the lie she would tell. *I wonder if she will blame it on biology.*

"I had to visit the bio chamber," Cress blurted.

Annwyn inwardly smiled. Too easy. Maybe there were some relevant things her father had taught her after all.

"Next time, tell me." Annwyn sat back down again, her knees wobbling like rubber. Thank Larunda Cress couldn't see them under her robes. "I wish to finish my meal the chef graciously provided, then return to my chambers. You may wait over there"—Annwyn pointed across the room to a chair by the entrance—"for me."

"Yes, Emissary."

Annwyn knew her father would be proud of her now if he were there. She frowned and struggled to swallow her second bite of food, which now seemed like brittle grass. She didn't want to be like him.

Chapter Four

Damius returned to his quarters where Wren greeted him. The wolf weaved his large, furry body around Damius's legs, like he had to check behind him.

"Who are you looking for?" Damius asked.

A quick flash of a green-skinned beauty appeared in his mind. *Annwyn.* His skin flushed and he locked his legs and jaw, battling the burgeoning desire begging for release. *Not now.* He forced his legs to move and collapsed at his desk. He pressed trembling fingertips to his forehead and drummed them against his heated skin in a long-practiced tempo.

"Stop. She's not here," he whispered.

How could Wren do that? Wren was a blocker, not a bringer. Had she affected his ability? Was it Wren or himself? He completed two sets of deep breathing exercises. *Inhale...exhale. Repeat.* His body hardened while images danced in his mind of touching her...tasting her. Would she taste as fresh as the spring waters of Haevis?

A quick set of pings at his door jerked him from his questions. He shifted to arrange the lower half of his body under the desk. *Naiba.*

"Enter," he called out.

"Major." Lt. Mirbeck gave a quick nod as he entered the chamber. "I received the report from the first accident and evaluated the information." He waved at the chair opposite Damius. "May I join you?"

"Certainly." Damius leaned forward, resting his elbows on the cold metal surface of the large portodesk. Anything to distract him.

"According to the reports and my research, the ship involved in the first explosion served as a supply shuttle. Only the pilots were onboard and no passengers. This struck me as odd. There are always wait list travelers at every station looking for a quick hop from one place to another. Even undocumented ones. In this case, no other souls were on the shuttle." Mirbeck handed over a dime bar.

"Why?" Damius slipped the finger sized alloy memory unit—dime bar into the viewer slot and pulled up the report.

"The shuttle carried cargo disguised as waste management and consigned to a high priority rendezvous." He smirked. "Smart move as no one wants to sit next to those crates."

"Some still do, if they're desperate," Damius responded, scanning the information in front of him.

"True." Mirbeck scowled. "In this case, no one did." He leaned back and crossed his arms. "This tells me they set up a quarantine to avoid having anyone inquire about the contents or sneak on board."

Damius tapped his fingers on the desktop, matching the same rhythm as before. Wren curled on the floor nearby and snored in small bursts. Damius shot a glance at the wolf before returning his gaze to his logistics officer.

He waved his hand. "What else? I can see from your grinning face you've got more to tell me."

Mirbeck leaned forward with his palms flat on his thighs. "The cargo was to be combined with the supplies for Paramita 5 and the new contact emissary envoy."

Damius stiffened. His gut clenched. "Say that again?"

"You heard it right the first time, Major." He crossed his arms. "Whoever procured those supplies wanted them specifically for the new contact. Which means—"

"Which means," Damius said, "whoever set the bomb wasn't doing a test run. They're out to jeopardize new contact." And the emissary team. Annwyn could be in danger.

"Or one of the emissaries assigned to it."

"Do we know who contracted the delivery?" Damius fisted his hands.

"No." Mirbeck pinched his nose. "I tried all my contacts, and no luck finding any information." He rose, stepped toward the exit, then paused.

"What is it?" Damius asked. Mirbeck's hesitation tapped against his energy.

"Major, we must consider one of the emissaries being involved. A supply order like the one on the shuttle required authorization by an emissary team member…or its leader." He sighed. "Or someone posing as one. I'll keep looking."

"Do that." Damius rose once his crew member left and paced his cabin. Tapping his fingertips on his thighs, he did a quick mental run-through of the information he'd received. Images of Annwyn lurked in the background of his mind. After unhooking his jacket, he tore it off and flung it over his chair, then growled and continued pacing. *She will not be a distraction.*

༄ ༄ ༄

Annwyn stormed into her quarters, completely dismissing her guard, and froze. Gront had redecorated the main room in her absence. He'd altered the color of the long workstation sitting under the window openings in a turquoise and white-water print. Its appearance and movement made it seem like a still pond. Moss padding covered the seats, and various species of holoplants sat on the edges, hung from the ceiling, and covered one entire shelf. The aromatic dispenser floated scents of her home strong enough to surround her like warm-seasoned leaves.

She inhaled deeply, and her body immediately relaxed. A slow smile spread across her face.

"You've eaten," Gront stated, joining her from his private quarters within a few ticks.

"I have." She frowned. "Unfortunately, my meal was unsatisfying."

"Would you like me to prepare something?"

"No. I am no longer hungry," she said and walked toward the workspace. She waved her arm to indicate the room. "Thank you for this. I needed it this setting."

"Of course."

She sat and slipped her private dime bar into the viewer. She lifted her hand and pointed to the information on the screen. "Come take a look at this, Gront." She waited until he joined her at the desk. "I've completed all the tests on the explosive materials and…I must admit, it is a puzzle I haven't figured out yet."

Gront shifted closer to the viewer to read the itemized component listing along with the particle test results.

"It is poking at the back of my memory. See here." She pointed to one compound configuration. "I have seen this combination before."

Gront nodded. "It appears to be an older material." He stiffened and rose. "I believe I recently came across this in my interplanetary historical science records."

Annwyn glanced at him, then shifted her gaze back to the screen. "You're right. I remember this from my studies." She flashed him a grin. "You wouldn't't happen to have the record with you now, would you?"

He smiled. "Indeed I do. I brought all my records with me to study." He headed into his personal quarters. "I'll grab it and return."

"Perfect," she said and waited. Thank the trees, he loved to study.

Gront returned with two records. He handed one to her, and they perused the information.

"Here it is," Gront said. "You're right." He held out his record and pointed at one spot.

She leaned over, took it in her own hands, and scanned the information. "Mercury fulminate. How odd someone would choose something this unstable when there are more easily available substances to create an explosion."

"And not a common substance in this galaxy. Whoever created this bomb had to have known...or studied the scientific history of chemicals."

Annwyn stared at Gront. Exactly. With this specific component, they might as well have tagged their name on the blasted thing."

Gront cleared his throat.

"What is it?" Annwyn asked.

"The compound in your notes state SCN, not CNO. That means it wasn't mercury fulminate, but mercury thiocynate."

Annwyn checked and he was right. "Either one can be used in explosive devices."

"True, but fulminate is more shock-sensitive."

"Which would be less controlled than the thiocynate. Yes." She closed the record and handed it back to Gront. "Major Damius will want this report first thing after star rise when the squad meets."

Gront nodded. "I'll return to my quarters now."

Annwyn dipped her chin and returned to the viewer. She studied the explosion reports again and reviewed the re-creation display. *So, that is how it happened.* Tricky, but still a risky move using something so easily traceable.

She rose, punched in a request in the drink replicator, and returned to her desk while sipping on cool aloe water. Images of Damius flickered in her mind. Such a tall male...and bulky. He would not be able to hide among the men of her planet. She pictured her last court drawing. Short, muscular, but slim males all vying for the position of her life partner. She shuddered.

She sucked in a quick breath when an image of Damius's tall body wrapped around hers popped in her head. Heat pouring from him with strong surges of energy called to her. His eyes. Those eyes, she imagined, filled with desire could distract her into making a big mistake.

Unless she kept it simple. Would she be able to have a play with him without him wanting to win the game? Should she even consider it? No. She pursed her lips. No. She'd committed to working on the new contact, and that was where her future resided. Not playing with some Oya who had the ability to stir her senses.

Stir. She scoffed. He did more than stir. He whipped her senses and tossed them about like fronds during a storm. She shook her head. No. Not this one.

He will not be a distraction.

❦ ❦ ❦

Annwyn woke at the star rising and prepared for the meeting. She'd worked late preparing her report for the investigation. She washed her face with cooling cubes to wake up faster.

Why had Major Damius asked her to report to his personal quarters before the squad meeting? Her body shivered at the idea of being alone with him in a small chamber. She shook her head. No. She'd made her decision during star setting. *Purely professional. That's it.*

Within ticks, she'd arrived at Damius's quarters. She rose to the tips of her feet and dropped quickly. She bounced a few more times before clearing her throat and tapping the portal panel.

"Enter." Damius's loud booming voice carried through the bulkhead.

She stepped forward and the doorway swooshed open, allowing her entrance. Four steps in, she froze. Damius stood in the center of the main room facing the window. His stature was so large and muscular, it made this area seem like a closet. His quarters were half the size of her own, and his scent seemed to envelop her. She attempted to breathe through her mouth. It didn't work, and his presence dominated the area. He spun around staring at her, his gaze like spikes, piercing her in place.

She inhaled through her lips. "I am here. Will you explain why we need to meet alone before the meeting?"

Damius moved toward her as though he stalked a prey. Her heart hammered while her pulse pounded in her body. Heat spread from her feet up her legs and pooled at her lower belly. Run or remain? She remained, watching him come closer. Her skin tingled as she labored for breath. Any tick now, she'd begin to pant. What was he doing to her?

"Thank you for coming here before the squad meeting."

The tension between them was palpable. His pupils widened while his nostrils flared. Her body hummed with desire. Her fingers itched to touch him. *Stay focused*. She took a step toward Damius, closing the small space between them, when Wren came bounding into the room. She gasped for air as the wolf pounced, placing his paws on her shoulders to lick her face and knocking her over.

Damius jumped forward, his arms coming around her body, catching her. Wren licked his face then sat on the floor, looking at them both.

Her heart quickened as Damius growled. Wren growled back then turned to return from where he came. She leaned her head against Damius's chest.

"I am sorry. He has never acted like this before meeting you."

Me neither. She turned in his arms and looked up into his eyes. "I guess he likes me," she whispered. Blades, her body yearned for him.

"It's unprofessional," he said, his arms dropping from around her.

Her body shivered at the loss of his touch. "Everyone needs to relax from time to time." Perhaps if she did something to alleviate this burning within her, she could concentrate. Did she dare?

"Not while there is..."

She stepped closer to him. "Even during difficult times, a moment is sometimes needed to pause and rejuvenate. Don't you agree? As a team leader, you must know this."

She bounced up on her toes, her hand caressing his cheek before she moved it behind his neck, bringing his face closer to hers. "A short moment in time, perhaps?" Before he could respond, she kissed him.

※ ※ ※

Her tongue swiped across his lip, and the hunter in him took over. He wrapped his arms around her and lifted her off the ground. Her legs wrapped around his waist as his tongue claimed her mouth. Her heart beat as the drums of his tribe did during their celebrations and his responded. Together, the sound and cadence called to the deepest parts of his soul. As he pulled away from the kiss, their breathing was in sync as well.

"Is this why you wanted me to come to your private quarters?" Annwyn asked.

"You kissed me first."

"You wanted me to and were taking too long."

"Impatient," he muttered as he shifted her weight to support her with one arm. His other hand traveled up her body. Her breast molded to his hand as he kissed her again.

What was he doing? It wasn't like him to lose control. *This woman.* She made him want to go on the hunt with her as his prey. Why now? What had she done to him? Her body was soft and inviting. How long had it been since he felt a woman in his arms? How long since he desired to lose himself in another's heartbeat?

He felt the tug on his pant leg but ignored it, deepening the kiss with Annwyn instead. Wren howled, then tugged harder. The wolf rose up on his hind legs, nuzzling his way in between Damius and Annwyn. Wren head-butted him then backed down, sat in front of the door, and growled.

Thank you, Wren.

"I'm sorry." He lowered Annwyn back to the ground. "I don't…"

"And here I thought you were wanting to confront the issue head-on." Her eyes sparkled as her hand traveled up his chest.

"I do." Damius backed away from her toward his desk. What the naiba was with him? "We need to profile the other new contact emissaries, and I figured you would be the perfect person to help us eliminate potential suspects."

"Potential suspects?" Her playfulness disappeared instantly. "There is a connection between the envoy and the first bomb. Someone trying to delay or stop new contact. And you don't suspect me this time?" She cocked her head toward him.

Damius focused his energy on her. Wren moved silently beside him, and Damius rested his hand on his head. He stared at her, willing his outward appearance to remain the perfect example of a military admiral. His energy wrapped around her, and with Wren's grounding support, he inhaled and allowed her heartbeat to surround him as her essence filled his mind. A smile creeped onto his face. What he couldn't prove with physical evidence he knew now in his soul. She wasn't a part of the bombings. She was cunning and hiding something, but her soul's song told him she was innocent.

"You are not part of the bombing."

"No, I'm not. What changed your mind?"

Wren growled and went to the door again.

"For another time. Are you willing to create the profiles or not?"

"I am."

"Good. If you don't mind, walk with me to the meeting. I need to let Wren visit the solarico area."

"Woof!" Wren agreed.

Together, they strode toward the turbolift, entered, and waited in silence until they arrived at level four.

🐾 🐾 🐾

As soon as the portal swooshed open, Damius stepped out and she joined him. She shot a quick glance into the bay window of her alchemy lab as they passed it. Farther down the hallway sat the security rooms.

Right before entering, Damius's fingertips touched her arm.

"Remember, review your report as it's written. Add no commentary until everyone has relayed the findings of their own assignments."

That was it? He had nothing else to say to her after what happened in his quarters? She slid a quick glance at his face. No emotion. Nothing to indicate he'd touched her...or been touched by her. That was fine by her as she hadn't expected to get seriously involved during her term as emissary, anyway. *Liar*.

"I know what to do, Major," she snipped and jerked her arm away from his touch. Blades, the man tripped her up too easily.

With a soft swoosh, the doors opened to reveal Damius's entire squad seated around a large round surface. In the center, a beam of blue light shot upward toward the ceiling.

Everyone rose when they entered, and Damius waved them down.

"Before we begin," he said, "I want to formally introduce Emissary Annwyn Silk."

Annwyn moved toward an empty seat and sat. *He wants to act like nothing happen. Well, two can play this game.* She'd prove it too.

"Emissary, this is Lt. Nicheo, my second-in-command."

Annwyn tipped her head at the dark skinned, muscular male bearing the skin staining of the married males of Nama.

"That pink glittering female is Sergeant Cudala. She's our diplomat and has a way with words."

Cudala winked at her.

"That one over there scowling—Lt. Mirbeck— is our logistics man. As I explained, Annwyn will be our science liaison for this investigation."

Mumbled greetings were directed at her. She nodded to each but remained silent. She lifted her gaze and focused on Damius.

"Has the room been cleared?" Damius looked at Mirbeck.

"Affirmative. We are cleared."

"Let's get this going. Reports."

Annwyn sat silently as each member relayed the findings of their investigation. When it appeared to be her turn, she stood as the others did and reviewed her report. She chose her words carefully to help those unfamiliar with scientific jargon to understand most of the results of her part of the investigation.

"Excuse me," Lt. Nicheo said when she'd finished. "I'm sure you did your best writing this so we non-scientists could understand. But, I'm more of a visual guy. Can you explain this to me using the hologram?"

A rumble of laughter followed his question, and Annwyn grinned. Poor guy.

"Certainly." She tapped a few lit buttons, and a hologram of the shuttle appeared in the center of the table. "When mercury thiocyanate burns, it expands into a mass of ash tentacles. See here." She pointed to the underside of the shuttle where its black legs were spread. "The compound was hidden in a soylent shock buffer, which made it safe until the shuttle attempted to dock. When the clamps extended, the nanosphere reflector crystal shifted and allowed the components to rise farther, making contact and exploding."

"I've never heard of mercury thiocyanate before," Mirbeck announced.

Annwyn turned toward him. "It is old and unstable and not easily obtainable in this galaxy."

"Which both helps and hurts us. It is rare enough that once we locate it, it will be easy enough to prove a connection with the attacks." She flicked the hologram off." But so rare, it'll be tricky to locate. It won't be like locating a dime bar. We're going to have to do some digging on this."

The squad nodded in unison.

"I've sent a summary Annwyn wrote describing how to determine what mercury looks like and possible containers. It's not something one can carry in their pocket."

Annwyn sat and listened as each squad member discussed and argued how to continue the investigation. She studied Damius. He also sat and let his team make the plans for moving forward. So, he worked well in a team and they appeared to respect him, although maybe not always agreeing with him. He didn't appear insulted as her family would have reacted to such behavior. She inwardly smiled, then bit her lip.

Although everyone seemed willing to reveal their ideas and suspicions, it was something she had not yet become accustomed to. Her thoughts returned to Moiran. Why was he so interested in her? Did it have something to do with this investigation? She'd need to find out and if it did, let the team know.

Chapter Five

A chime rang before the door swooshed open, and Admiral Carmichael entered followed by her aide.

Damius and his men stood and bowed in greeting. *Politicians needed to learn not to interrupt.* Emotional waves from his team's frustration tapped at him.

"Admiral Carmichael," Damius said as he offered her his seat.

"Not necessary, Major. I shall not be staying. I wanted to let you know the new contact envoy has been delayed indefinitely. It appears not only are we dealing with a bombing, but with theft as well. My aide has sent the information to your devices. I believe the incidents are related. However, I trust you and your team to confirm this."

"Yes, Admiral."

"Good rising, Major." Carmichael turned toward Annwyn, who remained seated and bowed. "Emissary."

Before Annwyn could return the greeting, Carmichael turned and left the conference room.

A quick surge of anger from Annwyn hit Damius squarely in the gut. Wren stood and rubbed against his leg. Damius took a deep breath and focused his attention on the job at hand.

"I hate higher-ups," Cudala muttered, flopping back into her chair.

"At least she didn't stick around expecting a thank you for something we already knew," Mirbeck groused.

"Enough chatter," Damius said as he sat down, grabbing his tablet. "Nicheo, double-check the information the admiral sent us against what we already discovered. Send a communication to the outpost to see if the pilot is able to be interviewed."

"On it, sir."

"Cudala, speak with Madame Raine. I want to know everything about their protest by the end of the moon cycle. If we need to go to the surface, we might have an issue, as I've received reports of a corona cloud destabilizing. It may shift too much after star rise for us to get a landing for several moon cycles."

"She asked me to join the circle yestermoon." Cudala winked at Damius.

"Yeah, well, don't forget we have better benefits."

"I doubt that." Cudala rose and laughed as she headed out of the room.

"Mirbeck, get down to receiving. As soon as the package from Aeron arrives, get it to the Emissary's lab, and while you're there…"

"See what else I can find out. On it."

As his men filed out, he turned toward Annwyn.

"Do you have marching orders for me?" She raised a brow and smirked.

Did she think this was a game? He'd warned her before.

"Work on the profiles." Damius slid a dime bar toward her. "I've included some basic information for you. While you do that, I need to speak to Gront."

"I thought you decided I was innocent."

"You are, but as you pointed out, Gront has a history of theft."

The light left her eyes when she frowned.

His gut burned. *This is my job—investigate everyone. If she doesn't like it, that's her problem.*

"One time." Annwyn slammed her hand on the table, then stood, moving away from Damius.

"Regardless, I am on my way to speak to him now." *Oh yes, she is not happy.*

"I'll go with you." Annwyn moved back toward Damius.

"No, you won't. I want to interview him alone. Work on the profiles and have your lab ready for the fragments when they arrive."

Annwyn shifted between him and the portal entrance, rose on her toes, and poked his chest in cadence to her every word. "You are not going to interview him without me."

Did she really think she could stop him?

"You are not in charge here, Emissary. I am." Damius picked her up, moved her from his path, and stormed out.

Annwyn's swearing silenced when the door closed.

Damius strolled toward the turbolift with a grin plastered across his face. Her voice, especially angry, ignited a small fire inside him. Maybe avoiding that fire was the smart thing to do. His body disagreed. He shook his head and punched the button that led to Annwyn's suite.

Once there, he blanked his mind and tapped Wren's ear. "Let's see what we get here," he whispered.

A quick double-tap caused the muffled ring inside the suite to echo. Damius blinked and focused on any emotions nearby. Oops. He cleared his mind immediately when he received a couple's lovemaking in the suite across from Annwyn's. Odd he'd get it from that direction when he focused forward. He rolled his shoulders and waited. *Hmm*.

Politeness gone, he placed his palm against the door sensor. Did she think having Gront refuse to answer the door would keep him from entering? She obviously did not know the extent of his security clearance.

The door opened immediately, and Damius stepped into Annwyn's quarters.

What on Oya? Holoplants seemed to fill every space. He rubbed the back of his neck. The place reminded him of a holo-replicator trip experiment. He loved it. His muscles eased their tightness, and he turned toward the Hunee presently watching him.

"I make her comfortable in her surroundings which helps her work better." A male of a slightly larger build than Annwyn but with the same green-tinged skin and grey eyes stood near the drink dispenser.

"It is calming."

"As is its purpose." The male nodded.

"I assume you are Gront."

"Yes. I'm sorry for not answering the door. I told her it would do no good."

"She mistakenly believes she can tell me what I am and am not allowed to do."

Gront laughed. "She is unaccustomed to people telling her no."

Privileged. The word flashed in Damius's mind. It fit what he'd seen of Annwyn. Soon Nicheo's contact on Haevis would send more information on Annwyn's background.

"I understand you are enslaved to the Emissary for three of your life-seasons."

"Yes."

"Tell me, what have you been doing since you arrived on Penduli?" Damius waved his arm to encompass the suite. "Other than decorating?"

ꜟꜟ ꜟꜟ ꜟꜟ

"Blades," Annwyn grumbled when she read the message from Gront. She'd underestimated the authority of that frustrating...and attractive major. She replied, letting Gront know she understood his inability to avoid Damius. No sense blaming him. Still, she sighed. Gront needn't be dragged into this...whatever was happening. She'd need to minimize, or at the very least, keep his involvement unknown for his own protection. If word got back home... No, she refused to dwell on it.

Damius could have his way, this time. Although, she hated losing to him. Next time, it'd be her win. She grinned, then frowned down at the paperwork in front of her.

Emissary profiles bored her. Why did Damius want these reviewed? Her fellow emissaries appeared to carry credentials like her own. Although, they appeared like a bunch of boring scientists shooting for a way to get their names in the history records. The only two not claiming scientist status had stated agriculture and politics in their files. No red flags noted anywhere. She quickly prepared a summary. There, done. Now, she had time to focus on the investigation.

Blaring sirens filled the air. Annwyn jumped up. She ran to the portal as a deep voice echoed a warning.

"The station is under lockdown. Remain where you are unless instructed by Penduli security. Repeat, the station is under lockdown. Remain where you are unless instructed by Penduli security."

Annwyn's pulse raced as her heart beat against her chest. Another bomb? No. She didn't feel any vibration. Then again, being recently upgraded, Penduli likely had replaced their hull buffs. Either way, she had to get to the site as soon as possible. If it was a small-grade bomb, she'd need to gather materials. Why hadn't Damius called for her? No matter. She grabbed her bag, placing her tablet, dime bars, and collecting kit inside. The doors whooshed open when she neared.

"Lt. Cress," Annwyn said. "I'm ready."

"Emissary Silk, please, put your bags down. We will be remaining here."

Annwyn stepped back and stared. "If there was another bombing or an attempt, I need to get to the site to collect evidence." She moved forward, only to have Cress block her way.

"The station is under lockdown. We must remain here."

That did it. "Who sent you?"

"Excuse me?" Cress said with wide eyes.

"It's a simple question, Lt. Cress. Who assigned you to shadow me?"

"I am to protect you."

Liar. "Then you can protect me as I go to the site," Annwyn stated.

"I cannot permit you to leave."

Something snapped inside of Annwyn. The second person in as many hours was telling her what she could and could not do. She may not be able to move the mountain of the major, but she could handle Lt. Cress.

"Lt. Cress, I have had quite enough of you. I am part of this investigation team, as I am sure you are aware. I need to know what is going on. Take me to Major Damius or explain right now why you are hampering my position here."

"He has left for the planet."

Fiery heat ripped through her body and filled her face. He went to the planet without telling her? She'd deal with that later. She still had an investigation to do.

"Take me—"

"Emissary Silk, this is Lt. Nicheo." Nicheo's voice snapped over the com. "We need you to collect samples in cargo bay four. Can you find your way here, or should I send someone to retrieve you?"

"No, Lt. Cress is here on stalking detail. I'm sure she can show me the way." Annwyn glared at the guard.

"We will see you shortly, then. Nicheo out."

"Now, Lt. Cress. Take me there now," Annwyn ordered.

Cress cleared her throat and nodded, leading the way out.

The trip to the cargo bay was less complicated than she remembered from her previous escapades.

Not being treated as an equal by Damius and his crew grated on her nerves. Adding Lt. Cress into the mix, and it was as if everyone but her had control of her life. She could've stayed on her own planet to receive this treatment.

The large cargo bay hatch stood open with several guards outside. She paused a moment and turned to Lt. Cress. "You may remain here with the rest of the guards." Without waiting for a response, she rushed into the bay and stopped near Nicheo.

"Lt. Nicheo." She bounced on the balls of her feet, looking at the scattered debris filling the cargo area. "What happened here?"

"The items we were expecting were stolen."

"Wasn't Mirbeck in charge of making sure I obtained the item?" she asked. "He seemed very capable of handling that assignment."

"Yes. It seems he was given incorrect information on its arrival. Either by accident or on purpose, we'll find out. Luckily, the thieves didn't have the chance to detonate their bomb, and only took the item instead."

"They intended to bomb the area as well?"

"I believe it was an attempt to cover up the theft."

"I see." She glanced around. "Have you swept the area for bio evidence, or should I?"

"Usually, our alchemist takes care of it." His face reddened.

"Then I shall do it." *First, get rid of Cress.* Annwyn smiled at Nicheo. "Would it be possible for my serv—my assistant to join me in my lab?"

"Of course. Anything else you need?"

"Gront is sharing quarters with me. Would you mind asking Lt. Cress to retrieve him and escort him to my lab?"

"Certainly."

"Oh, Lt. Nicheo, Damius is on the planet, correct?" *Second, see how long the major will be gone. The jerk.*

"Yes, he and Cudala went on the last transport right before the theft."

"If I remember correctly, he won't be able to return until the moon after tomorrow?"

"Correct. A destabilized corona cloud formation won't allow travel until then," he responded, then tilted his head. "Did you need to see him?"

"Oh, no. Curious only. Thank you, Lieutenant." She tipped her head toward the bay. "I'll start collecting evidence."

She enjoyed the menial task of collecting bio evidence. It allowed her the opportunity to sift through the information she'd gathered so far. She sprayed on the protective gloves and started at the far end of the bay.

No matter how hard she tried to focus on the task at hand, her thoughts drifted back to Damius. Why did he go to the surface and not tell her? Did he have plans to keep her out of the main investigation? Maybe he didn't think she had the any skills other than alchemy to offer.

Another man, just like her father, underestimating her.

She blew out a breath and swabbed the space coat dropped by one of the thieves. She clipped a small square of the fabric and placed it in a bio bag before dropping the rest of the coat into a larger bag. She stowed it in her collection case and stepped toward the bomb. Three suited techs maneuvered and melted areas around the edge. Small droid bomb. She scanned the walls and the filtering system built in the ceiling. Even if it went off, nothing could have happened before the vacuum system kicked in and did its thing.

If Damius didn't think she was capable of more than just scientific explanations, she would just have to prove him wrong on her own. Besides, solving puzzles and conquering strategy challenges was what her people thrived on.

When given the all-clear signal, she tagged the bomb.

"Get this to my lab. Someone is there already and will sign the receipt," she told a nearby tech.

He nodded and lifted it, walking away.

She finished gathering samples, swabs, and particles, placing them within her two lab collection bags. She set her hands on her hips and leaned backward, stretching her back. Now she remembered why she'd rushed to get past this part of her training. Blades, her back ached.

She would need to get her analysis done quickly so she could explore other avenues of the investigation. She didn't understand why she cared what Damius thought of her, but she needed to prove herself to him.

"Emissary Silk," Annwyn jumped when Lt. Nicheo touched her arm when he greeted her, "have you completed your collections?"

"I believe so," she tried to calm her breath.

"I shall escort you back to your lab. Please, follow me," Nicheo said as he reached for one of her collection bags.

As they walked, Nicheo slipped her a piece of paper. "Read it, and then destroy it," he whispered.

Annwyn gasped, then unfolded the paper and read the message scrawled across the page. *Must check for listening devices in your lab and quarters - do not say anything substantial until rooms are cleared.*

Annwyn bit her lip. She always talked out loud to herself in the lab. She flicked through her memory before the emergency signal had alarmed. No. She had been quiet the entire time she wrote the profiles. She nodded to the lieutenant, while he walked faster than a leafeater in mid-stormcast. She would not run but she wanted to beat him there. Oh well. Maybe another time.

She arrived at her lab and waited with the door open for Nicheo to enter. As he passed her, she whispered, "This place is being watched. I found out last setting."

Lt. Nicheo's head tipped slightly as he moved past her.

"I will have a report ready by our next meeting," she said in her normal volume. *Let them see what happens when a Hunee is in on the game.*

Chapter Six

Annwyn joined Gront at the bio box holding the bomb. He carefully removed the outer lining with floating bio-hands inside the container. For several moments, neither spoke. Gront hummed as he worked the second layer of lining loose. Annwyn flipped the switches along the side of the box, which allowed a large screen on the side wall to show details of each layer's alchemical properties.

"It's as I determined." She sighed. "Common low-grade bomb." She spun around to grab one of her bio bags and began unpacking her samples. "Any being can make those with ease.

It doesn't help us at all. Perhaps we can find more with these samples."

"Pri—"

"Gront." She cast a glare at him.

"Excuse me," he whispered.

Annwyn scanned the walls and ceilings for the hidden devices she'd known existed. Nothing seemed obvious as a camera or listening device.

"Gront, finish dissecting it and write it up. Then, return to quarters."

"Understood," he said and returned to his work.

By the time he'd finished, Annwyn had all the bio samples separated and running through the standard testing. She bounced on her feet while staring at the chemical containers lining the far wall of her lab. She'd focused on Emissary Leader Moiran. Although he was behind Annwyn being watched, there had been no indications of why. However, being so far up the galaxy political ladder, there were numerous connections to untangle. Annwyn tapped her fingertips together. Admiral Carmichael appeared to have a penchant for reassignments, though. She'd have to check into it further.

The beeping on the testing bar jarred her thoughts. She turned, twisting the sample to the side, closed the compartment, and hit the button which began the second round of testing. It would take much longer to complete. She scanned the lab once more, then left. She'd left her reports in her quarters. The admiral needed a second look

Cress nodded upon her exit, and Annwyn headed for the turbo-lifts, ignoring the officer's presence. She almost tripped when the image of Cress arguing last setting popped into her head. Of course. Cress could be the key, couldn't she?

❦ ❦ ❦

Damius slipped out and got behind the moss-covered dome building, placing himself, Cudala, and the lead security officer from Penduli in the shadows of Chalar's tri-level receiving arena. The place left little room to breathe with all the tourists jammed inside arguing over delayed or delisted departures.

Damius faced Lt. Balder. "Is it normally like this?"

"Absolutely. Every moon cycle, every solar phase since Chalar joined The Directorate for the Larunda Legacy."

Damius paused as a glider slid to a halt above and passengers departed. He watched them walk single file down the descending plank on one side, and another group filed on the ascension plank to enter the glider. Within ticks, the hyper-drive initiated, and the glider peeled away.

He studied its direction. "Balder, we're grateful for your help finding contacts on the planet. The Circle was not forthcoming, and as a native Chalaran, you were our best hope for contacts."

"I have some reputable and some not-so-reputable contacts on the planet. This is definitely better than attempting to infiltrate the Circle for information." Balder shrugged. "Besides, rumor has it, they've had some issues with their leader lately."

"Sometimes those of questionable behavior have the best insights into what is going on in the underworld of a planet. I won't ask how you know them." Damius grinned "Where to now?"

"This arena is mainly for tourists. We need to get into town, which is a bit of a hike. However, any form of transportation other than walking will draw too much attention from the Circle."

"Just how much does Silvergrass Circle's power carry over into the locals?"

"They are the prime religion here on Chalar, which of course gives them spiritual and moral power in the local areas. But their real power is the tourists. The tourists visit Silvergrass, but they tend to stay and shop in the city. Economically, the locals depend on Silvergrass for the tourist traffic."

Damius nodded and shifted away from the walls of the building. "You know the way, so I'll follow you. Does everyone have their coms off?" He scanned the faces of the small group.

Balder nodded, along with Sergeant Cudala. Balder headed toward the twenty-foot-high wall of dense plant life. Damius gazed up and noted most of the taller sprouts sported smaller limbs with orange and yellow buds. He strode behind Balder into the dense foliage, and within ticks, they reached a wood-like covered trail.

Balder turned south and called over his shoulder, "We have a bit of a walk. This is the safest route. Only locals come along this trail, and they rarely question others. We won't run into any of the Silvergrass members until we get closer to the city."

"The Silvergrass Circle runs the tourist trade?" Cudala inquired.

"No, the locals do. It was decreed during the sector creation. The Silvergrass allow the locals to process and run public tours of the open areas of the Sanctuary. However, there is instruction and information provided to all tourists, male and female. It states during the tour, a selection may be made for certain tourists to go inside the more secured private Sanctuary of the Circle. This area is off limits to the public." Balder winced. "Female tourists only are chosen for such a special treat."

"Why is that?" Damius asked.

"I believe it's for their selection process," Balder responded.

"Selection process?" Damius raised a brow.

Cudala spoke up from behind him. "Every time a new group of tourists arrive, five women are chosen to be tested and allowed the option to join the Circle."

Damius frowned. "And those who decline the invitation?"

"They are returned to the city to live their life as they so choose," Balder said. "But, you have to understand, to the people here, it is an honor to be invited into the Circle. It is like being accepted into royalty."

Cudala grunted. "Royalty. That's a joke. They may not have to worry about income. But their every move is dictated by the Circle Tomes."

Balder shrugged. "You're from Nushao, right?"

"Yes."

"Your planet has deeply rooted spiritual beliefs and sects. The Circle here is similar, with a few more rules. And, yes, they're all written in Tomes, as is their history."

"And the exclusion of men."

"Most of the male population here on Chalar have lived this way for decades and respect the Circle. Some have traveled to other galaxies, as well as applied to work on the station to find mates due to a lower female population count.

However, most return here to live and raise their families."

Damius wiped his forehead and tugged at the shirt clinging to his body. The foliage and heat reminded him of the holo-rooms he'd experienced during his training.

An image of Annwyn popped in his head. This would be a place she'd love, with it mimicking her home planet.

A rumbling noise ahead of them grew in volume as it drew closer.

Balder pointed to the side of the path. "Get out of sight," he ordered. "Quickly."

All three dived into the plant life lining the path and ducked behind large purple and green leaves. Damius shifted to crouch behind a dark green round plant and peered between the stalks. A small convoy of approximately ten males chained together at the ankles walked in unison in the direction of the tourist buildings. Behind them marched four uniformed women. Damius inhaled quietly until the group passed.

Balder stood, returned to the path, and motioned for them to follow.

"They're headed to the compound, correct?" Cudala asked when they resumed their hike.

Balder nodded. Damius shot a glance at Balder, then Cudala.

She stepped closer and spoke under her breath. "Prison."

Damius scowled. "Who governs the law enforcement here?" No need to get them involved if it could be avoided.

"The locals have their own form of organization which includes a leadership liaison with the Circle, as well as other areas of most cities," Balder responded.

"Will we be using them?"

"No. Even though their main objective is to keep order and peace within the city, they do still report to the Circle."

"Who chooses punishments of the law breakers? The Circle?"

"Oh, no. The local law enforcement does such things. However, like I said, they are required to submit reports of all proceedings to the Circle."

"How involved does the Circle get in the everymoon running of the city?" If there were too many Circle members running around in town, their plans could fail.

"They don't. They're not really interested in the city, except as… How can I explain this?" He faced Damius and Cudala. "Like a parent of an older child. They keep tabs and only get involved when needed."

"I see," Damius said and waved for Balder to continue their trek. It still could cause problems for them. *Naiba. What a mess.*

Damius grabbed a quick sip from his liquid tube, then replaced it.

Cudala slipped beside him and spoke under her breath. "I feel like we've been walking for eons."

"Just a little farther, and we will be taking a route toward the city."

Cudala shrugged and took a sip of her liquid, too, before placing it in her pack.

Balder pointed to the right and stepped off the path onto a thin rocky road. Damius and Cudala followed. The humidity surrounding them threatened to suffocate him.

"Here we are," Balder announced, stepping through a wooden archway.

Damius followed and paused as his muscles relaxed. The sudden coolness of wind blew about them. He scanned the area where they'd emerged. It appeared to be a large, flat sandy section of the planet surface. To the right, a bridge of mud shaped into bricks reached a grassy plain where small circular structures spread out against farmland.

"I had not noticed this on my prior trip to the Circle." Cudala pointed in front of them where five large pools of water shivered and reflected the bright colors of the plant life surrounding them. She turned toward Balder. "Why is this not visible from the Circle plantation?"

"The Circle does not care to visually keep tabs on the city."

Damius stepped forward and pointed toward the farmland. "Is that our destination?"

"No, we will take the little bridge over there." Balder pointed to their left where a large moss-covered hill ended with a plateau several kilometers high. Atop the plateau sat dome structures built within and above tall columns of clear material. Each column connected via a walkway. At the base of the columns, the city constructed smaller domes like buildings along the edge of the plateau. Several hover crafts flew above the city and around the tall buildings.

Damius nodded and lifted a palm toward the city. "Lead the way."

The trio hiked the short distance to a wood-crafted grate. Balder lifted the grate and indicated for Damius and Cudala to go down the ladder on the side of the pit. Damius went first, placing his booted foot on the rungs and descending into the darkness. The damp air surrounded him while the sounds of their footsteps alone echoed within the circular walls of clay. He opened his senses and received nothing except trepidation from Cudala, which was normal for her. He received determination from Balder. *Good*.

The lower he moved, the damper the air became until a cool wind pushed up from below. His foot hit solid ground, and he stepped off the ladder. A weak light filtered from behind them. He waited until Balder joined them at the base of the ladder. He followed the officer down a cave-like tunnel for less than half of a kilometer before it opened and revealed a small shelf off the plateau's edge. He stepped toward the edge and looked over the precipice to note the surface planes of this planet contained several cracks which dropped far down onto a web of rivers.

Damius scanned across their location and studied the large waterfall, which spilled from the edge of the farmland plateau down below. His gaze followed the edges of each plateau he'd seen from above. All had large waterfalls from their surface feeding the rivers underneath. Their waters generated an echoing rushing sound all around him.

"Major Damius, I presume?" a dark-skinned Scargilian shouted out.

Damius spun around. His eyes widened, and a huge grin split across his face. "Noden." He reached out a hand and got it slapped away.

Noden grabbed him and pulled him into his arms. "No handshake, Bo. Long time, no see." Damius's former second-in-command spoke in a loud voice. He gestured for Damius to follow and the group rounded a large rock where a small camp hid. They headed into a large tent, where

Noden sat at the head of a large wooden table and gestured toward the group.

"Join me. We shall eat and make plans. Balder has filled me in on what you are looking for, and I have had my scouts out for the last moon cycle gathering information. Let us deal." He laughed heartily.

"I'd wondered what galaxy you'd escaped to. It's good to see you, too. Thanks for helping out here." Damius followed the robust male.

Noden wore what appeared to be some type of leather material strapped around his body with several hooks holding hand weapons, and his pockets bulged. *Likely ammunition.* Markers hung from rope near his waist.

"Of course! As soon as Balder mentioned your name, I agreed." Noden pointed at Balder. "Didn't I?"

Balder smiled. "He did so. Then he broke my wrist and made me swear not to reveal his identity to you before we arrived."

"Bah, bones heal," Noden mumbled. He turned toward Damius. "So, the High Priestess refused to help, I assume?"

"We tried that path," Cudala said. "She's refusing visitors right now."

Noden shook his head. "She should. She's sick or something, as word has it. There's problems in the Circle, and you'd be best to do what you need without involving them."

Damius nodded. "Understood." He leaned forward. "So, what have your sources found out?"

"We've only began reaching out. I've several of my scouts who haven't yet reported in. They will, but only once they have information." He waited while a large plate of a dark meaty substance was set in front of him. Noden glanced at the young male who delivered the food and nodded. He lifted his chin, and the boy served the rest of the visitors.

"It'll be another moon cycle before the corona cloud patterns shift to allow your return to Penduli. You might as well camp here until we get all our reports in." He swallowed a large amount of his beverage. "You and your team are safe here. We're hidden from all, and I keep it that way."

Damius bit into the food before him and swallowed quickly. He gulped several mouthfuls of his drink before coughing. Dear *Larunda, it was hot.*

Noden burst out laughing. "A little too spicy for you, Bo?" He shook his head. "You've gone soft on me."

Damius waited while the liquid cooled his scorched throat. He'd forgotten how much his friend loved spices. Another moon cycle before he'd be able to see Annwyn again. He'd forgotten to leave word they'd left. He mentally shrugged. Nicheo was the one in charge of telling the others where he was, though Damius doubted that Nicheo saw her as part of the team. He took another swallowed of liquid. He'd contact her as soon as he returned...maybe.

Chapter Seven

Two moons. Two whole moon cycles without seeing him, and he had the audacity to send a message via com announcing the team report meeting time was set for earlier than normal? Had he lost his mind? She'd spent the last two cycles reviewing all the notes available via the dime bar he'd given her. Even with the updates scanned in by Nicheo and Mirbeck, something was missing. Just as she suspected. They'd intentionally withheld information. Likely on his orders. Orders or not, she was not military, and by Larunda, she intended to inform them of their mistake.

She glared at the com notice. She'd have preferred to instruct Major Damius without his team present. However, considering his rearranging the meeting, he'd receive it along with everyone else.

Besides, in her review, she'd noticed several interesting facts, which, it appeared, no one decided to investigate. Facts which could and should reveal the location of the perpetrators.

"Gront, I'll be back immediately following the meeting. Collect the results and our rising meal, and I will meet you here."

"I live to serve," Gront responded, bowing and avoiding her gaze. His behavior had been different since the last time they were in the lab. He'd hardly said a word to her.

"I want to discuss the results with you," she said, hoping it would smooth whatever was going on between them.

"Of course. Wouldn't it be better to do such a thing in the lab, not to overstep my bounds?"

"The lab…" Annwyn stopped herself. Though their quarters were swept for bugs, she had no way of knowing if someone had placed devices since then. She looked around, not seeing anything obvious, but then again, she had yet to find the ones in the lab. What if Damius's men had actually placed devices here instead of sweeping her quarters? "Actually, I'll meet you in the dining facilities. Bring the dime bar with the results."

She could see the hurt look on Gront's face. She reached for her tablet to write to him but thought better of it. She saw Gront's drawing papers on the table and reached for one, then scribbled on it quickly. "There, now you can't get my rising meal order wrong. I'll send you a com when I am on my way."

She turned and exited her quarters, hoping Gront would understand the message and forgive her curtness. She knew Gront would be able to search their quarters and find out if they were now bugged.

Once outside, she took a deep breath. No Cress stalking her, it seemed. She walked toward the turbolift and decided to go through the solarico on her way to the briefing room. She hoped Damius would be there with Wren, but she found herself alone walking the trail. She breathed in deeply, missing the smells of real atmosphere instead of the artificial one on the space station. She was jealous Damius had been to the surface and had set foot on ground once again. He was infuriating, yet she longed to wrap her legs around his hips once again and feel his lips on hers. As if on cue, she felt Wren licking her hand.

"Wren, behave!"

Wren stopped licking her hand but sat next to her, looking up at Damius as he walked up behind them.

"Go. We don't have time for this."

Wren took off for the generic greenery sub-room and disappeared inside. Annwyn looked at Damius, her heartbeat quickening. Why did he have to be so damn tall and well built? The aroma of her home planet mixed with his personal scent filled her senses. She scanned the outline of his biceps through his tight military-issued shirt. She wanted to run her hands on them again, mapping them. His strength both scared and intrigued her. The things they could do together, if given the time or chance.

"Good rising, Emissary. I am sorry for Wren's behavior."

"Good rising, Major. Nice for you to grace us with your presence again." Her voice sounded rougher than she intended, but she was trying to stay mad at him and not get lost in her need to feel her body making contact with his.

Wren came bounding out of the sub-room and inserted himself between them as they walked.

"The corona cloud shifted earlier than expected, forcing us to delay our return."

"I hope you enjoyed yourself, while we were up here working trying to solve this crime."

Damius stopped in his tracks, and this time Wren stayed next to him instead of continuing with Annwyn. "I did have moments I enjoyed. I would be lying if I said I didn't, but most importantly, we made progress in our investigation."

"That's nice." Annwyn warred within herself—stay mad at Damius or tell him?

"I need to tell you…"

Wren howled and took off running back toward the exit of the solarico. Damius drew his weapon and grabbed her by the arm, pulling her close. A second later, an alarm rang out, and his com sounded.

Damius tapped his ear piece. "Report," he growled as she tried to pull away from him, but he held her close to his body.

"Where?" he growled. He looked down at her and whispered, "Don't make me throw you over my shoulder again."

Heat rushed to her face, and she clenched her jaw. Why must this infuriating man make her want to both tell him off and be ravaged by him, possibly at the same time.

"I'm on my way. I have the Emissary with me. The hit may have been meant for her. Have Lt. Balder meet us there. Damius out." He tapped his earbud again, holstered his gun, and pulled her into an embrace. His lips brushed her temple, and then he released her. "I'm sorry for my…"

She looked in his eyes and could see the fear and worry inside of them. Maybe she wasn't the only one warring with feelings. She pressed her hand to his lips, stopping his apology.

"What happened?" her voice cracked breaking whatever was happening between them.

They stood in silence and stared into each other's eyes.

"Security Officer Cress was found dead outside of your quarters." Damius looked down, shaking his head. "Gront was covered in her blood when the officers arrived."

❦ ❦ ❦

For one brief second, Damius could sense Annwyn's horror at Gront killing Cress. She stumbled then, but he caught her, and together they quickly returned to her quarters.

Despite his best efforts, Damius couldn't tap down his sensing. Annwyn's emotions washed over her. Like an ocean's tides turning, she went from horror to disbelief and made it hard for him to concentrate. She ran toward Gront when they arrived at her quarters. One of Balder's men stopped her.

"Let me by."

"Emissary, you must remain apart from the suspect."

"He is not a suspect. He is my assistant."

The station's Security Major Astole, appeared suddenly. "Emissary, he is your slave because he committed a crime, and he is paying for the crime he committed against you by being your servant. Isn't that correct?"

"Yes, he is my servant, and as such I have a right to speak to him."

"No, you don't. As a matter of fact, both of you will need to be brought to the holding cell for questioning. Being he is your servant, it is, of course, possible you ordered him to kill Cress."

"I don't believe it will be necessary, Major Astole." Damius knew he needed to defuse the situation immediately, before Annwyn carried through on her thoughts of punching the Astole.

"Major Elkwood, there is no need for you to be here. This does not concern your investigation."

"I beg to differ. How do you know the Emissary, a member of my team, wasn't the target instead of Officer Cress?"

"Well then, she would be lying here dead instead of my officer."

Damius stood to his full height, dwarfing Major Astole and most of those around him. When he desired, Damius could fill the space around him, projecting his energy, making himself seem even more imposing. "Why wasn't Officer Cress with Emissary Silk this rising?"

"How do we know she wasn't?" He put his hand on Annwyn's arm and started to pull her toward him.

Damius had had enough. Astole was touching her, and that must stop. "Unhand Emissary Silk right this moment. Admiral Carmichael appointed her to my team, and since she is on my team, she is under my protection and jurisdiction."

"Very well." Astole pushed Annwyn toward Damius. "But I am taking her slave with me."

"No!" Annwyn yelled, lunging for Astole.

"Stop!" Damius pulled her roughly back and indicated for Lt. Nicheo to join them. "Take the Emissary to our meeting room. I will be there presently, and we will get this sorted."

"But. . ."

Damius turned his back to Astole and whispered to Annwyn.

"I know you are upset, but you will have to trust me. You need to get out of here now, before he decides to throw you in a cell, as well. If he does such a thing, we'll be limited on contact until my team can prove you're innocent."

Annwyn jerked her head in a quick nod before looking away.

"Go," he ordered.

Nicheo guided Annwyn away from the scene. With her gone, Damius could focus his sensing and control his own emotions more. He looked first at Gront, and sadness rolled off him.

"What happened?" Damius asked.

"I heard a commotion outside of our quarters, and when I looked to see what was happening, I found Officer Cress on the floor," Gront said.

"Why are you covered in her blood?"

"I called for help, and then tried to revive her. Prin—Emissary Silk's father insisted I have emergency medical training if I were to travel with her."

Major Astole turned toward the closest medical and other officers investigating the scene. "How did she die?"

"Stabbed several times. Even someone unfamiliar with her biology couldn't miss hitting a major organ."

A howl broke through the questioning.

About time, Wren.

"What in the blazes?"

"My wolf. He's found something."

"Why wasn't I notified about a wild animal on my station?" Major Astole asked.

Damius clenched his jaw, sucking in a harsh breath through his teeth. He scowled while struggling to calm the irritation climbing his neck. It failed. "First off, this isn't your station. You are simply the Security Major in charge." He straightened to his full height. "Second, Wren is a member of my team and"—he glared as the man opened his mouth—"as such was on the roster you received prior to our arrival. Now,"—Wren's howls grew louder and longer—"Wren has found something. You can either come with me or stay here. I do not care." Damius spun on his heels and stormed toward the sounds of his wolf's howls.

❦ ❦ ❦

"Wren found the weapon...a large knife, which probably killed Cress," Damius said when he burst into the conference room, then jerked to a halt. "Have we...?" Damius pointed toward the ceiling.

"Affirmative, the room is clean."

"Thanks, Nicheo."

"What is happening with Gront?" Annwyn had paced the entire time Nicheo held her captive in the conference room.

"I talked Major Astole into letting Gront clean up and change, but he is in holding until the testing is completed on the knife."

"He didn't do this," she stated. "A quick bioscan can confirm his prints won't be on the knife."

"I know. His story checks out but getting Astole to admit it." He shook his head. "That is another problem. He should be out by star set, next star rise, at the latest."

Mirbeck and Cudala entered the conference room and sat.

"Let's get this started, before something else happens," Damius said.

Annwyn sat in the chair Mirbeck pulled out for her. Her leg bounced under the table as her gaze swept across everyone's faces. She didn't know who to trust.

The door to the conference room swooshed opened, revealing Emissary Moiran.

All the officers rose from their seats and bowed, but Annwyn stayed seated.

"Annwyn, your father is on the com. He heard what happened and has requested your return. He does not believe you are safe."

Blades. How the hell did he know so fast?

"I will speak to him." Annwyn rose to leave.

Emissary Moiran turned to Damius. "I will not be replacing Emissary Silk at this time, as the mission is on hold, but you will need to find another alchemist."

Annwyn paused. "No, he will not. I'm not leaving."

"Your father—"

"I don't care what my father said. I am of liberated age, I passed the initial interviews on my own and I make my own decisions." Annwyn hated interrupting, but they must understand her position.

"I will dismiss you from the new contact party," Emissary Moiran said.

"I'm sure my father would pay you to do that, but I'm still a part of the investigation team, aren't I, Major Elkwood?" She lifted a brow and stared at Damius.

Damius bowed her way, and she bowed back. "Yes, you are a part of my team." He slid a quick look at the Emissary. "Though before we go further, perhaps it is best if you speak with your father. I don't believe anyone should keep someone like King Silk waiting."

Her heart thudded. *He knows I'm a princess.*

Chapter Eight

"You are not safe, child," Annwyn's father said. "I demand you return immediately."

"We have discussed this, many times. I will not return now, and your attempts to buy my return will not work. Unless, of course, it is your intention to have me kidnapped?" she asked.

"Of course not. I will not lower myself to such an act."

"What about hiring someone to set off explosions?"

"Must I remind you to whom you are speaking, child? I am not only your father, but I am king. I suggest you monitor your words more carefully when speaking to me."

"Am I speaking to my king or my father?"

"Annwyn," he sighed. "I am, and always shall be your father first. But I do have the right to your respect, as well."

"Father, I am remaining here as part of the investigation team into the recent bombings. I'm sure you've been updated?"

"Of course. Although our agreement was limited to allow your position as a new contact emissary only, not as an investigator. Which I may remind you, I know about your current situation from my spies. I am forced to use them to learn about your well-being, since you do not contact me regularly."

"You would hear from me more often if you would but give me some trust, Father." She sighed. "I promise to contact you within a reasonable amount of time."

"Your definition or mine?"

Annwyn laughed.

"Gront should be returned. He is involved in a death—"

"No," she interrupted. "He's innocent and only tried to help. He remains with me. I will not argue with you on this, Father. You know my position on this."

"Very well, then."

He disconnected. No goodbye, nothing. She bit her lip, then shook her head. No. She would not let him make her feel guilty. She stretched her arms and checked the time. She'd likely missed the full report on Damius's trip on the planet. Blades, she hated being late. But she'd get the report eventually. Of course, it was sure to be altered to only allow her information they deemed necessary for her to know. Her pulse picked up when she thought about seeing Damius again.

What in Larunda was happening to her? She blew out a long breath while tapping her fingers as she arrived at the lift. When it arrived, she slid inside and scooted so her back pressed against one side. She stated her destination and waited while the slow hum brought her to the correct floor. Once the doors opened with a quiet whoosh, she stepped out and searched the corridors. Empty. Good.

Annwyn searched for a virosphere, then stopped, closing her eyes and picturing the directions she needed to return to the conference room. Once the image solidified in her mind, she grinned and made her way through the silent passageways.

As she drew closer to the conference room, Damius's voice pierced the silence. *Uh-oh, he's not very happy.* She slipped open the door and paused, keeping her breaths soft and quiet, while remaining just out of sight from the team inside.

"She will not be included on the suspect list. I've already cleared her, and now I am wondering why I'm having to repeat myself."

Silence. Annwyn frowned. Who wanted her on the list still? Hadn't she proven herself to everyone?

"The last time I checked, I am in command of this team. If you do not agree with me, I'll be more than happy to have your relocation orders delivered before you can clear your tablet. Do I make myself clear?"

"Sir, if I might make a suggestion?" Cudala said.

"Go on," he responded.

"I have absolute trust in Emissary Silk...err...Annwyn. Since there seems to be something going on within the Circle, and they allow female tourists more access into their Inner Sanctum, why don't you let me take the Emissary to the planet for a little undercover work?"

"What?" Damius barked.

"Sir, please hear me out. She and I can go on a tour. As two unescorted females, the chance we're chosen for the special tour into the Inner Sanctum is increased. From there, we can both gather more information on what is going on."

"And the Inner Sanctum is where the choosing is completed," Damius said.

"True. However, Balder confirmed not all the females must accept. If she is chosen, she can refuse."

"And yourself?"

"It's the beauty of this plan, sir. Since I've gone on the tour, the only way I can get back in those secured areas is if I'm with someone who has not been there yet. I can send a com to my contact and arrange for a meeting as well. I'd like to get Annwyn's opinion of the situation. I believe she has skills we've yet to use, and I, for one, am more than happy she's on our team, as everyone should be."

Annwyn peered through the crack in the door. Damius's entire team around the table shifted while everyone except Cudala bowed their heads. Cudala rose and stood facing Damius. At least Cudala trusted her.

Annwyn scanned everyone, searching for the one whose face might reveal they distrusted her. It was a waste of time with all their heads bowed. Obviously, it wasn't Cudala, from her statement.

Wren growled and trotted toward her.

Blades.

She finished opening the door and strolled into the room as though she'd recently arrived. She glanced around, lifted her brows, and faced Damius. "So, what did I miss?"

"Did you make the communication?" he asked.

She tipped her head to one side. "I did. I will be remaining here as part of your team to assist with the investigation." She cleared her throat and refused to make eye contact with anyone but Damius. "That is...if you still wish it so."

"I do," he stated.

"Good." She sat in her normal spot at the table, glancing at Cudala who sat at the same time. She returned Cudala's smile before returning her gaze toward Damius. "If you don't mind updating me on what I've missed?"

Annwyn's feet bounced on the floor beneath the conference table while Damius did a quick review of his trip to the planet and Cudala's suggestion. Although she tried to keep her focus on Damius, she repeatedly did a surreptitious scan of team members. Nicheo's attention remained steady on his notes, typing onto the pad, then moving items around. He sat farthest away from her, which prevented her from reading his notes. Cudala kept still and attentive on Damius with an occasional smile tossed her way.

Mirbeck's eyelids closed, his body stilled and his breathing barely perceptible as though in a meditative state. Was he avoiding her gaze or simply sleeping? A logistics officer should pay attention to the plans Damius outlined for the team, even if it was for the second time. Wren's paw planted itself on one of her feet, holding it motionless. She paused her bouncing for him and could have sworn he purred. Did wolves purr?

She studied Damius as he switched between reading off his tablet and staring at her. Blades, his eyes heated her body. Images of their intimate moments quickened her pulse. She waited until his attention returned to his tablet, then allowed her gaze to skim down his muscled body. Once again, she wondered what he'd look like under his uniform. Would his muscles be more defined? Would she be able to trace each indentation of his skin? She bit her lip to keep from shivering.

"Are you agreeable?" Damius asked.

She'd lost track of what he was saying. She stared into his darkened eyes with wide pupils. Had he'd known what she was thinking? A strong pull tugged her. Wren pushed against her leg and she blinked. She cleared her throat, about to speak, when Cudala interjected.

"I'll be with you the entire time," she promised.

Annwyn shook her head. "It's not that. I'm sure we'll be safe. I'm curious as to why the need to determine what the issue is within the private business of Silvergrass. Is it your belief it has something to do with the bombings?"

Damius shrugged. "I don't believe so. However, it is our position that all avenues must be investigated." He placed his tablet on the table, along with both his hands, and leaned forward. "By now, everyone on the station and on the planet is aware of the explosions, theft, and...at least on the station, Cress's death. Whoever is behind this has a very well-informed contact." He blew out a breath. "Which is why we must be vigilant in our security and censorship of our words when not in this room." He straightened. "Nicheo has been checking and removing recording devices found in your lab and everyone's private quarters."

Annwyn gasped. "My private quarters are being monitored?"

"Not yours," Nicheo said. "Due to your...err...standing, there is limited access there. Only you, Gront...and one other has access."

Annwyn lifted a brow. "Who is the one other?"

Nicheo's face darkened, and he coughed, glancing toward Damius.

Annwyn faced Damius. "You, I suppose," she snapped. All the conversation she and Gront had engaged in since her arrival rushed through her mind. *Blades.*

Damius shrugged one shoulder. "Yes."

"I see," she responded. He knew of her royal status and Gront's position. There weren't any other secrets to keep from him. Except...she tipped her head a little to one side. "Are you constantly monitoring it?"

"No. In fact, my access is for entry only. There are no cameras or recording devices in your private rooms. Nicheo and I confirmed it."

A small breath escaped her lips. Good. Her father had monitored everyone's private quarters at home. She'd hoped to escape that as well as his dominating presence.

֎ ֎ ֎

"Nicheo, finish checking the information we received from Noden. Mirbeck, we'll need to schedule another trip to the planet, after we get Gront released. We'll go now and see if we can get some sense knocked into Major Astole." He faced Annwyn and Cudala. "You two, prepare for a trip to the Circle for a tour. However, we'll have to wait until the destabilized corona cloud allows another transport."

"You travelled." Annwyn rose. "What is the difference?"

"We are required to submit a travel itinerary for each trip. Our most recent was done covertly, and only one other person on this station was notified." Damius stepped around the table to get closer to Annwyn. He'd held his body in check from the moment she walked in and nearly lost it when her sexual pull hit him. "Since the trip you and Cudala will be taking will be public, we must follow regulations. Besides, your status requires it since you two intend to gain entrance into the Inner Sanctum of the Circle."

He stopped within feet of her, inhaling her scent. His body hummed with silent craving to touch her...taste her. A slip of his desire pushed past his defenses and shot out from his mind.

"Sir." Cudala jerked his attention away from Annwyn.

"Yes?"

Cudala gasped.

Naiba, he must control his desire. Clenching his jaw, he focused on reining back his desire.

Cudala's body swayed toward him.

Get over here and do some protection, Wren.

Wren whipped around Annwyn and pressed his full body against Damius's legs while shielding him.

Cudala shook her head and blinked several times.

"You have something to add, Sergeant?" he asked. *Snap out of it, female.*

"Um, yes." Cudala pressed one hand to her temple. "My apologies. I meant to add I could meet with Annwyn and explain in more detail what will be expected once we reach the planet and go on the tour."

"Do so," he said.

Cudala faced Annwyn. "If you have time now, we can return to your quarters to discuss plans. I'm afraid my own may be monitored, and I do not trust the dining facility either."

"I understand." Annwyn nodded. "You are more than welcome to join me there." She lifted her face toward Damius. "And Gront? Will you be able to secure his release soon?"

"I cannot guarantee a time. But I will promise to get him released."

"Sir," Mirbeck called.

Damius fought to hide his frustration. He wanted—no, needed—to be closer to Annwyn. Dear Larunda, what was she doing to him?

He looked over at Mirbeck typing away at his station. "What is it?"

"We've been denied an interview with Gront until this setting." He scowled. "And only after we meet with Major Astole."

Damius jerked his head in a quick nod. "Fine. Set it up." He turned toward Annwyn and Cudala. "Meet this setting. I've received notice the pilot we retrieved from your arrival has regained consciousness. Annwyn will need to accompany me to medloc to complete the interview."

"Why?"

Damius stared at her. "Why what?"

"Why do you need me in on the interview?" she asked.

He pressed his lips together for a moment. First, she complained about not being included, then she demanded to know every little detail of the reports he sent her. So, what if he redacted some of it? It wasn't like she needed to know it all. After what he'd found on his research of her, too much information could cause her to attempt to do things on her own. If she did, she could get hurt. If she got hurt... *Stop. Wren.*

Wren moved away from him and leaned into Annwyn.

Naiba.

She stroked his head while keeping her gaze on Damius.

"You indicated you wished to be included. As part of my team who is not otherwise scheduled for a specific task, you will join me."

"I have a task." She waved toward Cudala. "We need to plan this trip."

"You have only to be informed of what may happen there. The planning portion is Cudala's assignment." *Stubborn female.* He shrugged. "However, if you do not wish to accompany me to gain more information on what happened to the transport on which you almost died…"

Annwyn's body stiffened and she began tapping her fingers together.

She's thinking about it. That much he'd figured out. He'd wait.

She nodded. "I do want to know, and I will be helpful too." She nodded to Cudala. "I will meet you this setting." She returned to Damius and lifted her hand to wave toward the door. "Lead the way, if you would, Major."

Damius lifted the corners of his lips as he headed toward the doorway. Of course, she couldn't resist the lure. And now…now he'd have time alone with her.

Wren bumped the back of his leg, but he refused to acknowledge the stubborn wolf.

Chapter Nine

"**H**ow was your father?" Damius inquired, allowing Annwyn to fall into step with him. Wren inserted himself between them, and Damius swore he felt jealousy coming from his companion. And not because of his connection to Damius.

Traitor.

No surprise there. If he had feelings for Annwyn, Wren would pick up on it as well.

"My father is fine."

"And agitated," Damius added. He had read enough intel on King Silk to know their father-daughter relationship was far removed from his harmonious one with his father. Where Damius experienced support and understanding, it appeared Annwyn met with roadblocks.

"He's always agitated, particularly with me."

"Because you do not follow the rules."

"No." The air escaped Annwyn's lips in exasperation. "Hmm, maybe you are right. I have never been very good at rules."

"Except in the lab." The connection between them vibrated inside him. It'd become almost second nature for him to start sensing around her. She was like the star on an overcast moon cycle, lifting the veil he kept firmly in place to block his ability of feeling and hearing those around him.

"Well, yes, and in games. I do believe in playing fairly."

He couldn't say why, but he knew instantly she was keeping something from him. "What is it you are not telling me?"

"I have told you everything."

"No, you haven't. You were starting to say something to me in the biosphere. What was it?"

Annwyn's hand on his arm forced him to stop. She looked around before pulling him into her body. He didn't have time to object before her lips found his.

Almost from the moment they touched, he started to lose himself in the energy they produced together. She was far from the first woman he had kissed, but there was something different. Maybe it was because she was Hunee, or maybe it was because she was Annwyn. Regardless, his body hummed when their lips parted.

"Not here," she whispered as she rose on her tiptoes, trying to reach his ear. "Later, after I finish with Cudala."

He inclined his head toward her, when Wren inserted himself between them, pushing them apart. A few ticks later, Balder rounded the corner and walked toward them.

"Good, I was hoping to catch up with you," Balder hollered as he approached Damius. "Major Astole wanted to inform you the analysis on the knife will need to be run on the planet, as the only people available on the station have been compromised from working in the lab with Emissary Silk."

"Compromised? I hardly know them." Annwyn threw her arms up.

Damius sensed her anger rolling off her in waves. Wren leaned into his leg, steadying him.

"Regardless, Astole will only trust the lab on the planet to run an unbiased test."

With Wren's help, Damius switched his sensing over to Balder. As before, he could sense nothing from him but honesty. "Walk with us, Balder. We are going to interview the copilot who survived the crash."

"She is awake?"

"Just within the hour."

"I should inform the Major Astole, but I shall do so after my lunch break."

As they rounded the last corner before the med center, Damius felt a dime bar pressed into his hand. "I should be going. Be careful, Major Elkwood, these are dangerous times." Balder lowered his voice. "Noden's men have gotten word to me to be wary. There is a traitor on the station."

Damius nodded. "Please, inform Major Astole we understand his precautions, but I will be escorting the knife to the lab on the planet and will be present at the testing."

"Oh, no, sir. I'll let you tell him yourself. I wish to continue at my post." Balder turned toward Annwyn and bowed. "Emissary."

"Lt. Balder." Annwyn bowed to Balder who turned to depart.

"Hmm," Damius muttered. "You like the underdog."

"I like to see justice prevail, and frequently the underdog is the one needing justice the most."

"Fair enough. Shall we have lunch after this?" Damius inquired as he placed the dime bar from Balder in his pocket.

"Maybe."

"Maybe?"

"I have to keep you guessing," Annwyn teased.

"I thought you liked to play fair."

"This isn't a game."

Damius winked at her and said, "Don't be so sure about it."

🜲 🜲 🜲

She swore if she didn't have so much on her mind about the case, she would enjoy the back and forth word sparring she and Damius engaged in. As it was, she still wasn't sure why he needed her present at the interview with the copilot.

"Because she is a female."

"What?" Annwyn asked.

"I needed you here because she is a female, and the only other female on the team is Cudala and she needed to make arrangements."

"How did you—?"

They'd arrived at the med center, and Damius pushed the com button before she could finish her question. "Major Elkwood to interview Darvia. I was told she was conscious and able to communicate now."

"Yes, Major, please bio-scan and enter," the voice instructed.

Damius placed his hand on the console, and the door opened in front of them.

The med center's bright, white lights made Annwyn cringe, and Wren whimpered beside her. The constant whirl sounds from the equipment buzzed in her ears. The starkness of the space was jarring, as was the lack of anything organic. The entire room was as sterile as one of her testing benches.

"Major Elkwood, I am Doctor Buehl. Pilot Darvia is my charge."

Damius bowed to Buehl, and Annwyn did the same. "Can you lower the lighting? Both my eyes and the Emissary's are not designed for such harsh conditions."

"Normally, yes, but Darvia is Nushaoian, and her skin requires special lighting to heal. I do have some protective glasses. Let me get them for you. You may wish for your animal to wait outside."

Wren was still whimpering, and Damius pointed him toward the door.

"Wait outside," he said.

Wren licked Annwyn's hand, then bolted out the door.

"Here you are."

Annwyn took the blocky looking black rectangle glasses from the doctor. She slipped hers on and looked up to Damius. How did he do it? She was sure the ridiculous glasses made her look anything but attractive, but they made him look even more like a Krizlarian God.

"Darvia should be awake. She tires easily, so please keep your questions to a minimum."

Annwyn followed Damius into the screened-off area the doctor indicated. Her eyes adjusted, and finally she was able to look around at the sparse area. Panels lined the walls with labels indicating the equipment hid from view. She looked over the panel to the left of Darvia's head and could see the beats of Darvia's two hearts. Her translucent skin was reddish tinged instead of the pink Annwyn had seen in other Nushaoians.

"Pilot Darvia, thank you for speaking with us."

Annwyn listened as Damius went through the basic investigative questions. She cataloged the area and the items on Darvia's side table. Nushaoians rarely left their planet because of their delicate physical nature, so she wondered why Darvia had decided to become a pilot.

"Can you take us through the events in the cabin which led to your injuries."

"Yes." Her voice was weak, but there was fire in her eyes. "We were preparing to dock, going through the standard actions, when I noticed Pilot Triani wasn't following protocol. He appeared to have a box of some sort in his hand. When I asked him why we were deviating from the norm, he pointed a blaster at me and started spouting the segregationist litany. We struggled, and he detonated the first bomb before I got the blaster from him."

Damius closed the distance between them as Darvia spoke, and now was pressed against her. She could feel the tension emanating from him but couldn't tell what was going on behind his protective glasses. He held his tablet as it recorded the interview.

"How long had you known Triani? Had you worked with him before?" Annwyn asked.

Darvia's heart rates changed on the screen, barely perceptible, but there was a difference.

"That was my first run with him. He was actually a replacement."

"He was not originally scheduled to pilot?"

"No. A fellow Nushaoian was scheduled with me. She had spiritual commitments which prohibited her joining us."

The screen moved behind them, and Doctor Buehl joined them. "I'm sorry, Major, but it is time for Pilot Darvia's treatment." She waved her hand in front of a side panel, and a set-up with a gel-like substance and bandages appeared.

"I need to get a bio signature on her statement first."

Annwyn saw movement out of the corner of her eye. An attendant was cleaning equipment in the main area.

"I'll wait for you by the door, Major Elkwood," Annwyn said.

Damius nodded as he tapped the screen and held it out toward the copilot.

👑 👑 👑

Annwyn walked quickly toward the attendant. "Hi, I'm Annwyn."

"I know who you are, Emissary Silk. I helped to administer to your party after the bomb."

"My apologies for not remembering you."

"I was assigned to Emissary Moiran. We did not cross paths directly."

The attendant continued to open wall panels and check on various pieces of equipment, ticking and making notes on her tablet.

"I see." Annwyn drummed her fingers on her leg. She had to hurry before Damius joined her again. "I'm working with Major Elkwood."

"I know."

"Well, then, you wouldn't mind telling me if someone visited the copilot."

"No, I wouldn't."

"Well…"

The attendant looked behind her to the patient cubicle and lowered her tablet. "The Lead Emissary has been to visit several times since she awakened. He was here moments before you arrived."

"And the doctor doesn't mind?"

"I don't believe Doctor Buehl thought she was able to rebuke him."

"Thank you."

"I have said nothing."

"Of course."

Annwyn joined Damius as he walked toward the door, throwing their glasses in the contamination bin as they left.

As the door to the med center closed behind them, Damius knelt and put his forehead on Wren's. The wolf nuzzled him before Damius stood.

"He is more than a wolf, isn't he?" Annwyn realized too late the words she'd thought had been voiced.

"Wren is…" Damius glanced down at the massive grey-furred animal. "He keeps me grounded and reminds me of home."

"We all need connections to where we come from."

"Walk with me, Annwyn."

The sound of her given name spoken by him sent an unexpected heat through her body. Wren walked behind them as their hands kept gently touching.

"I do not believe the pilot is telling us everything," Damius said.

"No." Annwyn made the snap decision to tell him about the attendant. "She's had visitors."

"Who?"

"Major!" They turned to see Lieutenant Nicheo running toward them.

"Nicheo."

"There is a private communication from the planet which requires your attention."

"I'll be there shortly," Damius said.

"Major, it's from your brother."

A look passed between the two military men.

"I thought you were an only child," Annwyn said.

"We are all brothers to each other," Nicheo said to her.

"Wren, go with Annwyn to her quarters."

"I am perfectly fine on my…"

Wren moaned pitifully, while Damius took hold of her arm and turned her to face him. "Need I remind you there was a murder outside of your quarters which very well may have been aimed for you? You will allow Wren to remain with you until Cudala joins you."

The impetuous child in Annwyn wanted to explain to Damius no one told her what she could and couldn't do, but she could see the worry in his body language and eyes.

"Ok. I enjoy Wren's company."

"Protect," Damius said to Wren as he pointed toward Annwyn. "I will be by as soon as I can."

The two soldiers ran back in the direction of the station's command center. Wren licked her hand to get her attention and started to walk toward her quarters. Or at least the direction she thought her quarters were in.

⚉ ⚉ ⚉

When Damius and Nicheo reached the command center, Nicheo pulled up the incoming report on the central monitor and stepped away. Damius sat, punched in his code and read the brief note from Noden, before connecting the com link.

"Are you sure?"

"Enough so I would bet my mother on it."

Damius winced. "Your mother is dead, Noden."

"Well, if she was alive I would bet her—or at least my Aunt Rhona." Noden chuckled then continued, "Look at the information Balder gave you. I'll have more for you on the connections to the planet later. Another visit may be in order."

"Let me look over the files. Cudala and another team member are scheduled for a trip to see the Circle's Inner Sanctum, and I have to escort a murder weapon for analysis."

"I'd love to get a look in there," Noden said.

"You'd love to be surrounded by all those females."

"Well, yes, how could they resist me?"

"Cudala suggests easily given how they commune with each other."

"Ah, Bo, you are underestimating my charms."

"You keep believing that. Got to cut com. Don't want anyone poking about."

"Understand. Send word when you are on planet. And let Balder know my offer stands."

"What?" Damius asked.

"Got to go," Noden said, then closed the communication.

Damius stared at the black screen. What had Noden offered Balder? A position in his organization? Damius couldn't blame Balder if he took him up on it. Working for someone like Astole couldn't be a good situation.

As he skimmed the files, it was evident Noden was right. There was much more to this than just a bombing.

꙳ ꙳ ꙳

Annwyn immediately relaxed when she entered her quarters. Gront had done an extraordinary job at creating an atmosphere which reminded her of home. Wren jumped up on the chair with her, laying his head in her lap.

"You know, you are a bit too big for a lap wolf?"

Wren snuggled closer, so she grabbed her tablet and started to search for information on Darvia.

"Something isn't right." She absentmindedly petted Wren as her frustration increased. "Did she not exist before she became a pilot?"

The door chimed, and she dismissed the information on her tablet before she rose to answer it. When she opened the door, Damius rushed in.

"You should know who is at your door before you let them in," he scolded her.

"Wren would've let me know if it wasn't safe."

Wren raised his head, looked at them, and then lowered it.

"What have you done to him?" Damius sighed. "It doesn't matter. I'll deal with him later. I know why the ship was targeted for bombing."

"Why?"

"Someone wants to block new contact."

Chapter Ten

"What? Why?"

"We haven't figured it out yet. You're still scheduled for the Circle?" Damius asked.

"I am." Annwyn tilted her head. "Do you think the Circle is involved?" Why would they want to stop contact?

Damius shrugged one shoulder. "At this point, all we know is what I've told you."

No, it wasn't. She searched his face. Nothing. "I know Cudala mentioned some dissension within the Circle. Perhaps, there's something there that will enlighten us."

Damius frowned. "Or it could be an inner political issue."

"Or it could be connected to the bombings." She bounced on her feet and spun to pace her quarters. "It could be something significant." She faced him. "I also think the pilot is hiding something. We should question her again."

Damius nodded. "I agree. But after you return. We need to eliminate possible Circle involvement before pursuing other leads."

Annwyn frowned. "One at a time?"

"If need be. There's too many questions needing answers. With Astole breathing down our necks, I want to be very careful in this."

"Understood," she said.

He hadn't moved from his position near her door while he periodically switched attention to Wren in a way that appeared they were mentally communicating. She glanced between the two. She waited, watching both males. After a moment, Damius glanced at her. He cleared his throat and turned. He was leaving? The door swooshed open.

"Wren, come," he ordered, and the wolf followed.

They left. Her shoulders dropped while she glared at the door. Left without another word.

Blades. She shook her head and returned to her tablet.

Annwyn plucked at the light blue fabric draped over her with one intricate knot sitting on her left shoulder, leaving the other shoulder bare, with matching knots gathering the hem at her ankles.

"Why am I wearing this?" She lifted the pleated skirt to reveal a slit from ankle to thigh. She glared at Cudala. "Is this necessary?"

"Yes, it is. Many of the female visitors will be wearing similar outfits. It is the traditional outfit to indicate interest in the inner sanctum." Cudala stood beside her, and they both studied each other's reflections in the floor-to-ceiling mirror of the dressing room attached to the Silvergrass Reception square. Excited chatter seeped through the metal sliding door.

"What about your attire?" Annwyn waved at the light pink flowing knee-length pantalets covered by a long, matching jerkin, under which a snug white shirt covered her skin from neck to wrist. "You're not showing as much skin as I am. Plus, you can hide a weapon in that outfit. I cannot."

"The color of your gown accents your skin and will be immediately noticed. Most of the women will be in colors like my own. By not wearing a gown, yet in the accepted colors, I am indicating interest in seeing the Inner Sanctum only with no interest of being chosen."

Annwyn shrugged and tugged the snug waist belt, then bounced on her toes. Not even a small knife would fit comfortably. She peered at her nearly naked feet and exposed arms, then groaned. "How can I hide a weapon in this? I'll have no protection if there is a problem."

"There won't be any trouble within the Inner Sanctum...err...any physical trouble, I mean."

"Clarify," Annwyn demanded.

Cudala blew out a breath. "There will be no trouble which will require a weapon. My contact advises there have been some concerns with regards to Madame Rain's behavior of late."

Annwyn dropped her shoulders. "I see. Should we be concerned—"

A loud musical ring interrupted. What was that? She raised a brow toward Cudala.

"It is time to board the gliders," Cudala explained while quickly gathering their travel clothes. She stuffed them in a carry bag and shoved it into one of the provided locker units. After punching in the code, she tapped Annwyn's arm. "Let's go."

Together, they left the dressing room. The Reception Square had filled in their absence. Annwyn scanned the crowd and noted nearly twenty women were dressed in various pastel-colored outfits similar to hers. But none bared a shoulder. She slid a glance toward Cudala. The woman had turned away and spoke to a family of four standing nearby. Several children giggled in groups near the tall windows as a glider tube aligned itself next to the opening of the hyper-drive which matched the opening of the building. Within the tubes, long benches of silver leaf-shaped pads stretched down the center, allowing passengers to view the clear walls of the hyper-drive.

The ring hummed softly while the doors whooshed open and the tourists entered. Cudala walked by her side as they entered the glider tube and tugged her toward the end where a smaller bench sat empty facing the air tracks. A bell sounded, then the doors closed. The faint sound of strong winds pulled the glider away from the building.

"For a rather young planet, I'm surprised they've incorporated hyper-drives here."

"For now. I'm sure their technology will improve with time. Sometimes it's hard to believe Chalar joined The Directorate twenty…" Cudala pursed her lips. "Hmm, twenty-nine or so life-seasons, I believe is how it would be defined on Haevis, correct?"

Annwyn smiled. "Yes. Not long at all."

"They'll catch up."

Annwyn nodded, then gazed out toward the city, watching the buildings shrink while the glider rose higher along the drive embedded within the trunks of what appeared to be a mountain-sized tree. She blinked when darkness descended and then stiffened. Within ticks, the tube's inner lighting brightened, and she noticed they had entered a section covered with living plant vines. She smiled. So much like home. She leaned forward to study the plant life when the tube stopped.

Cudala leaned in and whispered, "We have arrived at the first stop. There are six along the way, and each will have a guide from the Circle providing information of various points of the Circle's lifestyle, food, work, city interactions, and such. At each point, some of the women may be given a card…invitation," she corrected. "When we reach the sixth stop, the women carrying the invitations are escorted to another glider and given a tour of the Inner Sanctum. The men, children, and the females without invitations tour the housing areas." She pointed to smaller, thinner tree-like buildings surrounding the Circle's main tree.

Annwyn rose as the last few tourists headed toward the exits. Cudala paused until they entered the first stopping area. The large wood floor showed signs of usage, as did the worn rails surrounding the stop. The roof consisted of woven dried leaves of a plant she'd only seen in books. She inhaled the scent of natural plants, and grinned when a soft spray from a nearby waterfall danced along her skin.

When they boarded the glider to the sixth stop, Annwyn shifted closer to Cudala. "So, after this next place, we'll be taken into the Inner Sanctum?"

"I haven't received my invitation yet. Likely, Tercora will have it delivered during the last stop," Cudala said.

"I've noted two colors of the invitations. Do you know what it means?"

Cudala nodded. "One is the general invitation to tour the Inner Sanctum sanctuary areas, such as the learning centers. They'll receive more in-depth information on expectations for those chosen."

"So, the choosing doesn't happen right away?" It differed from what she'd read during her research. She frowned. If she couldn't get closer to Madame Raine, then how could she discover how, or if, the Circle was involved in the bombings? Annwyn tapped her fingertips together. There had to be a way.

"The pastel invitations indicate the Sanctuary tour and the possibility of being chosen. The white invitations indicate those who are chosen immediately."

Annwyn gasped and forced her hands not to clench tightly on the white card she was handed when they entered the glider. Her body stiffened and froze. *Chosen*.

The abundance of floral activity exploded around them. Scents permeated the glider and called to her. Her heart swelled while her mind swirled with memories of home. She jerked her head and pushed away the images.

This is not home. This is a mission and nothing else. She squeezed her lids closed, conjured Damius's face to mind, and focused on his eyes. Her muscles eased their tightness, and she rolled her shoulders to loosen them more.

"How can a woman consent to being chosen without even knowing the training and lifestyle? I mean, why don't all the women go through the Sanctuary first?"

"Because it is an honor to be chosen immediately without having to go through the screening process. Those who go there must show their commitment. It is not uncommon for a woman to go the general route several times. It is one of the ways a Chalar female can request entrance into the Circle."

"And the rest, like me, are expected to make a decision immediately?"

Cudala nodded.

Blades.

The bell rang while the doors whooshed open. Several guides appeared in this last stop. One approached Cudala and slipped her an envelope. They gathered the tourists into the center, and one female guide turned, faced the group, and spoke in a loud voice.

"This stop is the separation point. Those without invitations need to follow the path to my left to complete your tour of the housing sections of the Circle." She paused while all the men, children, elderly, and a handful of women shifted and headed in the direction she pointed.

How would they know who had invitations? Annwyn searched the remaining women and found they all held their invitations in front of them. Of course, it was an honor, so why would they not wish for their invitations to be visible? A guide wearing a bright multicolored robe approached her and Cudala.

"If you will both follow me, please," she said in a soft, singsong voice.

Annwyn nodded and slid a glance toward Cudala, who winked in response. One guide per two women moved down the path to the right. The ground cover along the path exuded fresh plant aromas as they walked.

When a few women began whispering, Annwyn turned toward Cudala. "Where are they taking us?"

"To the Circle Ceremonial Plateau," she pointed up. "We'll tour the surrounding gardens, then they divide the group. The general invitees will go do their thing in the Sanctuary, while the chosen ones will be taken to the top where the Ceremonial Plateau is located. That is where the senior Circle members meet daily for meditations, ceremonies and the like. We may be allowed to watch or participate in a ceremony...maybe."

Ceremony? Interesting.

The group continued until the dirt path turned to multi-hued stepping stones. Annwyn blinked as the colors appeared to swirl when she placed her foot on each stone. Fascinating. She lifted her head, preparing to ask Cudala, when the group stopped near an arbor of braided wood.

"Your guide will take you among the gardens here at our sacred plateau. Please remain with your guides."

Annwyn and Cudala followed their guide past others to the farthest point of the plateau, around large stone towers aligned into a circle. Annwyn peered between the stones, but long braided vines blocked her view into what had to be the ceremonial circle.

As they reached a patch of various blooms, Annwyn leaned in and inhaled. "They are marvelous."

"Thank you. Please do not inhale these." The guide waved an arm over a smaller grouping of plants, which appeared to be burnt near their roots and contained a white crystalized substance on their leaves. "This is the same plant, however we have not—"

"Rawanna, you are needed within the sanctum. Sister Neela has injured herself," a voice behind them whispered.

Our guide, Rawanna, nodded then left.

Cudala grinned and spun around. "Tercora. Glad you could make it." Cudala hugged her friend. "I was getting a little worried here." She handed Tercora her pastel-colored invitation. "Can you get it changed for me?"

Tercora shifted her attention toward Annwyn and lifted her hand." I am Tercora. Secondary of the Silvergrass Circle."

Annwyn raised her hand, and Tercora pressed her fingertips on Annwyn's wrist. Cudala's friend was taller than her but just as slight in figure. Tercora smoothed her long silver hair behind her ear and pointed toward the card in Annwyn's hand.

"I see you have been chosen." She turned toward Cudala." I have no other invitations."

"I'd hoped to at least get invited into the Sanctum. She cannot go in alone."

Tercora frowned. "She will not be alone. Have you forgotten my position already?"

Cudala's face darkened. "No. I'm sorry."

"I'm teasing you, my friend." She laughed softly. "She will be safe with me. I promise."

Three rings of bells sounded.

"Cudala, you must go to the Sanctuary. I will ensure Annwyn's safety and have her join you at the Reception center as soon as possible."

Cudala nodded. "I trust you. But you must be careful as well."

The bells sounded again, and Cudala strode toward the braided wood arbor they'd entered earlier.

Annwyn raised a brow.

"The chosen are to have an audience with the High Priestess. There will be no ceremony, only a visit." Tercora scanned the area and lowered her voice. "Of late, Madame Raine has displayed a very aggressive personality and undesirable behavior. She has made some poor decisions in which the Circle coven representatives are investigating. There is a possibility of her being replaced."

Annwyn swallowed. "By you?"

Tercora nodded, then began walking. "Follow me, please. I will place you with my trusted guide and see you at the Circle center. No harm will come to you while with her."

"Understood." Cudala had said no weapons. But what could happen? She followed the guide

Tercora assigned to her and watch the Secondary stride away. Annwyn studied her confident walk. It made her appear to float along the ground, rather than touch it.

The Secondary reached one of the tall stone pillars and proceeded to walk through the stone. When she and her new guide reached the stone, the other woman tipped her head to the side.

"You must trust the way."

Annwyn shrugged. Why not? "I must," she said, then moved forward.

Please let me pass. A coldness washed over her, and she shuddered before opening her eyes wide to the large circle of twenty-six white, sparkling stones engraved with symbols. In front of each sat a woman dressed in pale-colored robes. Between every third stone sat a grey stone with similar markings.

Another guide was waiting and turned and smiled at her. "You trusted the way. Take a seat on any grey stone."

Annwyn moved toward the closest stone, only to be stopped when another woman sat first. She turned and went around the circle. Before she could reach another grey stone, her guide grabbed her hand and led her to an empty one near the farthest end of the circle. Annwyn sat and studied the area. Foliage of various species surrounded and crawled upon the large stone pillars. Some appeared to move into a twisted braid and draped along the tops.

In the center of the circle stood a small platform and a large round wooden table with various instruments, candles, and plant clippings strewn about its surface. Tall silver chalices burned with bright flames lighting the area so brightly, no shadows existed. Within ticks, the women on the white stones began humming, and small torches surrounding the plateau lit, bringing in additional light.

Annwyn blinked at the brightness. Suddenly, the humming stopped and the torches and chalice flames dimmed when an older, slim woman with long silver-and-black-streaked hair entered the circle. She stepped once, then paused, then stepped again. Her body swayed, and her hand pressed against her temple. She shook her head and continued until she reached the center and grasped the table.

Her knuckles whitened as she seemed to stare at the women around her. She blinked, then her lips lifted in a small smile. She raised her hand and waved above her head once, then dropped her arm to grab the table again.

Annwyn peered at the women sitting among the Inner Circle. Their faces appeared pinched and some frowned. One closed her eyes and dropped her head.

Tercora joined the woman at the table and laid a hand on the older woman's back.

"Welcome to our Circle. Those of you here, have been chosen to join us." Madame Raine clapped her hands, and several younger women came forward carrying trays of drinks and fruits.

"I am Madame Raine, High Priestess of Silvergrass Circle," the older woman called out." You are the chosen ones. Join us and we will be your new family where…"

Tercora leaned in and whispered. Annwyn could not catch what she was saying. She shifted on her stone and noticed a redness covering the forearms of the priestess.

Madame Raine collapsed onto the ground. Everyone gasped. Several of the inner circle women rushed to help lift the woman and carry her away.

Tercora stood in front of the circle guests, "My deepest apologies, chosen ones. Madame Raine has taken ill. Our most trained healers will take care of her. Do not despair. Please, we must end our visit. You will be escorted to the Reception room if you wish to refuse our choosing. If you agree, you will be taken to your new living quarters."

The remaining inner circle women gathered the chosen together. Annwyn frowned, but joined the group preparing to leave.

"I know your answer already, Annwyn. I wish to discuss this with you a moment," Tercora said and waved away the guide who approached them. She lowered her voice. "Here take this." She handed over a dime bar." It is evidence which proves the pilot in the hospital is not the innocent one."

"What?" Annwyn gripped the item.

"The one who lived is responsible for the explosion," she said before spinning around and walking away.

Annwyn stepped to follow her when a frowning guide grabbed her arm.

"That is the wrong way. It is time to leave. Follow the others." She pointed toward the chosen group.

⚘ ⚘ ⚘

Annwyn arrived at the Reception square still holding the dime bar and gritting her teeth. As soon as she announced she would not accept being chosen, she was shipped off to a small tube glider and whisked back to where Cudala awaited her. Not one of the three visitors in the cramped space spoke a word until the tube stopped and they all rushed out of the doors.

Annwyn updated her companion on everything that happened. Cudala stared wide-eyed and open-mouthed.

"Please, gather your items from the dressing room. The Sanctuary is closing immediately. The last glider will leave in three minutes," one of the female Sanctuary guards informed them.

Cudala grabbed her arm and pulled her toward their locker. "We'll have to change clothes on base. Do you know what that means?"

"Raine is ill?"

"No, not that. Listen, only the High Priestess can speak with guests present." She frowned. "If Tercora spoke, then she has made claim to the position. Madame Raine may no longer be in charge."

"That's a good thing, don't you agree?"

"I can't agree. If she's no longer in charge, or if she's gotten ill, then we'll never know for certain if she is involved in the bombings."

"Does it matter if she's involved, if we can't do anything about it? I mean, how much authority does Penduli Force have?"

"We have more authority than you know, so it does matter. Well...not as much as what's on that dime bar."

Annwyn glanced at the small alloy unit in her palm. *What all is on this little device?*

Chapter Eleven

Damius slapped his palm against the call button.

She was to report to me as soon as she docked.

He counted to three while his foot tapped against the floor. No. Damius entered his override code to open the door.

"You were to report to me…"

Damius stopped and the door closed behind him and Wren. His eyes traveled down Annwyn's body. The green sarong made her skin glow.

"What are you doing in here?" she asked.

Wren butted his head against Damius's leg then turned and lay in front of the door.

"You didn't report."

"I thought it would be inappropriate to report wearing this." Annwyn's arms fanned down her body.

"Oh." Damius started to fidget, looked back at Annwyn. "It looks good on you."

Wren made a groaning sound behind him.

Great. Even my wolf thinks I sound like an idiot.

"There is no place to hide a weapon. Too much skin shows. I mean, why must I have one bare shoulder and slit cut up to..."

Damius closed the distance between them in two strides. He slid one hand slowly down her bare shoulder, closed his eyes, and inhaled her scent. She smelled like the fields at home during the first growth of spring. Heat radiated from her body as his other hand wrapped around the back of her neck, tilting her head. His nose skimmed down her cheek. His lips hovered above hers.

"For Larunda's sake, kiss me."

"As you wish," Damius whispered. He wrapped his hand in her hair and tugged while his mouth descended on hers.

He stroked his fingers up her arm, causing her to shiver, and opened himself to her emotions. They washed over him like a spring shower. The sensations were overwhelming, and his grip on his own emotions slipped as he untied the knot holding her sarong in place.

He broke the kiss, pushing his body away from hers. She radiated confidence and control, one of which he was decidedly lacking.

"I shouldn't…"

"Stop. It's time we got this out of our systems and stop ignoring it. And this has to go." She reached and tried pulling his shirt apart. "Damn…indestructible…"

Damius smirked as he covered her hands with his and pulled, his shirt ripping easily down the middle.

"I can stop imagining what you look like now."

"Me as well," Damius said as he cupped her breast through the silky fabric. "This is not a good idea."

"It's a very good idea." As her gaze traveled downward, his skin heated. "Major Elkwood, are you embarrassed?" Her fingers slipped inside the band of his pants, teasing him.

"I want you."

"I deduced as much."

"Naiba," he growled pulling her body against his own and kissing her. Her sarong fell to the floor as he picked her up and headed toward the open door to her bedroom.

Damius tossed her on the bed and shrugged off the tattered remains of his shirt. He knew he was at the point of no return. Sex wasn't just an act for him. It was a joining of emotions that rolled through his body. In the past, he chose his partners carefully, but none of them invoked the primal feelings Annwyn did inside of him. Once he started making love to her, there would be no stopping.

He inhaled a long breath, waiting until she looked at him. Like a wolf stalking its prey, he placed one knee on the bed between her legs and crawled up her body, his tongue tracing a fine line between her breasts. He gently licked her neck, then nibbled on her earlobe, her body arching off the bed.

"Yes," she whispered.

He hovered above her mouth, his hardness pressing against her leg.

Ring.

The shrill sound of the door chime filled the air. Wren jumped on the bed, licking his face, then Annwyn's.

❦ ❦ ❦

"Annwyn, it's Cudala. Let's go! The major is going to be pissed we didn't go see him first," she called through the portal.

Damius rose and growled at Wren. "Thanks for having my back." He grabbed his destroyed shirt off the floor. "Where can I hide?"

Annwyn jumped off the bed. "Blades." She grabbed his arm, turning him to face her. "This is not over."

"Absolutely."

Annwyn hit the panel on the wall behind him and pushed him in the closet, then grabbed one of her jumpsuits. "Wren." She pointed toward the closet, and the wolf joined Damius.

The chime sounded again as she closed the closet door and strode toward the portal to her quarters.

"Hey, sorry. I was in the bio," Annwyn said as she opened the door for Cudala. "Give me a tick."

Cudala reached and picked up the discarded sarong.

"I see you couldn't wait to get out of this."

"Could you?"

Cudala laughed." Not fast enough."

Annwyn grabbed her tablet and returned to the portal.

"Got the dime bar?" Cudala asked.

"It would help, wouldn't it?" Annwyn headed back to the bedroom to grab it. She glanced at the closed closet doors. *Guess he'll have to figure his own way out of the closet.*

ᴪ ᴪ ᴪ

Annwyn inserted the dime bar into the computer as Damius and Wren walked into the meeting area. "We've been waiting on you."

Wren joined her at the computer bay, but Damius stopped, his hands on his hips. "I went looking for you when you did not immediately report."

"Do you always go looking for your crew?"

Cudala snickered next to her.

Damius sighed and walked toward her." Just bring up the files."

"Yes, Major."

"Open that one." Cudala pointed to a file on the screen labeled with her name.

My Cudala,

If you are reading this, I have deemed it necessary to take control of the Circle. Madame Raine has been growing sicker and more irrational, and I fear I may have to take charge before she harms the Sanctuary's reputation. It is my duty as Second.

I found the bombing reports in Madame Raine's papers. She had not shared them with the inner counsel, so I went on a bit of a scavenger hunt after you left.

There was a name among the injured which I recognized, and I fear it is the reason Raine hid the report from me. Darvia, the copilot, was once part of the Circle Sanctuary and my lover. She is not to be trusted. Over the course of three cycles, she managed to turn sister against sister. When I realized the extent of her malevolence, I spoke to Raine, and she counseled her to leave.

Darvia left us a cycle ago, but Raine has remained in contact with her. I have attempted to find the correspondence, but it is not on her drive. I've copied what I could find and will attempt to get into her private chamber.

Know this: She is a liar. Our entire relationship was built on lies. The life she told us about before the Sanctuary was lies as well. Do not believe anything she says.

I shall treasure our time together until such time I can enjoy your fruits again.

Until again...

"When I told you to get close to members of the Circle, this was not exactly what I had in mind," Damius said.

"Don't for a moment think I slept with her for you or the investigation." Cudala went to stand toe-to-toe with Damius. "I was with her for myself."

"Good. Otherwise you would be looking for a new troop."

Cudala's shoulders visibly dropped, and the tension of the moment fled. "Thank you."

"Next time you are up for leave, let me know the timing, and if you desire, we'll get you back here to see her."

Annwyn smiled to herself. Damius was a romantic. Not surprising.

"There's much more on here. It's going to take some time to go through," Cudala said.

"I'll leave it to the two of you. My ship departs in the hour for the planet to get the knife analyzed. Hopefully, this will get Gront cleared. I'll check in when I return this afternoon." Damius walked toward the door. "Cudala?"

"Yes, Major?"

"I would consider that letter personal correspondence. It doesn't need to go into the final docs. Let me know what you find. I want to be prepared when we interview her again."

And before Annwyn could rein in her surprise, he was gone.

☙ ☙ ☙

Annwyn arched her back. "How long have we been at this?"

"Too long," Cudala replied standing up next to her. "I have got to stretch my muscles. You want some lunch?"

"Can you bring me back one of their lunch sets? I need to go back to my chambers and check on something."

"You should take one of the guards with you. Major won't like you off without protection," Cudala said.

"I can take care of myself."

"I'm going to remind you a trained guard was killed outside your quarters."

She'd almost forgotten about Gront. How could she have let herself get caught up in digging through files? She paused. Perhaps she should go see him.

"Stop right there. You don't need to go near Gront without the major either. Why don't I walk with you to your quarters?" Cudala offered.

"Okay, but I can make my way back. I may need to get something from the lab." Annwyn bounced while her fingers tapped out a rhythm on her leg. Raine's illness, a saboteur in the ranks of the sanctuary—more pieces for the puzzle. Soon, she'd connect all of it. *Perfect.*

After their trip, Annwyn returned to her quarters and scanned the area. He wouldn't keep it out here. She entered Gront's private room and paused, biting her lip. No, he wouldn't mind if her intrusion helped the investigation. She sighed and began searching.

"Where did Gront put it?" Annwyn asked no one. She opened the second of Gront's trunks and picked up another bound book to scan. Gront carried original source material with them when they traveled. It drove the side of her who liked traveling light crazy, but now she was thankful for his quirk.

Damius should be able to free him once he got the bio trace results back. The puzzle of who killed Security Officer Cress intrigued her. Who would stand to gain by killing Cress? Or was she the target and Cress got in the way?

"Finally!"

The *Ancient Metals* book was heavy in her hand. Maybe it had a clue to trigger her memory. There was something about Madame

Raine's symptoms which bothered her. It was all connected if she could put the pieces together.

She grabbed a messenger bag and slipped the book inside, along with a packet of tea from her home world.

She paused, standing in front of the door.

What if someone is trying to kill me?

She knew too well she wasn't the center of the universe from her father's favoritism of her brothers, but could she be the target?

No, I'm not important enough. But why was Cress killed? Was she simply in the way?

Annwyn marched back into her bedroom to find her ritual scythe she'd brought with her. At the harvest, she and her mother used to cut the moonlight herbs together. How many cycles had it been since she had basked in her mother's presence?

Too much death.

Annwyn stashed the scythe in her messenger bag. She would use it for more than harvesting if needed.

⚘ ⚘ ⚘

Damius stretched his arms over his head and cracked his neck from side to side. Airbuses weren't built for his height. Wren moved his head to lay it on top of Damius's foot.

"Yeah, I know, buddy. Maybe we can go for a run planet-side before we head back."

Wren whimpered and shifted again.

Damius needed to be in the real outdoors. A run would give him an opportunity to meet with Noden. He'd mention it to Balder before the testing.

The airbus docked on the landing bay with a jerk. The other passengers rushed to the doors in some semblance of order. Damius waited until the stampede settled down before he joined Balder at the door.

"See if Noden is available for a run after we finish this. I need to stretch my legs," Damius said as he slung the travel pack on his shoulder.

Wren stuck close to his side, neither of them enjoying the chaos of the docking station.

"Will do." Balder secured the container with the evidence onto the transportation pod and pushed it forward toward an individual wearing a white coat.

"Lt. Balder, I presume?" the white coat said, keeping his hands on his clipboard while bowing in greeting.

Balder returned the bow and said, "Affirmative. Are you Dr. Lovett?"

"Yes. No time to waste. We have been very busy the last few weeks, and I have you slotted for this rising." Dr. Lovett attached a device to the handrail of the transport pod, and it started to follow him as he walked. "I don't understand why they could not do the analysis on the space station. This is a waste of my resources and time." Lovett stopped, and pointed toward Damius and Wren. "And I do not need supervision. Your *dog* is not allowed in the lab. Filthy creatures."

The image of Wren relieving himself on Lovett's leg popped into his mind.

NO! Absolutely not! He communicated with Wren, who huffed, causing Lovett to turn around and look again at the pair.

"To be clear, since apparently you are not educated on animal species, Wren here is a wolf, not a dog. They are related, but Wren is a wolf tamed from the wilds of my country to be my companion and to serve the Larunda Directorate. He is an officer of Larunda Force as much as I am and will be treated as such."

"My lab is a Chalar lab, and as such, your wolf will need to wait outside. The Directorate and their enforcers rule between planets, not on them. And if you don't cooperate, you both can wait outside. My lab, Chalar rules, and we do not trust outsiders nor their wolves."

"Dr. Lovett. I am a Chalaran. I can vouch for Major Elkwood and Officer Wren. I'm sure he will consent to Officer Wren enjoying some well-deserved R&R in the park next to your lab. Agreed?" Balder interjected.

Damius nodded.

When they arrived at the lab, Damius pointed Wren to the park, and he took off running.

Don't go too far. I'll join you when this is over.

"This is our sterile area where we test. Both of you can watch from the observation room in there." Lovett pointed toward a glassed-in area with nothing more than a bench, a monitor, and a communicator. "This will hopefully not take long. I have more important work to do."

"Dr. Lovett. That weapon was used to kill a Security Officer who was from Chalar," Balder said.

Lovett turned, his mouth agape and his face ashen. "I had no idea it was one of our own." He looked down at the box. "I shall be extra thorough."

Damius waited until the door to the observation area closed. "Cress was from Orias."

"She is? I guess I misunderstood." Balder grinned. "I'm going to make the arrangements for your run. Lovett may be a planetist, but he is the best."

"Understood. Thanks," Damius said.

Dr. Lovett burst through the doors. "I do not understand these results." He shook his head." There were no bio markers at all. You have wasted my time and the time of my lab when obviously this is not a weapon used to kill one of our own." Lovett slammed the evidence box down. "Are you trying to cover up the murder of a Chalaran? I will not allow this."

"W-what?" Damius stammered.

"Take your sham and get out of my lab. I will be reporting you!"

Lovett turned, leaving a stunned Damius and Balder in his wake.

⚘ ⚘ ⚘

The thick purple and green leaves felt good grazing his skin. Wren ran beside him. Damius could feel his contentment. They turned back toward the path and crossed the bridge to the sandy clearing. The meeting point was just up ahead, far enough outside the main city but close enough for a plausible run. He saw the slight movement in the overgrowth and headed toward it.

"You go cycles without a word, and now I can't seem to shake you, Bo," Noden said from within the foliage.

Damius laughed, bending over with his hands on his knees, his breathing labored. He opened his liquid tube and pulled a collapsible bowl out of his pack. "Here, Wren, drink."

Damius rose and waved Noden out. "We need to know how connected the Sanctuary is to the underworld here."

"Demanding as always." Noden stepped from his hiding spot.

"You know it. And see what you have on the security force on Penduli Station."

"That's why I sent you the message, Bo. I'm still checking into it, but I wanted to warn you to keep an eye on Astole. He's hiding something. I'll find out what, if I can," Noden said.

"When this is done, your debt to me is cleared." He clasped Noden's hand and shook it then placed Wren's dish back in his pack.

"Try again. I don't think my debt to you will ever be clear. You saved my life, Bo."

"And you're helping me save more here," Damius said.

"We'll see about that. Remember to watch your back on station."

"He can't hurt me."

"Perhaps not, but what about your team?" Noden asked.

Damius's stomach burned.

Chapter Twelve

Cudala glanced through the small portal window into the solarico. "Why would anyone want to spend time in there? It's hot, humid, and smells funny."

Annwyn grinned." My home planet is often hot, humid, and smells funny, depending on which season we're in."

"Enjoying a cool drink is more my style for relaxation."

"I'm not surprised. Enjoy your time." Annwyn turned and entered the space holding thousands of assorted flora species from her home planet. The scents of home along with those she didn't recognize reached her. Immediately, her body relaxed while she strolled along the soft-cushioned pathway which would take her toward the farthest corner and the designated area for Haevis and her favorite flora.

After entering, she located a bench created of twisting wood which shifted when she sat and closed her eyes, allowing the quiet hum of the aromatic plant life to surround and permeate her skin. So much like home. Damp air wet her throat. She filled her lungs and emptied her mind of everything except this place, right now. The bench snugged against her body as though fitting itself to her form, and the corners of her mouth lifted. This was a mirror of Haevis, and her heart swelled with memories of her home planet and the times she'd spent with her mother.

A short breath escaped her lips as the image of her family came to mind. Lifting out the small handheld scythe, she fingered the cover and slipped it into her waistband. Soon, she'd continue the ritual her mother had taught her. But not now. Now, she had to put the pieces of this puzzle together.

Damius's face floated in her memory. The taste of his mouth sent warm heat through her while her heartbeat quickened. Soon…soon, the memory would hold more than a sample to sift through.

She tugged out the large book she'd confiscated from Gront's quarters and flipped through the pages. There it is. The words confirmed her suspicions on the type of compound used in the bombs. She'd been spot on.

This investigation had become quite a deep deception by dubious players. Determined to deduce the culprits and uncover their connections, Annwyn replaced the book in her bag and leaned back. One by one, each person involved so far came to mind, and she manipulated them on an imaginary plot map like the ones used on Haevis.

She groaned. The map held many people and several overlapping lines. She straightened and stood, bouncing on her feet, and then paced, tapping her fingers together. The stakes were high here. To win gave more than boasting rights; it saved lives. So much more important than anything on Haevis.

She stopped and stood frozen. *This is what I'm destined to do. But I can't do this alone.* Her shoulders relaxed, her heartbeat slowed, and she sat on the live wood bench again.

What about this puzzle? There were too many variables to consider. Damius had gifts unknown to her and training and connections. Those connections had moved their investigation farther. *Blades.* All this time, working alone had hampered things. No more.

Damius called to her soul like no other male. Would he consider being her partner? Their strong physical attraction worked in her favor. Would it be enough, now? Would he consider something more? She was certain Wren would approve.

She chuckled. Physical satisfaction first and foremost. The rest... Well, she could work on it. After this investigation, she'd approach him with something more...ongoing.

Her shoulders dropped. What if the physical attraction was all he felt? What if he didn't want more? She frowned and returned to pacing.

Would it be enough? *Could* it be enough? She shook her head. *Stop it. Blades. Quit the questions.*

She checked the time and knelt before the bench, singing an ancient Hunee melody, then rose and continued the harvest hymn as she clipped moonlight herbs. Images of her mother along with other females of their city danced in her mind while she worked.

❦ ❦ ❦

"I have the report here. Whether Major Astole is available or not, is not my concern. Refusing to release an innocent from lock-up is against interplanetary agreements and is punishable by station lock-outs. I suggest you reconsider your position, Sergeant," Damius spat.

Wren pressed against his legs, drawing away some of the fury fighting to spew from Damius. The sergeant behind the desk jerked a nod and punched his com button, again requesting a response from the major in charge of security.

Damius blew out a breath and raised a brow toward the partition keeping him from grabbing the sergeant by his uniform. He forced his clenched hands to open and shifted his shoulders. No one refused him, and this would not be the first time.

He pulled out his own com, turned, and whispered, "Mirbeck, join me in lockdown, now."

He advanced through the main access door and punched in his own code, which overrode all security codes. Once the beep indicated clearance, the doors whooshed open, and he strode toward the cells where Gront was held. After locating him, he punched in the code to release him. Nothing happened. Damius frowned and hit the buttons again. No buzz, no beep, nothing.

Gront rose from the small bench and stood near the portal.

"My code isn't working. I'll get this figured out."

Gront nodded and returned to the bench. Damius growled and stormed back toward the sergeant's desk. It was empty. Naiba. What was going on here? No one should have a code that overrode his own.

"No matter your security clearance, you are not authorized beyond this point," Astole snapped from outside lockdown.

Mirbeck strode up behind him and lifted a brow.

Damius exited and stood within inches of Astole. "No one has authorization to override my security clearance. Not even you."

"Yet, I did." Astole lifted one side of his mouth. "Gront is my prisoner until my investigation is complete."

"I submitted the results of the bioscan. No fingerprints were found on the weapon. Which means Gront is innocent of charges. You cannot—"

"I can, and I will. The results do not exonerate him. It only confirms he must have worn gloves." Astole strode behind the security desk.

"You were there immediately afterwards, and you're stating he had time to clean up, remove bio-stained gloves, and wait in the room until someone noticed a dead body in the hall?"

Astole shrugged. "It's a possibility."

How did he get authority to override codes? Damius clenched his jaw and clamped his lips together when Wren butted his leg.

"It's a biased possibility." He spun around, jerked his chin toward Mirbeck, and together they walked away.

"Find out how he overrode my codes. No one has such authority on a local level. No bio-prints were found on the knife. And get all the information you can on Astole. He's too focused on Gront, and I don't like it...or him."

"Done," Mirbeck responded and turned at the next corner.

Damius headed toward his quarters. Wren grunted.

"I know. But you should have let me at least hit him. I'd have felt better."

Wren growled.

"I still would have felt better." Damius took the last turn toward his quarters and stopped.

Annwyn paced before his door, head bowed. His pulse sped up. Had she come to finish what they'd started? She stopped and jerked her head up, then stood there staring at him. Nope. He sighed and strode toward her.

"What is it?"

The glittering in her eyes told him she'd discovered something, and it had nothing to do with removing clothing.

Naiba.

༻ ༻ ༻

"Ah, good, you're back," Annwyn said. "I need to talk to you." His dark scowl made her hesitate. "Is this a good time?" She glanced at Wren who moved from Damius's side and nudged her leg. She reached down and stroked his head. At least Wren was happy to see her.

"Now is fine." He punched in the code, and the door swooshed open. He stepped back and waved her to precede him.

She nodded and entered. Such starkness. She should have requested he come to her quarters instead. At least there, the atmosphere welcomed relaxation. Then again, it was not the time to relax. Not after what she put together during her mediation. After the doors closed, she turned and faced him.

"I've found some information which eluded me before. I've put together the pieces, and we need to consider the consequences of what I've discovered."

"Consequences?" he said. "Of course we do. Do you wish for something to drink?"

Her eyes widened. This wasn't a social call. Yet, she nodded. "Thank you." Her heartbeat increased its pace, and she strolled over to the dining area and sat. When he joined her, she took a small sip of the cool liquid, then sat back and cleared her throat.

"When Cudala and I visited the inner sanctum, I noticed in the private gardens some flora which had turned color. The guide informed us it was dying, but the cause was unknown. It seemed familiar to me, but I did not make the connection right away. Later, when Raine had her...err...moment, we were rushed out of there so fast, I didn't have time to evaluate everything."

"I see. And now that you have?" Damius asked.

Annwyn leaned forward. "I believe Madame Raine has succumbed to mercury poisoning."

"What? How?"

"That's the part I'm not sure about. Her behavior is indicative of prolonged contact with mercury. She has to have handled it without protection." Damius opened his mouth, but she held up her hand. "Please, let me finish. Mercury poisoning causes confusion, among other ailments. It is deadly. Based on her condition, she doesn't have long. If we're to determine her connection with the bombings, we need to speak with her, or whomever is her contact with the bombings. Don't you agree?"

"I do. However, with someone so powerful, it won't be easy."

"Were you able to get Gront released?"

Damius frowned. "No."

"Why not?"

Damius explained what occurred in lock-up. "It doesn't make sense he'd easily get authority to override my own codes."

"Perhaps he didn't get authority?"

Damius stared at her. "I'm looking into it right now."

Annwyn laid her hand on his arm, pushing away the heat that called to her body. "You know of the competitions constantly held on my planet."

"I do."

"You also know, as the king's daughter, I was not...am not ever allowed to participate."

"I am aware of that."

"I was raised as though I would be. Which means I have the skills to piece together information rapidly and manipulate the situation to obtain the outcome needed to win."

Damius stood. "I've told you before, this is not a game."

Annwyn rose. "I know it's not a game. It is a puzzle, correct? A case to solve is obtaining pieces of a puzzle and placing them together, is it not?"

"True."

"And that is what I'm good at. It's where I excel. I cannot—no, will not—ever return home." She began pacing. How to explain? "I thought contact would be my calling. I've searched inside myself and discovered it's not something which would fulfill me completely." She sucked in a small breath. *Here goes.* "I want to be a full-time investigator. I want to figure out puzzles like you. I know I can be an asset to your team, if they would only trust me. If I could learn to trust them."

"Wait a tick. Do you trust me, Annwyn?" he asked, grasping her hand to keep her from pacing away.

She paused. "I do."

"Then you can trust my team. We've been together in worse situations than this. Our lives have depended on each other for too long not to have trust in one another."

"But would they extend such trust to me?"

"They will if they see it coming from me," he said.

She studied his face. He meant every word he'd said. "Trust goes both ways, Damius."

"I'm aware of that."

"You cannot fake trust. I have trusted you with my life, and now with the realization of what my heart and mind call me to do." She stepped closer toward him. "What have you trusted me with?"

Chapter Thirteen

Damius chewed on his lower lip. He looked down to Wren for support, but his companion turned his back and went to his bed.

Thanks, could've used some backup here, buddy.

Wren growled low in response.

He caught Annwyn's glance over to the grey fur mountain that kept him sane.

Wren. That was a secret he could share.

"Wren isn't simply a military animal."

"He is smart and very well trained. And you said before he keeps you grounded."

Damius shook his head as Wren turned and walked proudly over to sit in front of Annwyn.

"He is also an attention whore," Damius grumbled.

Wren rested his head on Annwyn's knee, staring up at her.

"Well, at least he is with you. Do you have treats hidden somewhere? I'm asking because he never has liked someone as much as he does you."

"He is so sweet. I'm sure all your lady friends have liked him," Annwyn said quietly.

Lady friends. Where did that come from?

"No lady friends. Usually he has to get to know someone before he would behave this way."

"You were saying he is more than a military animal."

"Yes." Damius downed his drink, wishing it could fortify him for what he was about to share. No one on his team knew this about Wren. He assumed most of them had figured out they had a connection, but not to what extent. Damius needed Wren to function; without him, he wouldn't be able to keep his emotions in check.

Without him, Astole would be lying on the ground, still trying to recover.

Damius rose and started pacing. He could feel her energy. It was a frantic buzz of a bee around a field of flowers, flitting from one to the next. It was infectious, and he had to fight getting lost in it. It was the polar opposite of his steady small ebbs and flows.

"Wren and I are connected," he blurted out. "He helps to ground me in the moment and focus, which is common with animals and members of my tribe, but we can also communicate telepathically." There. He had said it.

Annwyn stopped stroking the top of Wren's head. Tick after tick, the silence stretched. Did she think he was crazy? That what he'd revealed were lies?

"Telepathically?" she finally asked.

"Yes. We can communicate."

Annwyn grabbed her tablet and furiously typed on it, her fingers flying across the screen so fast he could barely discern what they were doing.

"Here. Tell him this."

Damius looked down at a set of instructions typed on the screen. "You're testing us?"

"Of course. You're from the nomadic tribe of Krizlar. Your people do not have telepathic abilities, not even the tribal shaman leaders. So why would you?"

"I would if my mother was a non-nomad," he spat, the words tumbling off his tongue before he could stop them. He looked down at the tablet one more time, then to Wren.

She's testing us. Go to the bedroom.

Wren licked Annwyn's hand then trotted off to the bedroom.

Bring back a headrest from the bed.

Wren came running back into the common room with the corner of a headrest in his mouth.

Drop it at my feet.

Wren turned away from Annwyn and dropped the headrest in front of Damius.

Jump into my arms.

If Wren had been a humanoid, Damius was sure he would've rolled his eyes at his last request. Instead, he paused, cocked his head as if to say really?, and then jumped.

Damius caught him and was soon engulfed in wolf kisses.

"You can communicate with him."

"Didn't I say that? Why couldn't you trust me instead of testing me?"

"I...I..."

Damius let Wren back down. "You either trust and believe me or you don't. It isn't an 'I trust you until I don't believe you' deal. Most people do not know about my mother. My tribe has a special connection to the animals of our planet, but my mother's lineage gave me the power to connect on an even deeper level." Damius settled on the floor, Wren curling up in his lap.

"I found Wren as a pup, deserted by his mother. He was in poor health, and his paw was hurt badly. We've been together since he was moons old. I raised him. We take care of each other. So, no matter how much he cuddles up to you, he will always be my companion."

Wren looked directly at Annwyn, but then lowered his head into Damius's lap, indicating where his loyalties lay.

The com bell went off in Damius's room, making Annwyn jump.

She didn't mean to upset Damius by giving him a test to prove his telepathic abilities. Wasn't that what a scientist does when confronted with information which differed from the norm? Somehow, Annwyn did not think Damius felt the same way. Her whole life, everything was a game. Her parents played against each other. Testing, teasing, stabbing into each other with words and riddles. She had lived in her head since she understood her breath, always asking questions, always taught to doubt until there was proof. There was no room for faith or belief.

"Major Elkwood."

"Go ahead, Nicheo."

"You are needed in the command center. Mirbeck has some information for you, and we have a visitor from the Sanctuary."

"Very good. On my way. Elkwood…"

"Sir, if you can find Emissary Silk, she is needed as well."

"Will do. Elkwood out."

Annwyn admired the way Damius rose off the floor in a fluid motion, his muscles tensing beneath his tight shirt.

"I'm sorry if I insulted you about Wren."

"It's nothing," he said, walking toward the door. "We need to be going, Emissary. They are waiting on us."

He extended his arm through the open door of his quarters, and Annwyn walked out ahead of him. The coldness in his voice wasn't missed, especially by someone like herself who lived in her head most of the time. When would she learn everything wasn't a game outside of her planet?

They walked in silence until they reached the command center, and again, Damius paused and outstretched his arm, waiting for her to walk through ahead of him. Would his team notice the change in his demeanor toward her? Were they so perceptive? She had no way to know, but she needed to win them over if she had a shot of being on the team. Cudala, she felt, would trust her, but the men... It was like rolling the chance dice.

"Sir," Nicheo said. "We've swept the room. We are clear for communications."

"Good. Who is the visitor you spoke of?"

"The new Madame of the Circle..." Nicheo began.

"Tercora," Cudala filled in.

"Tercora sent a representative on the pretense of delivering a private message for Cudala."

Mirbeck whistled from his computer. "Lady charmer."

"Better than you any moon, you bakayarou," Cudala dug back.

"You're still jealous I went home with more women from the bar on our last planet-side R&R than you."

"Quality versus quantity, Mirbeck. How many times must I tell you. Take as many as you want home, but you'll never beat me."

"Enough," Damius snapped. "We all appreciate your ability to charm the pants off people, but back to the topic at hand. I assume it wasn't a personal message."

"No, sir." Cudala walked over to the display she and Annwyn had worked on previously and brought up the letter hidden amongst other files. "Along with a private letter, she included some historical documents. I don't believe they are of importance, though Annwyn might be interested. The important one was here and encrypted. It's on Darvia, the copilot."

Annwyn moved with Damius to the screen. It was correspondence between Madame Raine and Darvia, giving her a letter of acknowledgement to a group of planetists.

"Are the planetists a strong faction on Chalar?"

"Not sure, Major. I'll see what Balder knows when he gets back," Nicheo said.

"Where is he? I'll need to get this information to our contact on the planet."

"Trying to make time with the Sanctuary representative, if you ask me," Mirbeck murmured.

"He took her for a tour of the station. She should be in the dining hall getting a meal before checking for Cudala's return message," Nicheo continued.

"Good. I want to talk to the copilot before we send a message back. I fear the Sanctuary has more ties to our bombing. Annwyn discovered a connection to mercury and Madame Raine, which may link her to the bomb supplier or buyer," Damius explained. "Mirbeck, any luck finding out how the Astole was able to circumvent my security codes?"

"Not yet, sir. The coding on the station is a jumbled mess. Whoever wrote it was either an idiot or was using it to hide something," Mirbeck barely looked up from the screen.

"Keep at it. Jumbled mess or not, you're better," Damius said. "I'm going to the med unit to interview the copilot. Cudala, do a deep dive on Madame Raine, find out everything you can about her. Nicheo, if our visitor returns, keep her entertained until I finish with the copilot."

Damius turned to leave the command center, and Annwyn reached for his arm. He stopped and turned to look at her.

For the first time, she felt small in his presence. It was as if he were a tree finally reaching its full height, stretching as tall as possible toward the sun to loom over her. It was intimidating, but she would not let him get the best of her.

"Major."

"Yes?"

"May I accompany you to the med unit? I'd like to review Darvia's chart for the same symptoms I observed in Madame Raine," Annwyn said as she bounced on her toes. Her fingers drummed on the side of her leg as she tried to control the nervous energy making her blood feel on fire inside of her.

Damius didn't immediately answer but waited silently while Wren sat beside her. He nodded to his wolf. "Let's go."

ꙮ ꙮ ꙮ

Damius strode quickly, mindful of Annwyn's attempts to keep up. He was still trying to get his emotions under control.

This Hunee was going to drive him over the edge so far, he didn't know if Wren could even bring him back. Part of him regretted being cold and distant toward her, putting space between them, but another part knew it was self-preservation. He needed to focus on the case. Solve the bombings, then he could sort out his feelings and her feelings after it was over.

Maybe then he would know what was really motivating her to want to be a part of his team.

He stopped outside the med unit and touched Annwyn's arm for a tick. His fingers buzzed from the momentary contact.

"Do you think you could distract Dr. Buehl while I start talking to Darvia?"

Annwyn nodded. "I need to look at her chart."

"Good. If you find anything, join me, and I'll give you an opening to ask her. You know more about it than I do."

Annwyn nodded.

"I don't want her to know we are onto her until it is advantageous to reveal our hand."

Annwyn's lips lifted on one side and she whispered, "But it isn't a game."

"But it is a puzzle, and we will solve it."

Damius hit the com button and resisted the urge to enter his override code.

"Major Elkwood and Emissary Silk to interview Darvia."

"Please, bio-scan and enter," Dr. Buehl instructed.

He placed his hand on the sensor, and the door opened.

"Major Elkwood, another surprise visitor this cycle. The medloc unit is rarely this busy."

"Dr. Buehl, I need to speak to Darvia. Is she awake?" Damius asked.

Wren whimpered at his side from the brightness of the med unit lights.

"And I must ask you to lower the lights."

"I can, but only for a few moments, Major. Darvia is still healing, though she has made some progress. She should be able to answer a few questions."

"How is she healing?" Annwyn asked as Dr. Buehl brought up the light controls on one of the wall units.

Damius breathed easier as the lights were lowered to a normal level. Wren brushed up against his leg, and together, they walked toward the screened area were Darvia was recovering.

Suddenly, Wren ran, jumped, and hit him in the chest, knocking him back.

Damius heard the explosion a micro-tick before he felt the shrapnel as it ricocheted through the room.

Wren's cries of pain pierced his ears. They dropped to the ground.

Blood dripped from Wren's neck before everything turned black.

Chapter Fourteen

Blasts of bell-like alarms blared all around them, bouncing off the walls and covering the cacophony of voices calling out to each other. Annwyn shook her head to clear the ringing from her ears and searched among the debris surrounding her. Blood, bodies, glass, pieces of walls, ceiling, and flooring lay strewn on them, under them, and some pieces, she noted, staring at one body ten feet away...*in* them.

She performed a quick internal check of her body. Bruising and small cuts. She whipped around and crawled toward Damius. Med personnel flooded the hallway along with security. She ran her hands down his head and body, finding several cuts. She grabbed the arm of the nearest medical, who knelt beside Damius and ran a med scan on her portable unit over him.

"Cuts, bruises and a few shrapnel caught him. One moment..." The medical dropped the scanner and pulled out a small sealing unit. It suctioned the small metal fragments out of each cut into the little box connected to the unit.

"How bad is it?" Annwyn asked.

"Minor. With his health, he'll heal quickly." She turned toward Annwyn. "Let me get you scanned."

Annwyn waved her away. "I'm fine."

The medical leaned closer and began scanning." It's protocol. Everyone must be scanned, and it'll go directly into your med files for any further evaluation. Please don't argue. We have too many injured."

Annwyn remained still while the medical did her thing. Her head ached at the noise of the alarms and personnel pressing each other to get everyone checked.

Astole arrived and glared at her. She glared back.

"What happened?" he demanded.

"Explosion is all I know. Can you get these blasted alarms to shut off?"

Astole glanced at her and strode away. Blades, he made her need to scream battle against worry.

The medical rose and made to step away. Annwyn reached out and grabbed her arm.

"Wait. We need to check on Wren. He's a wolf," she said when the medical gave her a quizzical look.

"I'm sorry, only assigned personnel can be checked at this time. No pets."

"No, no. He's personnel. He's assigned along with Damius...err, Major Elkwood. Your files will confirm." Annwyn rose and searched the debris closest to the lab. She rushed over and shoved building fragments around, digging through the debris until she found him. She gasped. Blood pooled beneath his neck and streaked his once smooth pelt of hair.

"Here he is," she hollered.

When the med arrived, she shoved more debris off him while the scanning began.

"He's hurt pretty bad." The med tugged out the unit she used on Damius and began working on Wren.

Annwyn leaned down and whispered near Wren's ear. "You're going to be fine. Hang in there."

"Major!"

Annwyn jerked her head up when Nicheo's voice rang out over the chaos surrounding her. She raised her arm and called to him. "Over here." She waited until he reached her, Mirbeck and Cudala following. "Damius is unconscious." She glanced around, noting the floating carriers being passed out and used to transport the victims. She pointed in their direction. "Get two of those transports. Cudala, Mirbeck, you two get Damius back to his quarters. Medical is going to be overcrowded as it is. Nicheo, stay with me until we determine the extent of Wren's injuries."

Without argument, the three instantly followed her orders. She returned her attention to Wren and the med. The wolf had not budged, nor whimpered.

Annwyn bit her lip. "How is he?"

"I'm not familiar with wolf biology. I can only heal the obvious wounds, remove shrapnel, and stop the bleeding. Other than that...I'm sorry, but there isn't anything I can do." She glanced up and frowned at the scene surrounding them. "I doubt anyone here has such training, other than Dr. Buehl." She blinked. "I don't know what condition she's in. You're on your own with this." She reached down and stroked Wren's fur. "He's alive and I've sealed all his wounds. He has no shrapnel in him anymore. It's all I can promise you."

Annwyn nodded and the med rose and rushed away to help others. Nicheo arrived with a carrier.

She rose "We have to get him to Damius's quarters as well.

"He looks bad. They won't keep him in med?"

Annwyn shook her head." Only Dr. Buehl has training to deal with a wolf, and her condition is unknown. I'm not sure how much Damius knows about Wren's biology."

"Oh."

"Exactly. Let's get him out of here."

Nicheo nodded, and they carefully lifted Wren onto the carrier unit and worked their way out of the crowded hall. They walked carefully as each step caused the carrier to bounce.

"How bad is it?" Nicheo whispered.

Annwyn glanced down at the unmoving wolf then at Nicheo. "Very bad, I'm afraid."

Damius's team looked toward her.

She bounced on her toes a moment before speaking. "I know you need to figure out what happened and the intended target of the explosion. I don't believe we were the targets, but I know you need to be certain. There's nothing more to do for Damius and Wren until they recover consciousness."

"Mirbeck, check the records, monitors, everything you can access to find out what happened." Nicheo turned toward Cudala. "You go use your talent and hit medloc. See what all they know and how much security was set up there with that pilot." Nicheo faced her. "I am now in charge until the major recovers. Only I can access these quarters for now. For your own safety and because I'm assuming you'll watch over them, I'd like you to remain here until we figure out what is going on."

Annwyn tipped her chin. "Agreed." They all turned to leave when she reached her hand out to Nicheo. "Any chance to get Gront out and in here with me? He has training with non-humanoids which I do not."

Nicheo frowned." I'm afraid not. Now with the explosion, I'm sure Astole will be more difficult to work with. Try to figure something else out. Is there someone on your home planet who might be able to help? Although, I'm sure coms are being monitored as well."

"It's okay. I've got bio training, and I can research it on my own. I'll figure it out."

Nicheo nodded, turned, and left.

Annwyn stood alone in the quiet quarters. Wren remained unconscious. Damius stirred and moaned but had not awakened. The medical must have given them both something to make them sleep. *No. One does not give sleep tonics to these types of injuries. She frowned. Blades.* A medical she was not.

Damius jerked awake. He whipped off the blanket and sat up. His head hammered like an echo of a wolf pack's pounding paws against hard ground. He slapped his palms against his head and took slow, even breaths until it subsided.

Annwyn. Wren. He jumped up and swayed slightly.

"You'd best lie back down. There's nothing you can do right now." Annwyn spoke from the darkened interior of his quarters.

He sat and shifted to face her, then searched her face. She's safe. He reached out mentally for Wren. Quiet emptiness met him. His heart raced as he searched for the familiar connection. His breath caught when he couldn't find it. *Wren? Wren!*

"He's unconscious," she said.

Damius glanced at her. "What?"

"I'm assuming you're attempting to contact Wren. He's unconscious in the other room."

"How long?"

"A few hours. Your injuries were minimal. I had scratches only. Wren..." She hesitated a moment. "Wren's injuries were more severe. He's been sealed but remains unconscious."

Damius rose quietly and shuffled past her to Wren's sleeping area in the main room. White bandages contrasted starkly against his grey fur. He knelt and stroked a hand along Wren's ears. *Wren?*

"I've taken some bio samples and will have one of the lab assistants review them." She touched his shoulder. "In the meantime, I've been researching a wolf's anatomy." She stepped away, sat on the ground beside him, and tugged her tablet toward her. "I'm trying to see if there is anything the meds might have missed. It's been a very enlightening journey regarding your planet's animal life."

Damius nodded, his gaze remaining on Wren. "He's never been like this. I can't remember back when we didn't have a connection." He swallowed past the lump in his throat. *It's so dark.* He squeezed his eyes closed. "We have to do something…anything."

"I have an idea, if you're willing?" Annwyn whispered.

Damius jerked his gaze toward her. "What is it?"

"On my planet, due to our gameplay, we are often required to calm our thoughts and bodies to objectively consider all possible points of action and how to move forward. It is a type of meditation. I can show you how it is done. By calming your body and mind to its most serene level, you may be able to grasp some contact with Wren in his current state."

"Fine, let's do it."

Annwyn raised her hand. "You must understand when done between two people, it can sometimes open an intimacy which may be distracting. You need to trust me and not allow our attraction to overcome you."

Damius snorted. "I doubt that will occur in my current situation. Wren means more to me than physical release."

Annwyn's short gasp echoed in his ears. Naiba, he wasn't watching what he was saying. "Not that what is between us isn't distracting, I mean." He shook his head. "I didn't mean it that way, Annwyn." *Please let her understand.*

She flashed a smile. "I do understand. We're both still upset over what happened at medloc. That, along with what is going on now. I truly do understand."

"Thank you," he said.

Annwyn rose and held out a hand. "Come, it is best we do this in your sleeping quarters where it is darker and quiet."

Damius followed her. What all did this meditation involve? How would it affect him? It didn't matter. It had to be done. Wren meant too much to ignore anyway to improve their connection. He followed her and sat when she motioned to his bed. She nudged him to turn and face her. They faced each other, legs crossed, and she reached out and placed one finger of her right hand at his temple and the thumb of the same hand above his ear.

"Close your eyes," she whispered. "Empty your mind."

His skin warmed where she touched, and he pushed away all thoughts as best as he could. His pulse picked up, and he struggled to even his breathing.

"Your body will wish to move. Restrain it. Hold very still and keep your breaths as even as you can. Your connection with Wren is much stronger than I anticipated."

Instantly, memories flooded his mind of when he and Wren first met, their travels, their thoughts shared both during fights and while at peace. Images of Annwyn came to mind, followed immediately by Wren's emotions of caring, protectiveness...his awe of her. Damius pushed the images behind a wall inside his mind. Wren's heart pounding when Annwyn smiled appeared before him. Dear Larunda, but Wren was smitten with her.

Annwyn giggled when an image popped in his mind of his argument with Wren over whether to start a relationship with her. Wren wanted Damius to move forward. Damius did not. Wren had jumped him, wrestled him to the ground, and stood on his chest to make his point.

She saw it? She saw the images materialize in his mind?

"I do, but you must let me in order for this to work," she said in a low voice. She placed her other hand on his chest.

His muscles relaxed, and the images in his mind went blurry. Sleep called to him.

"No, stay awake," she whispered.

Damius twitched and focused on keeping a blank mind. His breathing evened out, and his pulse slowed. His body totally relaxed, and then he heard it. A whisper of a sound barely audible. A whimper. Wren. He opened his mind, waiting for more. Silence.

Annwyn dropped her hands. "That went well. You're calm, and you heard him, yes?"

Damius opened his lids and stared at her. "I did." He looked away, then back at her face, searching. She showed no fear, no joy, only peacefulness. An idea hit him. "Wren. Can you do this with Wren?"

She tipped her head to the side. "I don't know. I've never tried with an animal." Her face turned a slight shade darker. "You're the only person I've done this with."

"Please, will you try? I've heard calm can increase natural restorative chemicals in some animals. Would it work with Wren?"

She rose, and he followed her toward Wren. She stretched out beside the wolf then lifted her gaze to him. "You know what I saw with you. Things you saw and thought. Wren will have fewer filters, and because of his connection to you, he may let me see or feel more than you did. Are you okay with that?"

Wren knew how strong his lust for her distracted him. Would this be revealed? Did he even care at this point? Wren's life could depend on it. He nodded.

She dipped her head and focused on Wren. Placing her hands in the same locations as she'd done before, she hummed this time. Then her breathing increased. Her body shifted, and her panting breath came quicker. Her scent carried up to him, and his body reacted. *She's experiencing it.*

Wren whimpered and twitched against her. She hummed between pants and small gasps. *She's reacting to the emotions she's reading from Wren.*

She dropped her hands and rolled away from the wolf. Her eyes half lowered, and her mouth partly opened.

Damius sucked in a breath and clenched his fists. He wanted her here, now. He wanted her there on the floor, in his room.

Chapter Fifteen

Damius turned his back to Annwyn. "I'm sorry," he whispered. "Wren has to come first."

"I know," she said. "He lost a lot of blood, but he didn't show me anything indicating he had further injuries."

Wren whimpered beside her as his paw gently brushed against her leg.

Damius was on the floor with them before she could say anything. His hands tenderly cradled Wren's head. "Hey, buddy."

She marveled at the gentleness Damius was capable of showing. His hands delicately brushed over Wren's body as he cooed to him in what sounded like bird song.

"It's the native song language of my people. We speak words, but we sing sounds which have meaning."

"Beautiful," she whispered. She placed her hand on Damius's thigh as he continued to sing to Wren.

Wren started to lick his blood-stained fur.

"Stop." Damius batted his snout away from where his paw wound was mended. "No." He laughed and pushed Wren away again. "I know your fur looks bad, but she understands."

"Does he actually talk to you? You know, in your head, or how does it work?" Annwyn asked the question that had been gnawing at her curiosity since she accepted the two could communicate telepathically.

"Sometimes, a word or two. Mostly he shows me images. He doesn't like not looking well-groomed in front of you." Damius cocked his head. "So that is why you have been licking more since we got on the station."

Wren whimpered and looked away.

"And here I thought you had allergies!" Damius scooped Wren into his arms, rocking him. "Do you think it would be okay if I cleaned him up?"

A warmth spread through Annwyn's body. She could still feel the connection she shared with Damius. An unexpected benefit she didn't know would exist. "His wounds are sealed. From what I read, it is perfectly fine to clean the area of the wound after medical treatment."

"Shower time, old friend." Damius tried to stand with the wolf cradled in his arms, but instead landed on his butt and fell onto his back.

"Are you okay?" Annwyn scurried beside Damius who was prone on the floor, a wolf lying on his chest licking his formerly blood-stained paw.

"Except for my pride, yes." Damius sat up and Wren followed, standing. "I may need help. It appears the universe is still spinning a little bit in my head."

"Let's get you both in the shower and cleaned up. Then some water and nourishment." Annwyn took Damius by the arm to help as he stood. When their eyes met, she clearly heard his voice in her mind.

If you are on the menu.

It was as if everything stood still. Time. Space. Even Wren.

Damius broke the silence. "Did you..."

"Yeah..."

Suddenly, neither could look at the other.

"I'm going to go...clean Wren up," Damius said as he moved carefully toward the bio, Wren following at his side.

֍ ֍ ֍

For once, Damius was thankful for the upgraded officer living quarters. At Penduli Station, it meant he had a shower with multiple jets coming from the sides and ceiling, though all of them were off. For now, he was using the wand on Wren. After he was satisfied he was thoroughly cleaned, he planned on enjoying the shower himself.

He turned off the water and grabbed a towel, but before he could dry Wren with it, drops of water flew everywhere. Wren shook himself a second time, ears flapping, tail wagging, and water landing all over the bio area.

Damius used the towel for a few moments on Wren, then threw it on the floor to try to minimize the hazard from Wren's shaking. His link with Wren was stronger now, and he could feel the wolf's exhaustion.

"Go sleep."

Wren lumbered out of the bio room, and Damius took off his remaining clothes.

"Another shirt ruined," he mumbled as he tossed it into the bin.

The image of petite Annwyn trying to rip his shirt made his body ache with need for her. He moaned and stepped into the shower, debating whether he should take a cold one to cool his lust or a hot one to help with his aches and pains.

"I vote for hot."

Damius spun around in time to see Annwyn drop the last of her clothes on the bio room's floor. The light glistened over her skin, reminding him of the holoplants he'd seen in her quarters. Fire flashed through his body, and need clawed inside his gut. His nostrils flared as the scent of her reached him.

"You did want me to join you?"

"The thought had crossed my mind, but Wren..."

"He drank some water and is quietly sleeping...on the sofa."

"Good." Damius extended his hand to Annwyn, inviting her into the shower with him. "We may have use for my bed later."

There was no turning back now. If he were honest with himself, the point of no return happened during the meditation when her emotions for him crystalized in vivid images of them on her bed. He pulled her into the shower area, hitting the wall panel to close the glass door. His lips met hers as he tapped the buttons to release the streams of hot water from the other three walls and ceiling. She jerked against him when the water touched her body.

She laughed, wrapping her arms around his neck. She drew her finger over where the shrapnel had embedded in his collarbone, barely missing a major artery.

His hands explored her body, touching every inch. He grabbed the soap and turned it over in his hands. The smell of the aromatic woods from home filled the shower, mingling with a refreshing citrus smell.

Annwyn inhaled deeply with closed eyes and lifted lips.

"That is divine."

"It is made by the children in my tribe. They learn how to retrieve the essential oils from the woods and fruits and then make soap for the tribe. I always bring some with me."

"I can see why." Annwyn took the soap from him, twisting it back and forth in her hands before depositing it in the soap dish.

They explored each other's bodies, washing clean the blood from the attack. He cataloged her sounds and shivers. She pushed on his shoulders, and he dropped to his knees.

"You are too tall."

"Oh, really?"

"Yes."

"But there are advantages to me being this tall," he teased.

"Show me."

The gauntlet had been thrown, and he accepted the challenge.

Damius pushed buttons behind her to redirect all the water to the ceiling jets. The water cascaded on them like a gentle rain, washing away the last of the soap suds. Damius rested his head against the shower wall and cradled Annwyn to his body. His heart was racing, and his breathing labored, but he'd never felt more at peace. There was nothing but the two of them in his world for this moment. For the first time, her energy wasn't frenetic or confrontational.

No control left.

☙ ☙ ☙

Annwyn shivered when she heard Damius' voice in her head.

None needed. She thought back to him.

Annwyn gasped as he lifted her body and pushed her up against the wall. She wrapped her legs around his muscular body for support. His lips met hers and his tongue demanded entrance. This was nothing like the joinings she'd had at home. Pleasure turned into a contest between lovers to see who would submit first.

"Oh, that will be you, Mandis," Damius whispered.

Mandis? She titled her head at him.

Without answering, he bit the juncture of her neck and shoulder and sucked.

That's going to leave a mark.

Exactly, Damius replied as he slipped his hand between them. His fingers found her core and stroked, sending her tumbling over the edge of pleasure before she even knew she was at the precipice.

Heat filled her body, and all she could focus on was Damius's fingers and the humming they were creating at her core.

Shivers went out from her center, tingling up her limbs. Damius pulled her tighter against him, enveloping her with his heat. In a few ticks, they were breathing in sync. Their lungs filling, pausing, and then exhaling. She was adrift. Her mind completely cleared of thought.

She felt the growl as it rumbled deep within Damius before she heard it.

"Mandis," he exclaimed as he lifted her higher and tilted his body to connect with hers. He lowered her slowly until he filled her, pausing when her breath came too fast or when she cringed.

Never had it been like this. She was always in control before, pushing her partner over the edge before she found release, but not this time.

Damius moved inside her at an increasing rhythm, kissing her as they both gasped and toppled over the edge together.

Damius rested his head against the shower wall as he cradled her to his body. She could feel his heart racing against her chest and his labored breath against her neck.

He lowered her to her feet, kissed the top of her head and opened the shower door.

She reached for a towel, but he batted her hand away.

"It's my job to take care of you," he whispered as he brushed the towel over her body, kissing her before drying himself.

He picked her up and carried her to the bed, placed her on the mattress, then lowered himself beside her. His fingers traced along her jawline. "You are so beautiful, Mandis. It's okay to stop thinking, and simply be."

"You're in my mind..."

"I've been inside you, too. Lose yourself in us." Damius's hand drifted down to her breast, cupping it.

Annwyn's forehead wrinkled as she looked at him. "Wait. You've said Mandis twice now. What does it mean?"

"Mine," he whispered, holding her gaze.

"Oh..."

Damius settled onto his back, pulling Annwyn close to him. She felt him humming before she heard the sound. Damius hummed a melody with tones that rose and fell. Wren howled softly with him. The bed dipped when Wren snuggled close to them. Her eyes closed as the song echoed in the room and she let sleep take her.

✸ ✸ ✸

His com buzzed from the other room, and he held his breath, counting the beeps. Two. He slid a glance toward Annwyn and noted she'd not moved. She hadn't heard it. Good. He kept his own breathing slow and even to match hers. He lifted his arm, tapped the skin behind his left ear, and focused on raising the mental walls which would block mental communication. Thank the stars, Wren had taught him this trick long ago.

The com buzzed again. Nicheo must have obtained more information on the explosion. Damius shifted lightly while monitoring Annwyn and Wren. Both of his companions remained sleeping. As carefully as possible, he negotiated his way out of bed and padded naked into the center room. After punching the buttons which would allow him to read rather than listen to the messages, he scanned the contents of Nicheo's call and frowned.

Chapter Sixteen

Annwyn inhaled a deep breath, lifting her eyelids until her gaze met Damius's. He watched her awaken, and her body instantly responded to his scent. *Again.* His lips lifted at the edges before he leaned over and kissed her. *You heard me?* She waited for an answer, but when he pulled her over on top of him, his hands smoothed their way down her back.

"Again," he growled as his hand slipped between their bodies.

He had heard her, then. She straddled him, covering him with her body. They kissed, making her lids drift close again as the tremors of pleasure radiated out from where their bodies made contact. She freed her hands from his and placed both on his shoulders for balance.

Wren sighed, jumped off the bed, and lumbered toward the other room.

Annwyn lifted her body, her legs spread wide across Damius's massive hips and thighs. She grinned and lowered herself inch by inch over him, joining their bodies once more. They rocked in a steady rhythm. Heat built and spread through her body, while her pulse picked up and her breath came in short gasps. For a moment, she believed reality would stay within her grasp, but as soon as Damius was inside of her, that illusion was shattered.

Damius lifted his hips to match hers while he spread his large hands around her hips and slid them up to cup her breasts. His gaze remained locked with hers while their breathing increased. Their breaths synced, and her heart pounded against her ribs. So close...so close.

Damius thrust under her harder. "Now," he demanded in a low, deep voice.

"Now," she whispered and let go, spiraling along the waves of pleasure splashing against her.

Damius's shout confirmed his joining with her. His hands held her until the ripples subsided and she collapsed against his chest, listening to his heartbeat match hers. When their breaths slowed, she shifted to his side and laid her hand on his chest.

"Because of Wren, we were able to share our thoughts?" she whispered, needing to say the words out loud.

"Yes, he connected and strengthened the bonding."

"But…" She lifted to her elbow to watch his face. "How could he do that when he was unconscious…or asleep, rather?"

Damius shifted to his side and lifted a finger to caress her chin. "When you meditated with him, he connected to you. Since he is permanently connected to me, it allowed a bridge of sorts between us."

Annwyn frowned. "Does that mean this is permanent? Our ability to mentally communicate?" Would he be able to read all her thoughts from this point forward? That might not be a good idea. But then again, he wouldn't be able to hide anything from her either. It would be a new level of trust, and something she had to think about.

"No, it was only this one time because of Wren. He is the only one that can initiate and support the connection. Also, he was only able to do it because of your connection to him." He shifted his gaze away and shrugged. "It's something he can do. Not me."

"Oh, I see."

꧁꧂ ꧁꧂ ꧁꧂

Damius kissed Annwyn's forehead and rolled, rising from the bed to gather his clothing. "Nicheo called and left me a message. His report should be ready soon regarding the explosion."

Annwyn left the bed and discovered her clothing neatly folded on the desk corner. She picked them up and rushed into his bathing unit. "I'll be out in a moment."

Damius stared at the closed door and let the air he'd held in his lungs release in a rush. She believed him. *No one can know about this gift…ever. A pre-cognitive Moya would never be allowed to lead his father's Oya tribe.*

While she showered, he reviewed the reports along with a summons received from Admiral Carmichael. Perfect.

Annwyn arrived dressed near his side. Her fresh scent wrapped around him like a warm cloak. He clenched his jaw against the desire surging within him and cleared his throat to speak past the groan threatening to emerge.

"We've received a copy of the security footage. Mirbeck and the team reviewed every tick of the events leading up to and including the explosion in medical. The Circle messenger who gave Cudala the dime bar had made her way to medical. According to Mirbeck, the female named Eira appeared to have attempted to set a bomb for detonation and failed during the process, causing ignition before she could leave the area. Both she and the copilot were instantly vaporized during the blast. Cudala made a positive ID on the female from the vid com review. She has been with the Circle most of her life and worked closely with the highest members of the Sanctuary."

"Wren must have sensed something amiss, which explains him running ahead of us," Annwyn said.

"Agreed. Foolish wolf." Damius frowned. "I've sent you a copy of the recording should you wish to review it on your own." That will keep her busy for the time being. He needed time to get his emotions under control again.

"I do, thank you." She bounced on her feet. "How is Cudala dealing with this new information?"

"What do you mean?"

Annwyn stared at him." I mean she must feel badly that her contact used someone who could not be trusted." She waved her hand. "Or, perhaps, her friend was involved somehow with the initial set of explosions?"

Damius tipped his head to the side, considering her words. He shook his head. "No, I trust Cudala's sense of loyalty and ability to read others. She would not have aligned herself with someone who is deceitful."

"Aligned herself?" Annwyn smirked. "Is that what you call what we did last setting...and again this rising? Aligned ourselves?"

Damius blinked. What was she talking about? "No, we did not align ourselves." Then it came to him, and he crossed his arms in front of his chest. "I meant placing herself in danger with the wrong contacts. Her...personal actions are her choice."

Annwyn's face shaded toward a reddish green. "Right. I was teasing."

This time, Damius grinned. He reached for her and kissed her roughly, before placing her away from him. "Mandis, heed my words. We did more than align ourselves." And it worries me. He stepped back and punched several buttons on his desk. "I'm sending you a copy of the rest of the report for your review."

"Am I being dismissed now, Major?"

Damius snapped his attention toward her. "Of course not. However, we both have duties to fulfill. By the way you're popping up and down on your feet, I believe you're about to burst if you don't get to these reports soon."

She stopped and glared at him.

He laughed and reached out to guide her toward his door. He leaned down and whispered in her ear. "Again, as soon as we can arrange it?"

Annwyn smiled brightly over her shoulder while she stepped out into the hallway. "Perhaps."

The door whooshed closed, his own face returning a deep frown in the reflection of the metal. He rushed into the bio room to wash as fast as possible. With what he had to discuss with the admiral, lateness could not be allowed.

Once clean and dressed in his uniform, Damius made his way toward Wren and leaned down to speak in the wolf's ear. "I'll return shortly. I'm meeting with the station Admiral. You sleep."

Wren bumped his nose, then rolled onto his back and stuck all four legs up in the air. Damius rose and chuckled at the animal's present position. He sighed, then headed out toward the admiral's quarters. Once there, he tapped the com and waited for admittance. His fingers drummed against his thighs while the last image of Annwyn filled his mind.

She said the word "perhaps," like there might be a possibility of her refusing to be with him again. That would not...could not happen. His body shuddered as images of their mating flashed in his head. He blinked. Mating and his subsequent humming of his tribal song. Oh no, what had he let her do to him?

Before he could summon another thought, the doors before him slid open silently, and a guard addressed him.

"Stand and prepare for scan."

Damius lifted his arms out to his sides and spread his legs while the guard ran a small metal tube around his body.

Once complete, he nodded and stepped back, allowing Damius to enter. "Admiral Carmichael will see you now."

"Thank you," Damius said and entered the well-furnished main room of the admiral's quarters.

"Back here, if you would," Carmichael called from his right.

Damius followed the short corridor which led to an extremely large office-style room. One huge desk sat right inside the entry. Admiral Carmichael waved toward one of the two chairs sitting in front of her desk. Damius sat and leaned forward to speak.

"One moment, if you please." The admiral tapped on her desk, and the four screens in front of her evaporated before Damius could catch any words displayed. "Now, I've received your complaint and reviewed it thoroughly." She leaned forward. "For the record, everything discussed in this room is recorded. I have nothing to hide."

"Neither do I, ma'am, and I did not file a complaint, but rather an inquisition."

"Inquiry or complaint. They're the same to me and understood. I believe what you reported, and you should believe me when I tell you, I never authorized any override of your security clearance codes. Your work is for upholding the Larunda Legacy as the Directorate writings decree, not Penduli Station, and as Larunda Force are the highest security order in the galaxy, I would not even attempt to override them. After reading your report, I had my own personal assistant check the security codes of our station. Your codes were, in fact, overridden."

Damius nodded. "Do we know how and by whom?"

"I'm fairly certain a man of your intelligence can determine who overrode them. The 'how' is not clear yet." The com buzz in the other room sounded. Damius raised a brow. "I have requested Major Astole to join us, so we may get an answer to your question."

Damius rose. "I do not trust him, ma'am."

"I am aware of that. However, he is head of security and has never betrayed me. I owe him enough to allow him to defend himself. It is only fair. Don't you agree?"

"Well, maybe."

"If it were you in my seat and your team member was accused?"

"Yes, ma'am. I understand." He didn't have to like it though. He scowled and leaned back against the side wall when Astole entered.

Astole glanced toward Damius for less than a tick before seating himself in one of the chairs and faced the admiral, ignoring his presence. So that was how he intended to behave? Keeping his grin inside, Damius strolled over and sat next to the completely blank-faced man.

"Major Astole, thank you for joining us. I'm sure you know Major Elkwood." Carmichael leaned back in her tall chair and clasped her hands in her lap. "Can you explain why a Larunda-appointed major's security codes did not work in lockup?"

Straight to the point. Damius liked this officer more every tick. He shifted and slid a glance toward Astole, waiting for his answer. What kind of excuse could this man give?

Astole leaned forward, placing his hands on the desk. "Admiral, the slave scum—"

"Gront," Damius said. "His name is Gront, and he is not a slave scum—"

Admiral Carmichael snapped forward and slammed her hands on the desktop. "Enough," she demanded.

Damius jerked his head in a nod.

Astole studied his hands before he continued. "The indentured servant named Gront is our main suspect in the murder of one of my security crews, ma'am." He rose. "Although of higher position in the galaxy, Major Elwood must agree that the local security has precedence in a case such as this." Damius rose to argue, but Astole held up his hand before facing the admiral again. "As well as the suspect is indentured to a member working with him, I've no doubt Major Elkwood would proceed with the same security preventions as I have done."

"I would not, Admiral. I would leave the investigation of any person to whomever the highest investigator deems necessary."

"Sit back down, both of you," Carmichael said. After they were seated, she leaned back again. "Astole, your work on Penduli Station has been exemplary…until now."

"Admiral!" Astole exclaimed.

"No one on this station nor any other station in the Penduli galaxy has authority over the Order's own security members. Not even myself. If I do not have authority to override the major's code, then by Chalar, neither do you." The admiral rose with her face flushing. "You know better. Why would you do something so stupid?"

Astole pursed his lips and stood stock-still while silence filled the room. "Are you asking for my resignation, Admiral?" he asked softly.

"Blast it, Nort. I am not asking, nor will I accept your resignation. But it is required I place this incident on your record. You will release your overrides." She turned toward Damius. "I have also reviewed all the files involving Officer Cress's death. Due to the timing and lack of evidence, we must adhere to Penduli writings. This Gront fellow will be released immediately into your custody. Only you or your team members may escort him from lockdown." She turned toward Astole and pointed. "You stay here. We have more to discuss." She waved her hand at Damius. "I have not had this much trouble on Penduli station until your team arrived, and that disturbs me. Remember that, Major Elkwood. Now, go get your man and be sure he remains in his quarters until all this mess is cleared up."

"Yes, ma'am, I will," Damius said.

"You're dismissed," Carmichael said.

A guard arrived silently and escorted him out of the admiral's quarters and back into the hallway. Once the doors closed, Damius rolled his shoulders, stretching his neck muscles.

Annwyn would be pleased with Gront's release. Too bad Astole wasn't relieved of duty. His team could have had a short little celebration over that.

He frowned when he remembered the scene of Cress's death and Astole's behavior during that mess. Would Astole push to find out who killed her and why? Too many questions and very few answers.

An image of Gront sitting quietly in his cell flashed in his mind. He growled and stormed down the hallway to get him released—now.

Chapter Seventeen

The door to Annwyn's quarters slid shut behind Damius.

He barely looked at me when he escorted Gront in.

"Thank you for seeing to my release," Gront said as he tapped her arm, catching her attention.

"Major Elkwood pursued the matter."

Annwyn wondered if Gront could tell her and Damius were lovers. Maybe that was why he had been so cold and detached.

She felt like a schoolgirl wondering if the handsome boy in her class truly liked her. *What isn't there to like?* Her release-seeking turned into something much more complicated. Sleeping with Damius had not stopped her thinking about him; if anything, it had increased.

Gront tapped her arm again. She needed to get her head back in the game. She had an entire file to review.

"Are you okay, Princess?"

"Gront, I have told you not to refer to me by that title. My real name or Emissary is fine."

"Emissary," Gront said, dragging the pronunciation out, "you seem distracted."

Get your head back in the game.

"I'm happy you are released and here. Also, I was hurt in a bomb blast yestermoon."

"I think it is more than that. Perhaps Major Elkwood?" Gront said smugly.

"Why would you say that?"

"Because you are still staring at the door he walked out of, and your breathing increased when you saw him."

"If you have something to say, I suggest you say it," Annwyn snapped out.

"Be careful, Emissary. He is not one of our kind. He doesn't understand how our minds work."

"Stop making assumptions." Annwyn turned from the door and handed Gront a tablet. She needed to do something she could control. She needed something to keep her mind occupied, so it would stop drifting back to the image of Damius naked in the shower.

"Is this the video footage from the bombing?" Gront asked.

"Yes. I would like to review the rest of the feeds from the station and try to track the courier's movements. She was with Lt. Balder for part of the star rising."

The door chimed, startling Annwyn. For a moment, she wondered if Damius had returned to whisk her back into bed, but she knew that was not possible now that Gront was confined to her quarters. She nodded toward the door, and Gront went to answer it.

"How may I assist you?" he asked.

Annwyn recognized the man at the door from the new contact shuttle. He was a part of Emissary Moiran's entourage.

"I have a message for Emissary Silk."

"I shall see that she gets it."

"It is verbal."

Annwyn rose to join the standoff at the door. "Yes?"

"Emissary Moiran requests your presence at a meeting."

"We are in the middle of an investigation. Besides, I thought new contact was delayed."

"Regardless, Emissary Moiran wishes to speak to you."

"After I finish reviewing these films, I will see him."

"Emissary Silk, this is not a request. You will come with me, now."

"What? You have no right to order me anywhere." What was Emissary Moiran doing? He hired Cress to follow her, and now she was dead. What was his game?

"Actually, Emissary Silk, he does. You are authorized to be on this station because of your status as an emissary for new contact. Given that new contact is postponed, there is no need for you to be on the station. You will either come with me to speak to Emissary Moiran, or he will have you transferred back to your home world."

"I am working with the Larunda Force team."

"That may be true, but your presence on this station is based on your status as an emissary. You are not officially on the team."

What? Didn't Damius make her a part of the team? What game is Moiran playing?

"Fine. I will go with you."

"I shall accompany you," Gront said as he moved to leave.

"No. You are confined to our quarters until further instructions from the admiral. It was one of the conditions of your release. I will be fine," she said.

"Emissary, we do not want to keep him waiting."

"I doubt we do." She waved her hand before her. "Lead on."

ψ ψ ψ

Damius waited for the command room door to close behind him before he spoke. Simply being in Annwyn's presence for a moment had his system on overdrive. Without Wren by his side grounding him, resisting the call to take her back to his quarters and to not leave until they were both so satiated they could hardly walk was almost unbearable.

What is wrong with him?

Three bombings and four souls dead and he was unable to focus because a green-skinned, luscious Hunee was taking over his thoughts. It didn't help that physical distance was not dampening his gift's ability to connect with her. He breathed in to center himself. *Must focus on the task at hand.* He pictured walls surrounding him, blocking out the extrasensory data that his mother's heritage allowed him to experience.

Focus. Ground yourself.

He looked around, and his team was staring at him.

"Major, it is good to see you upright again," Mirbeck said from his computer station.

"How is Wren?" Cudala asked.

"Resting."

"Were you able to look over the reports?" Nicheo inquired, taking his place at the conference table.

Damius could tell his team was tired. They had worked all setting on the report while he slept with a member of his team. *How the mighty have fallen.*

"Yes, Cudala, any communication from Tercora?"

"No, there has been no word from the Sanctuary nor confirmation that they know of Eira's death."

"Good. We can use that to get you back in the Sanctuary." Damius picked up his tablet and scrolled through the report again. "Okay, no remains. What about personal effects? Anything we can work with?"

"She left her travel case in storage?"

"Okay, let's get what could pass as remains and see if..."

Lt. Balder entered the conference room. Damius had forgotten to lock the door behind him.

"We just got word there has been an incident at the Sanctuary. Reports are coming in of an uprising," Balder reported.

"That does it. Cudala, grab what we have of Eira and something that will pass as remains. We are going to the Sanctuary."

⚑ ⚑ ⚑

Annwyn followed the Lead Emissary's minion down yet another corridor. Penduli confused her sense of direction. The walls were all too similar. It was as if she were a rat in a maze trying to find her way out.

She used her override code on the door and locked Gront inside. He would be angry when she returned, but she couldn't risk him leaving her quarters and Astole using it as an excuse to arrest Gront again.

This whole situation with Moiran didn't feel right. Never before had someone from The Directorate sought her out specifically. She sighed. Her father. The Haevis representative on The Directorate followed orders from the King. Had he spoken to Moiran? Did her father have a role in this little play going on in front of her? She wouldn't put it past him. He hated not controlling all the pieces in a game, and everything was a game he must win.

Annwyn drew in her breath sharply as she realized where they were. It was the corridor where she had overheard the initial conversation between Emissary Moiran and Cress.

"Emissary Silk." Moiran floated out from the shadows and bowed to her.

"Emissary Moiran," Annwyn said as she bowed in return. "To what do I owe the pleasure and deception?"

Moiran smiled at her and waved his hand at his minion, who quickly disappeared.

"Please, walk with me. We have much to discuss."

"Let's start with why you had Cress spy on me?"

Moiran paused for a moment, and she registered his paler skin. He didn't know she knew about his investigation of her.

"It was necessary."

"Why?"

"None of your concern."

"It is my concern, especially since Cress wound up dead outside my quarters."

"I don't believe that is connected."

"You don't believe..." Annwyn was finding it harder to control her emotions. Emotions helped drive her forward, but it was her mind, her intellect, that helped her sort through information and determine the truth. She clenched her teeth. Resisting the urge to grab the taller Moiran and shake him, she continued. "If you want me to continue this conversation, you are going to have to tell me why."

"Emissary Silk, may I remind you that I am the reason you are allowed to stay on Penduli Station and not return to Haevis to resume your duties as Princess Silk."

"Fine. I will go pack my things." Annwyn turned, hoping that Moiran would fall for her bluff as she truly had no say in the matter. If he didn't, she'd have to find Damius. How bad did he need her cooperation?

"Wait." Moiran's voice rose. "Insolent children. In my youth, we did not question our elders."

Annwyn turned to face Moiran and crossed her arms, refusing to move.

"Come here, child, and I will tell you more than maybe you are ready to know."

The hair stood up on her arms, and she could feel the nerve endings inside her body pulse with a combination of fear and curiosity. She walked toward him, staying outside his grasp.

"As you know, this was not the first bombing, and I fear it will not be the last. There have been other disruptive events spread throughout the Larunda galaxy. My assignment to lead new contact was to facilitate the investigation into this disruption, as well."

"And how does this involve me?"

"Well, not you, but your father. He is one of the people under surveillance. I assume given the nature of your relationship you will keep that to yourself."

Annwyn inhaled a quick breath. Attempting to control her was one thing, but disrupting the plans of The Directorate? She shuddered. What would her father have to gain by preventing new contact?

"Your father is still not cleared. Originally, I thought he encouraged you to join the new contact party, but it has become obvious that he wishes to keep you on Haevis under his watchful eye."

"Yes, my father did not approve of my leaving."

"But it isn't your father who I need to speak to you about. It is Major Elkwood."

Annwyn's skin heated with the mention of her lover's name. "Why?" she asked and winced at the sound of her quivering voice.

"Do you know of Major Elkwood's heritage?"

"I know he is from Krizlar."

"Yes, he has a background very similar to yours, but he is next in line to be the leader of his people."

"He's a prince?"

"Krizlar's ruling system is a bit different, but his father is the current Shaman of the Oya, the nomads of Krizlar. It is expected that Elkwood will follow in his place, but it is not his father that concerns me as much as his mother."

"He mentioned that she was different." Annwyn bounced on her toes again, her fingers tapping incessantly on the side of her leg. What was it Damius had said about his mother?

"She was from the non-nomads of Krizlar— the Moya. They chose not to follow the sun and exist in near darkness for most of the solar phase. They are known for their mental adeptness and their ability to influence others."

"Wasn't the new contact envoy hoping a Moya would join us to help with negotiations?"

"Yes, they excel at negotiations." Moiran looked around them. He took Annwyn by the arm and guided her farther into the shadows. "We must hurry. This section of the station does not have recording equipment, but a station officer makes rounds every hour." He slipped a dime bar into Annwyn's hand.

"I have uncovered evidence that the initial bombers are from Krizlar. I need you to stay close to Elkwood. Do not let him go planet-side without you accompanying him. I do not believe he can be trusted. He may be influencing others or under influence himself."

She stopped moving, her gut tightening into knots. Could Damius be responsible for the bombings? And what did Moiran mean by influencing? Was that why she couldn't shake her insatiable need for his body?

The sound of a whistle jolted her out of her thoughts. It grew closer, and Moiran linked their arms and said louder than necessary, "Emissary

Silk, it appears we have lost our way again. Now, let's see where the virosphere is." Moiran scanned the walls, as if he were looking for something.

The whistling stopped when one of Astole's men turned the corner and approached them.

"May I help you?" He asked.

"Yes! What magnificent timing! My colleague and I were headed to the cafeteria for a mid-meal but seem to have lost our way. Perhaps you can guide us back on track?"

Annwyn bit the inside of her mouth to keep from smiling. What a thespian the Lead Emissary was. Perhaps she should take some acting lessons from him.

🜲 🜲 🜲

Damius sprinted to his quarters. He needed to pack his travel case and check on Wren. He entered, and an excited Wren licked his face and then growled.

"I take that to mean you are coming with me?"

Wren's howl reverberated off the walls.

"I know, but we don't have time to tell her." Maybe he did. Damius hit his communicator as he packed a few moon's worth of supplies. "Annwyn Silk." He frowned when she didn't respond. "We'll try again later," he told Wren while tapped the keys by his doors, authorizing Annwyn entrance. "Let's go, boy."

Chapter Eighteen

Annwyn reviewed her report while tapping her fingers together. More details than she'd ever considered were included in this report than any of her others. She shifted in her seat. Why hadn't Damius gotten her reassignment on record? Had he changed his mind about letting her be part of his team?

A breath escaped her lips when she leaned back and tipped her head to stare at the ceiling. Images of their intimacy flashed through her mind. Her body tingled from her toes to the top of her head. It had simply slipped his mind with everything going on.

She returned to her report and realized she hadn't included anything Lead Emissary Moiran had revealed to her, nor from the dime bar she'd scanned earlier. She couldn't include that information in her report. She tapped her foot. No, best not to put that information where it could be accessed by anyone. She stood, stepped to the liquid dispenser unit, and filled a tube with a hydration mix. The drink cooled her throat and body while she blanked her mind, allowing the liquidation to seep through her.

She returned to her seat and activated her com to contact Damius. She'd meet him in person and let him know about her private meeting and the current situation the emissary leader revealed. Trust. She must give it to receive it, and deep down, she'd gotten no indication of Damius attempting to deceive anyone. She waited for an answer and received the automated response. Hmm. Where was he that he couldn't answer his com? She rose and headed toward the door, then paused. Considering what Moiran provided her, she might be wrong.

"Gront, I'll return momentarily. I need to speak with Damius, and he's not answering his com. I'm going to his quarters."

"I understand," he said.

The doors whooshed open, and she turned toward the lift, pausing to glance at the virosphere. When would she finally have the station's floor plans memorized? Confirming her destination, she rushed and entered the recently arriving lift then waited while it transported her to Damius's floor. Once there, she exited and hurried to his quarters. She tapped the com pad and bounced on her feet while she waited for him to answer. Nothing. Odd. She tried once more without success. Where was he? She considered contacting the team members, but after checking the time, she shook her head. It was late, and they might become suspicious of her search for their major at this time of star setting. Their major...who was supposed to be her major.

She shrugged, spun around, and stomped back to the lift. She'd return to her quarters and wait until rising to speak with him. Where had he gone? Why hadn't he at least left her a message of where he was going? It wasn't as though she had a right to know his whereabouts always. Yes, she did. His team never failed to have immediate contact with their leader, so why shouldn't she?

As she stood in the lift, she tapped her foot and scowled. She'd tried to talk to Damius without success. She didn't need his permission to make a move. She wasn't on his team after all...not officially. *No. She, Princess Annwyn Silk of the Hunee does not chase...or rather, will not chase anymore. Enough.*

She squared her shoulders, and when the lift doors slid open, she stomped back to her quarters. She'd bested the best of Haevis game players, even if she kept the scores to herself.

When the door of her quarters whooshed open, she strode in and paused. *Now, it's time to put these pieces together.*

"Gront," she called out.

Gront joined her in the center room. "Pri...err, Emissary?"

"Gront, I need several holo-displays of my reports brought up right here." She waved her arms in front of the exterior bulkhead.

Gront scooted to her desk, tapped several buttons, and five holo-screens popped up.

She stepped forward to read the displays. "I've not used these often. How do I maneuver them?"

Gront joined her and lifted one finger to the far left display. As soon as his finger met the image, it glowed. He shifted his arm, and the display moved in the direction he indicated, placing the display to the far left.

"I see, thank you."

"Of course," he said, then turned to leave.

"One moment, please."

Gront faced her. "Yes, Emissary?"

Annwyn placed her hands together and tapped her fingers while she studied him. He bowed his head and stared at the floor.

"How is your family? I meant to ask before."

His head snapped up and he smiled. "They're doing well, thank you."

"Since we still have two more life-seasons left on your service, I thought I should let you know I've decided to resign my position for new contact. I think my skills are best used in investigations, rather than communications. As soon as this situation is resolved, I will be submitting my request for a position on an investigation team."

Gront tipped his head. "And how will this affect my service?"

Annwyn dropped her hands. "We both know why I've kept you with me instead of leaving you in the palace with my father."

"Yes. Even now, during my latest communications, I have learned your father has become even more severe with his treatment of the servants. I am grateful you chose to bring me along with you." He stiffened. "Are you intending to return me to Haevis?"

"No, no. I don't wish palace servitude on my enemies." His shoulders dropped. "However, since your family arranged for your education... I know I've never asked, and you have always been honest with me. I've been wondering why your family arranged for your alchemic training."

He coughed and looked away. "We intended for me to apply for player assistant."

Annwyn tilted her head. "But, for that, you'd have had at minimum a life-season training in game analytics."

Gront looked straight at her. "Indeed."

Annwyn gasped. "Why have you never told me?"

One side of his mouth lifted. "Because it's against the law for a lower social Hunee to train in it without permission?"

She grinned. "True," she said, then pivoted toward the screens. "In that case, we're going to work together. I have recently discovered the benefits of working in a team allows me to evaluate information from a different point of view faster." She maneuvered the screens in order of her initial ideas of importance. "Take a look at this. It appears to me as though everything overlaps everything else. I want to see if you come to the same conclusion as I did. The insurgents arranged for your training, didn't they?"

"Yes."

"That's how they knew to kidnap your mother, rather than someone else, to obtain those notes from my office." She tapped her fingers. "You sacrificed your future doing that."

"I did," Gront said.

"At least now your family is safe." She waved her hand at the screens. "What do you think?"

"It appears Madame Raine is being manipulated and very ill," he said.

"Go on."

"I would say she has had several meetings with whomever built the bombs. In fact, she had personal meetings, as it appears she is suffering from mercury poisoning. The rashes, anxiety, odd behavior. It could be a combination of exposure to the mercury along with coercion, so to speak."

"Why do you say coercion?"

"Although originally Chalarans, Silvergrass Circle only allows those who have accepted and live by Piradian beliefs. Those beliefs do not condone violence of any kind, nor would they put themselves in a position to handle, let alone be exposed to, an element such as mercury. Ergo, someone or something is forcing or coercing her to do so. It appears from your reports, she is too far gone for any kind of healing or redemption."

"I agree. What do you think about the information from the Lead Emissary?"

"Although Major Elkwood—"

"Call him Damius while it is only us two here."

"Although—Damius is not full-blooded nomad, he is in line to take over once his father steps down. The fact that his mother is non-nomadic is disconcerting, but we must consider he may carry her abilities of empathic communication. However, based on his prior service records, it's highly unlikely that he has allowed, nor will allow that gift, if it exists, to hinder his loyalty to The Directorate."

"So, you agree he can be trusted?"

"No. The opposite, in fact."

"Why do you say that?"

"Some men will do anything for their mothers. Assuming that may not be an issue here, he has potentially withheld the information if he does have his mother's gifts from his superiors." Gront pursed his lips. "That alone is distrustful. Compound that with his being Oya…"

"You should know, his mother is dead. So, while you would do anything for your mother, he does not have that option any longer, Also, we have no idea what his classified file contains, yet." Annwyn took a deep breath. She was harsh to Gront, but a part of her had to defend Damius. "What do you think about the bombings?"

"I agree with your reports. There must be a group of rebels on the planet supplying and planting the explosives. I cannot fathom why, but I have come to the same conclusion as you have. Someone is trying to prevent new contact."

"Exactly." Annwyn spun around and retrieved a drink. After taking several swallows of cool liquid, she returned to Gront. Together they stood studying the information and maps on the displays.

"Will you do it?"

"Do what?" Annwyn asked.

"What the Lead Emissary requested?"

"I will not be a spy. I will, though, keep an eye on everything for our own safety." And for protection from giving in to false beliefs and promises from a man who spoke too earnestly and had a lovely wolf by his side. "I've reviewed the communications he gave me. There is no proof that any of those came to, nor from, Damius."

"Is there another Oya...or Moya on the station?"

"He is not Moya, and there are several Krizlars here on the station and some on planet."

Gront opened his mouth to speak, but Annwyn held up her hand.

"As there are on Haevis, Nushao, and all the planets in the Larunda galaxy."

He nodded.

"I believe my next step is to locate Damius."

"I will research Krizlar and their politics, as well as the remaining emissary representatives' home planets. That information may shed some light on who may be behind the manipulation of Madame Raine, and if there are others being coerced as the Lead Emissary indicated."

"Good idea. Although he has provided significant information, there is nothing on what should be done next."

Gront touched the screens, and they all disappeared. "With your permission, I will retire to my private room to begin my research."

"Of course. And remember, everything we've discussed and whatever you find will be kept between us. Use my personal code to lock your information from anyone attempting to see what you're doing."

"Why would anyone suspect your servant of knowing anything?"

"They shouldn't. But I'd rather us take precautions against anyone getting any ideas."

Chapter Nineteen

Damius shifted his position in the flight seat. Wren was asleep at his feet. He was glad for his companion's company, but he knew the wolf wasn't at his full strength. Maybe there was an animal specialist on Chalar that could examine him. His gaze travelled across the aisle and he focused on Cudala sitting there with her hands clasped in her lap. The sparkle of her skin dulled somewhat which he remembered happening when she worried. He lowered his defense a moment to check on her.

Cudala's energy washed over him in waves. The news of the Sanctuary uprising caused her energy to start cycling. Her relationship with Tercora was more serious than she'd let on. She dressed in the traditional wear of the Sanctuary like the sarong-like dress he'd stripped off Annwyn. What if it was Annwyn caught in an uprising? He doubted he'd be as contained as Cudala.

Even though females were a part of the Larunda Force, few made it to the top tier teams. His team was Larunda Two, with only one team ranked higher. When Damius was promoted to Major, Cudala was the first he'd listed. Her diplomatic skills ranked only second to her piloting skills.

Another thing he needed to talk to Annwyn about—joining his team. It was much more complicated than her asking and him saying yes. There was training and exams. Not that he didn't think she was up to the task, but there were forms and rules and things that made his skin crawl and Wren grumpy.

The ship jerked then came to a halt. Another trip survived. Now, to talk their way into the Sanctuary.

He grabbed his travel case and put it, along with Eira's case with her remains, on the air cart. He grabbed Cudala's bag from her.

"How are we playing this?" she asked.

"Eira's remains are our ticket. I'm assuming at some point I will be refused entry. You are to assess the situation and protect Tercora if needed."

"Thank you, Major."

"Nothing to thank me for. We are Larunda Legacy Force, and we protect her rulers, citizens, and the planets equally."

Damius was refused transport to the Sanctuary until he flashed his credentials. The pilot was still reluctant but consented to take them to the entrance.

The airbus was empty except for he and Cudala. Good thing Astole chose Balder to accompany them to the planet.

"What is Balder doing?" Cudala asked.

"Making contact with Noden."

"I got a good feeling about him, boss. I think we can trust him."

"I agree. I'm sure Astole only allowed him along to have us watched." Damius studied the view as they glided past greenery surrounding the buildings. When this was all done, he needed to make sure that Balder was compensated for helping his team. And Noden. Maybe he'd check into getting Noden's record cleared...if everything went well and he wasn't somehow caught up in this mess.

It was significantly cooler inside the airbus than when they walked to meet Noden. Damius could appreciate the planet's unique structure and greenery better this way.

"You been here before our investigation?" Cudala asked.

"Not on planet. It's very different from my own." He slid a quick glance at Cudala and realized they hadn't had too many personal chats before. "My planet is more tepid, and my tribe moves with the seasons, to never be very hot or cold. Or immersed in the darkness. The Moya, the others on my planet, seem to embrace the darkness of our planet in a way I've never understood."

Memories of his younger seasons flooded in. The barren fields and lonely hours made him tired and sad. Maybe his mother had felt the same way. Maybe that was why she'd fled, and maybe that was why she'd passed when he was only a few seasons old. He remembered his father watching him, studying him to see if he would not able to tolerate the extended time in the light, like his mother, or her people.

Naiba. If only his mother's heritage had manifested that way. But no. Instead, he fought always to keep control of his emotions, as well as those pressed on him from others. That burden and gift was what she gave to him. He frowned and forced the memories away.

The airbus stopped at what was usually a busy square for tourists in the Circle compound, but this star rise, it was quiet with only two lone guards.

As soon as Damius, Wren, Cudala, and their air cart was unloaded, the airbus sped away, leaving them facing the guards alone.

"The Circle is closed to visitors. I do not know how much that airbus driver scammed you for, but no one can visit at this time."

Damius flashed his credentials. "I'm Major Elkwood of Larunda Force. This is Sergeant Cudala, a member of my team. We request permission to speak to Madame Tercora to deliver her the remains of her messenger, Eira."

"Eira!" The guard on the right dropped to her knees, staring at the urn. "Is...is this all that is left of her?"

"Yes, Sanctuary sister, this is all. She was killed in an explosion on Penduli Station," Cudala said.

The other guard went to comfort the first, then looked up at Damius. "Please, come inside the Welcome Center. I will contact the Second and ask what she would like done."

"Please, tell her to relay to Madame Tercora that Cudala is here."

The guard stared at Cudala for a moment then nodded her head.

Damius had yet to visit the Welcome Center at the Circle. It was designed to take the tourists from the crammed airbuses into a cool and calming environment. He could see the structure's nooks designed to make visitors feel like they were in a much smaller party than they were.

Cudala was adjusting her dress, and Damius put his hand on her arm. "It'll be fine."

"For the Circle to shut down the intake of visitors, it is bad. They haven't had an unscheduled closing in over ten solar phases. They depend on the tourists' money to keep the sisters fed and the Sanctuary profitable."

"I had no idea that finances were a concern."

Cudala lowered her voice and moved to stand in front of Damius. "The sisters do not work outside the Sanctuary, and though there are some artists among them that sell their wares, keeping the Sanctuary out of debt is a top priority."

"I see." Damius reached into his pants pocket, pulled out a container, and offered Wren some of the contents.

"How is he?"

"Stubborn, but better. I had hoped to find someone who specializes in animals while we were on the planet's surface."

"I'll ask Tercora. They keep animals here as well."

The second guard walked back over to them. "A representative from the inner circle is coming to speak with you, Major Elkwood, and she will escort Sergeant Cudala to see Madame Tercora.

We will have to ask you and your companion to depart."

"Understood."

After the usual greetings, small talk, and explanations, Damius was thanked and dismissed. There was a small airbus waiting for him when he exited the Welcome Center.

He sighed with relief. He had not looked forward to hiking back to the city's center. He entered, sat in the back, and Wren laid down next to him on the seat.

"Greetings, Major Elkwood. Noden sent me. He has some information he believes you will find interesting," the driver said.

"Thank you for the lift."

"I serve as Noden instructs."

That was the last the driver said to him as they zipped through the green undergrowth. The path was not the same as the bigger airbus that brought him to the Sanctuary. This one skimmed the ground at times, then would soar above one of the many waterways, the water spray coating the windows.

Damius thought he recognized the clearing where the driver sat the airbus down.

"Is Noden over that bridge?"

"Yes, Major Elkwood. He said you would not need directions."

"He'd make me hunt him anyway." Damius grabbed his travel pack and indicated that Wren should exit. "Thanks for the lift."

"I will be here if you need transportation back to the city center. Advise Noden. He will contact me."

As the door closed, the small airbus whisked out of sight.

"Bo!" Noden shouted out as he walked over. He pulled Damius into an embrace. "About time you got here."

"I needed to go to the Sanctuary."

"How did that work out for you?"

"I got to the Welcome Center."

"Yup, and no farther. I know all those women are tempting, but there is some crazy going on in there."

"I left Cudala to see what she can find out."

"I assume she is carrying some defense with her?"

"I'm sure. I've never known her to be without something. Honestly, she is the best of my team at hand combat."

Noden laughed deep in his belly. "Probably from fighting off her admirers. She is quite the looker."

"She is quite the sergeant."

"Always the professional," Noden joked, then suddenly was silent. He raised one eyebrow at Damius. "Some curve has your attention."

"Later."

Noden nodded. "We have much to talk about."

"What were you able to find out?"

"One of my men contacted the group and infiltrated. He is still with them but was able to get a message out to us. There is a hit expected this setting."

"Any idea where?"

"You aren't going to like it." Noden stopped in front of a table with a map of the city.

"Sanctuary."

"That is what we believe. There are people on Chalar particularly outside the city center who believe the Sanctuary has too much power."

"And how do you feel?"

"Bo, not my planet. It is what it is. They provide a moral compass here and help keep the peace."

"Doesn't that put them on the opposite side from you?" Damius was still trying to figure out exactly what Noden was doing on Chalar.

"Why don't you simply ask me what you want to know?"

"What are you doing here?"

"There, now you've asked it. Feel better?"

"I will when you actually answer the question."

Noden shook his head at Damius. "You are predictable. I deal in the finer commodities. Nothing specifically illegal."

Damius let his shields drop a little. Wren rubbed against his side. Noden was obfuscating, but not lying. "What is the real reason, not the fabricated story?"

"You have always been able to read me, Bo. Not all Larunda Force is official."

The two men shared a knowing look.

Wren went and rubbed up against Noden, and he squatted down to pet him.

"We definitely need to share a drink when this is over," Damius said.

"Agreed, but first, we need to set up our raid and get my man out of there." Noden pointed to a section of the city on the outskirts. "This area is known as No Land. There is an underground drug trade and black market."

"It seems every city has one."

"Here is the market, with the usual merchants. This whole section is teeming with people except for the late hours. To avoid civilian casualties, we will have to strike then."

"I was afraid of that, but it gives me time to get the rest of my team down here to assist."

"We are going to need to get some strikers on the rooftops."

"I'll get my people inserted before things shut down for the setting. The more troops we can get in the market before it shuts down, the better."

"Any accommodations?"

"There is a couple of traveler quarters." Noden pointed to a building a block out from the warehouse they were raiding. "I think this is the best one. Let's get you changed into something a little less military-like, and you and I will hit the town."

"Wren?"

"Not many animals down there, though there are some stragglers that roam the streets at setting. Can he meet us?"

"Yes, but I'll need someone you trust with your life."

"My man that drove you here."

Damius pictured the driver in his mind. His loyalty for Noden was undeniable. Damius nodded in agreement. "Let's get my people here."

※ ※ ※

Damius had to admit the clothing Noden outfitted him with was better suited for the planet than his own uniform. The fabric allowed his tough skin to breathe and his body to move without encumbrance.

He looked around the table at his team, minus Cudala. Mirbeck and Nicheo sat with Balder who decided that if his "assignment" was to follow Damius around the planet, the least he could do was add another man to the raid.

They had grazed for over an hour, partaking of the strong tea and hookah. Nothing that would dull their senses, but enough to fit in with the local crowd. Noden's reputation preceded him. Whatever his cover was, Larunda Force had inserted him into the locals without suspicion.

"So, Noden, tell us a story of the Major—Damius from his training times," Mirbeck said, almost slipping up with his rank. "There has to be one story where he lost it."

Damius was enjoying the relaxed table. He didn't get to do this enough with his team. There was always another mission, or they were on separate breaks. They worked like a well-oiled machine, but settings like this cemented teams. Balder was fitting in nicely as well. His mindset fit theirs better than that bakayarou Astole.

"I have bad news, my friends. Damius toed the line."

"More like I kept your ass in line."

A waitress arrived at their table. "We will be closing soon. Do you require anything else?"

Noden smiled up at the Chalaran female and handed her a titanium slip. "Keep what is left for yourself."

She looked down at the slip and smiled at Noden. "Please, come back again."

Noden winked at her. "Drink up, friends."

They walked out of the dining establishment and into the cool tropical breeze of Chalar. "Gentlemen, I have secured us a star setting stay just down the street. We'll be able to hit the markets first thing at rising to try to secure your business interest."

"Lead the way." Damius knew there were likely listening and tracking devices throughout the market. Noden's code was as smooth as ever.

Once at the traveler's quarters, Mirbeck swept for listening devices. "Clear."

"We can try to catch a few ticks' rest before we have to go seize control of the warehouse. We'll be entering the front, and my men have the back and rooftops."

The door to the central room opened, and all but Noden drew their weapons.

The driver from earlier stood in the entryway with Wren. "Maybe you should wait to see who it is before you draw on someone," Noden said.

"Maybe someone should knock first," Damius snapped.

"I didn't want to disturb. I deliver your companion. He has been quite good company this setting."

Wren trotted over to Damius, who knelt on the floor and petted him.

"Anything else before I take my position, sir?" Noden's man asked.

"No, hopefully we won't need you," Noden responded.

"The clean-up crew is always at your service," he said before bowing to Noden.

Damius watched the man leave. *Bowing*? He lifted a brow toward Noden who grinned.

Chapter Twenty

Nicheo tapped a few buttons on his com tablet, and a hologram of the warehouse appeared above the large round table in the central room. Damius's team gathered around and studied it in silence.

"No rest?" Noden asked.

"Nope," Mirbeck said with a grin. "Too much adrenaline to rest."

Damius pointed to the four walls of the building glowing before them. "Noden's team has all of this covered from the adjoining rooftops."

Noden pointed to a small entry point near one side. "That is the back portal. I've got two men on point with that. One on point at the front portal." He pointed to the large flat portal doors on the opposite side of the building. "That portal is from the early moon cycles. They're doors which slide on mechanical wheels to open. It's rarely used and a poor escape route. We'll need to enter via the back portal."

"Agreed," Damius said.

"How many are inside again?" Nicheo asked.

"Last count was eight...nine including my man."

"Should be a quick hit," Mirbeck said.

"They're not expecting it, so it'll definitely be a surprise. But they're trained and will not be taken down easily. Since the hit is scheduled for this star setting, there will be explosive materials on hand."

"We need to be sure we take everyone down except Noden's man. I'd rather no one died. Whoever we can capture can give us more information, and the rest can be dealt with per Chalar protocol."

"My man will know everything they know. He's very good at his job. No need to leave anyone alive to warn others, Bo." Noden shrugged. "Besides, the Circle isn't going to dirty their hands on a handful of rebels outside of the Sanctuary. That's the locals' job."

Damius considered his friend quietly. "The locals kill rebels?"

Noden snickered. "There's no rehabilitation on Chalar, Bo."

Damius jerked his head. "I still want one other than your man alive." He scanned his team, and they each nodded in agreement. "We'll go on point through the back portal."

"I'll enter first so as to point out my man," Noden said.

"I'll cover your back, then the rest of you will follow through. Watch your backs and keep your aim on bodies, not boxes. We don't need to have an explosion while we're inside."

Everyone stood and straightened their gear.

Wren gave a low howl, and Damius turned toward him. *You wait here, boy. It'll be better for me to know you're safe and healing while this goes down. I'll reach out once we're done.*

Wren loped to the far corner room and curled up on the cot, sitting off to the side.

Damius returned his attention to the team. "Set it and strap it, men."

"Let's hit this like a true Larunda squad," Mirbeck said.

Nicheo shut down his tablet and tossed it in his bag. He tugged out a smaller version and clipped it to his side. Damius switched his com from his lapel to his ear hook. While everyone else copied him, he tapped it on.

"Com line four, check," Mirbeck said.

"Come line three, check," Nicheo responded.

"Com line two, check," Noden whispered.

"Com line one. Okay everyone, let's get this done," Damius said, then lifted his chin toward Noden, who then tapped his wrist controls.

The rooms went dark. Damius followed Noden out, and his team did the same. They walked quietly down several corridors between buildings until they reached a small winding road. Noden pointed to the right, then patted his hip.

All of them bent low, rushed toward the right side of the road, and squatted in the small ravine that lined it. At least Noden remembered the hand signals.

Damius scanned the area and held his breath, listening. Only the sounds of late star-setting travelers reached him. Noden whistled, and the team all rose and began to jog along the road until they reached a small flat building. There, Noden stopped and raised his hand.

Damius studied the man as he switched com channels and pressed the small microbutton. Within ticks, his own com emitted a short static tone, indicating additional lines. He raised a brow at Noden, who nodded.

"Spotters check in," Noden said.

"Top one, check."

"Top two, check and clear."

Damius listened as five voices came through the com. He glanced back at his team and they nodded. He sidled next to Noden and scanned their targeted building. No activity outside. He pointed toward the left of the portal where two slit openings revealed lighting inside and shadows moving near it. Noden nodded.

Damius motioned a circle with his hand, pulled out his SL6, and checked the setting. *Kill.*

He'd have preferred to take everyone alive. He frowned and glanced back. Each team member had pulled out their weapons and stood in preparation for his orders. The distance to the building would leave them open and vulnerable for ticks only.

Annwyn's face flashed in his mind, but he pushed it out. *Not now.*

A low howl pierced the air from a long distance away, growing louder then descending in volume. *Wren.* Damius grinned.

But when he caught sight of Noden's weapon, his jaw dropped. Silver rings circled the barrel and several switches lined the grip.

"What the hell is that?" he asked.

Noden flashed his teeth. "It's the latest model. Faster and more powerful than those security issue Shanes your team carries. You still using the SL6?"

Damius nodded. "Where'd you get it?"

"I have my connections."

How did Noden get a newer-modeled laser weapon? "You buy it somewhere?"

"Um, Major," Nicheo said. "You two going to stand here and compare barrel sizes, or are we going to raid this place?"

Damius grunted. "Go."

They rushed toward the back door and flattened their bodies against the exterior walls. Damius held his weapon before him while Noden lifted the keypad and cut wires. He held his small blade under one wire and shot a quick glance at Damius before cutting the last wire.

The portal door whooshed open. Noden rushed in, lifting his own SL4 and began blasting. Damius ran in and toward the side. His team's footsteps followed.

"Green shirt is my man," Noden yelled over the laser fire shooting at them.

The smell of burnt flesh hit him along with screams of agony when a laser hit home. A burn on his left shoulder jerked him, and he dove behind a large crate. Peering out, he lined up on someone ten feet away firing from atop a large stack of metal boxes and shot. The man fell to the ground. Yelling and screaming rose as one by one a laser hit its mark and moved on to another target.

"I got your man," Mirbeck said over the com line.

Damius whipped around the crates and rushed across the warehouse toward the front where two men struggled to lift the large metal doors. He trained his weapon on one and yelled, "Don't move!"

The man crouched and rushed him, grappling him and punching him as they fell, hitting the floor like a ton of rocks. Damius punched the man and received one in response. He jerked his arm to release the man's hold on his weapon and got an elbow in the gut. He growled and bashed his head into the man's face. Blood spurted out onto them both. A scream from beside them preceded a thump as the other man was hit.

Naiba. No one gets his laser from him. Damius roared and shoved his arm against his opponent's neck, shoving him onto his back. He pressed hard against the man's throat with one arm and slammed his hands on the ground, trying to get the guy's grip to loosen. His blood pounded inside him. A red-hot rage rushed through his mind while he tightened his grip on the laser and twisted it. He hit the pulse button as soon as the barrel hit the man's head. He jerked back and rolled with the blast of the laser, ignoring the searing burn under his chin.

He jumped to his feet and crouched behind another crate as a laser ricocheted off a metal container and whipped past his leg. He fired in the direction of the shot, and a grunt followed by a moan echoed back. Damius catapulted over the crate toward where he'd shot and found his target dead on the floor. He scanned the room, ignoring the quick blasts of lasers and subsequent muffled screams.

Silence fell.

Through his com, Damius heard fast breaths. He waited a few ticks then closed his eyes and focused his mind on Wren. *I'm safe. Be back soon.*

"Report," Damius ordered.

"Clear, all enemy souls terminated," came Nicheo's voice.

"Stand down. Clear out men," Noden ordered.

Several voices confirmed.

Damius stood and stepped out from behind the crates. Several bodies lay strewn around the room. "I thought you only said eight were here. I'm easily counting twelve plus rebels."

Noden strolled from behind a tall metal post and shrugged. "So, I'm off a little."

Damius grimaced." What do we have?"

Nicheo joined them and tugged out his tablet and scanner. "Let me check these crates and see what they've got here."

Mirbeck arrived supporting a limping man.

Noden rushed to meet them. "Koda, you're hit."

His man chuckled then responded, "I got tagged right before the raid, and they decided to try using me as a punching bag for intel. It didn't work."

Balder entered the portal. "No one made it outside. But the sound effects in here have stirred up some locals. We need to get this place marked and locked to avoid interference."

Damius nodded. "Nicheo, mark it and call it in." He turned toward Balder. "Let's get out of here." He turned toward Noden. "Your men can get this cleaned out and send me an inventory."

Noden grinned. "If I take it, it's mine."

"All but the evidence I need. You can have the rest...for helping me out here." He waved his hand, indicating the warehouse. "But we can't have anything left behind to come back at us."

"You got it, Bo."

"Major, you're hit," Balder said, pointing at the streaks of blood streaming down Damius's clothes.

"I'm fine," he said and turned toward Koda. "Anything we need to know before we head out?"

"There's a buy going down. Mercury-laden explosives. They make them in a hidden room below this warehouse to supply some other group in the galaxy. Not for local use," he said.

"You got a name for this buyer?"

Koda nodded. "He's a delivery middleman. He's delivering it to someone off planet."

"We need to stop that sale and find out who is waiting for the bombs."

"The delivery man will know, I'm sure."

"But whoever is supposed to meet this guy is dead on this floor," Damius said.

"But the delivery man has never met him. We can slip in one of yours or Noden's men as the seller."

"Let's all get back to the safe room, and then we'll talk."

"I have it marked, Major," Nicheo said.

"I'll arrange to have the contents removed and eradicated evidence in here and below."

"You're taking the mercury bombs for yourself?"

"Bo, I'm not stupid. I'll secure up a couple for your case, and the rest will be dust with this building."

"Good idea." Within ticks, they'd left the building and taken the same route back. Damius ignored the burning in his shoulder and leg. "We'll regroup at the travelers' quarters."

Chapter
Twenty-one

"**M**y man should have the warehouse secured within the hour. It seems an abandoned building down the street caught fire, and some leftover fireworks caused a commotion that sounded like lasers," Noden said as he plopped in one of the chairs in their room.

Damius nodded. He hated relying on someone else to cover his tracks, but he knew Noden and his men were more than capable. Wren was waiting by the door when he arrived and almost jumped in his arms. With all the shots fired, he was glad Wren stayed behind.

"Major, I need to take a look at your injuries," Nicheo said as he pulled out the medic kit.

"Treat Noden's man first." Damius pointed toward Noden's guy.

"Yes, Major. But you are next. You can delay, but you can't hide."

"The name is Koda Ouray," Noden's inside man said as Nicheo scanned his injuries.

"Where is the drop taking place?" Damius peeled off his jacket and shirt as he talked with Koda. At least this time it wasn't his own clothes destroyed.

Noden tossed him a fresh shirt. "Wait to put that on until your man has a look at you. You're burned pretty bad."

Damius turned and looked at his arm in the mirror. Noden wasn't kidding. He looked worse for wear. And he smelled like burned flesh as well.

"The drop is to take place in one of the back alleys of the market. Not in the open air, but close enough to blend in if things go south," Koda said.

"Have they dealt with this buyer before?"

"Same buyer, different agent man."

Mirbeck popped up the map of the market place. "Where is the meet?"

Koda looked over at the display. "Pan to the left a bit... There—between those two buildings. It has multiple entry and exit points. Lot of potential places to hide and escape."

"So, they have no idea what the seller looks like, only a name?" Damius asked as Nicheo dabbed his wounds with antiseptic. He could hear Wren whimper, lying down beside him. The cleansing agent stung like a million flying pollinators from his home world. Little tiny pricks at his skin as the liquid agent cleaned and sealed his wound.

"None."

"Good, let's get a plan together, and I'll go in as the buyer. I'll wear a disguise of sorts to blend in with the locals." Damius winced as one wound after another sealed.

"Now, Bo, I was thinking that should be me, not you, as I have all my skin attached," Noden teased.

"Not a chance. You're already a known commodity here even if you don't want to see it. You and Mirbeck get a plan together."

"How long until the meet?" Nicheo asked.

"Right after star rise. The market will be opening, but there is enough traffic to provide cover," Koda said.

"Yeah—for both sides. As of now, we are on radio silence. I don't want anyone to know about this that isn't in this room or trusted by Noden. We still haven't figured out who is behind the warehouse, and until we do, we can't trust anyone," Damius announced.

Everyone in the room nodded their agreement and turned their communication devices off.

"I'm going to try to catch some rest. Let me know what you dream up."

"Will do," Koda said.

"Wren, come." Damius walked into the connecting bedroom and lay on the bed without disrobing. Wren jumped up and curled next to him. "It was closer this setting than I liked."

Wren grumbled.

⚜ ⚜ ⚜

Annwyn hustled to catch the airbus to the market. The sky platform was jam-packed with early-rising tourists and workers headed to jobs. There was standing room only, and Annwyn tapped her foot to keep from moving too much. She gripped onto the pole by the door as the airbus came to its first stop. She was too short to reach the handrails, and it was all she could do to stay upright and not launch herself to the other end of the airbus.

Artificial floral scent was piped in, but she guessed it was better than the body odor of all the people crammed together. Her stop was halfway through the circuit, and she had to push through the crowd to disembark. The light was starting to turn the sky a brilliant pink tinged with red.

The market stretched out in front of her. She inhaled delectable cinnamon, clove, and coffee that greeted her, and her stomach rumbled from its lack of nourishment. The market was welcoming with its brilliant colors, and merchant buildings and tents lined the streets. It was different from the main city center, less clean and perfect. More off-worlders that weren't tourists gathered here. She had rushed to catch the first shuttle to the planet after the Lead Emissary arranged her passage.

Her last communication from Balder had said the team was staying in the outskirts of the market with their contact. What was Damius up to in this place?

Why was his entire team down here but her? Was he keeping her out of the loop because he didn't trust her?

She didn't want to accept what the Lead Emissary and Gront thought about him. Logic and reason were the keys to her understanding what was happening. She needed to keep her emotions about Damius locked away until she could decide which side he was playing. Her father had taught her all too well that the outside face of someone was not always who they truly were.

She spied a bakery down a side street about halfway through the market. She tapped her communicator and tried reaching Balder again but to no avail.

I might as well get something to eat. How will I ever find them in this place?

Balder had given her no indication of where they would be in the market, and now he, along with the rest of the team, were silent. Annwyn walked toward the bakery stand, the sun blinding her momentarily until her eyes adjusted. Before her stood a maze of open doorways, lifted platforms displaying wares and children chasing each other, laughing and weaving through the crowds. Aromas of various eatables reached her, and her stomach growled. She should have eaten more.

She paused at one stand covered in brightly decorated fabrics and ribbons and studied the fluffy brown tops of what appeared to be some sort of biscuits. She pointed out a dark green palm-sized nugget and tossed a few credits at the vendor who nodded and wrapped her prize in a large soft leaf.

Annwyn bit into it, chewed, and swallowed quickly. Close but not quite the flourents from home. She frowned and wove between the tourists and vendors through a thatch-covered building. A darkened corridor opened to her right, and she moved forward until reaching the end. Several males entered and exited different portal doors at the edge of the building. There, she reached a gated wall. She lifted the handle to open it, but it did not budge.

Blades. Nothing was going her way. She was in a sketchy area of town by herself. The team she thought she was a part of obviously left her out of their latest dealings, and now she stood before a locked wall. *Damius, this is all your fault.*

Annwyn turned around and wandered aimlessly, muttering to herself. Suddenly, she realized she had drifted away from the merchant section of the market and into what seemed to be housing. She was lost.

A low conversation reached her, and she glanced around the corner to find two men down the connecting street to her right engaged in conversation. Maybe they could point her back toward the main thoroughfare.

She walked closer to the two men, the bigger of whom covered in a hooded cloak and in the process of presenting the contents of a case to another shorter man.

Annwyn stopped and looked for a place to hide. She ducked into an entrance alcove where she could still observe the two men.

A small breath escaped her lips as she willed herself to be as quiet as possible. The men had not noticed her yet, and she wanted to keep it that way. Her research on the market had alluded to the underground economy. If you needed almost anything, the Chalar market had it or knew where one could get their hands on it.

It's the perfect place to sell weapons.

꒰ ꒰ ꒰

Damius tightened the cloak he wore and tugged down the hood. The rising star steamed warmth against his stiffened shoulders. They needed to take this guy alive, but after they made the buy. Otherwise he wouldn't be able to file charges and go the legal route. Though he was sure Noden would help if the buyer needed persuading.

"Smit?" The buyer glared at him. "I pictured you smaller...weaker."

"You look exactly as I pictured you, Gauthos." Damius wondered how a rail-thin man could find a shirt too small. Gauthos's shiny black shirt threatened to rip at the seams at his belly. He even had matching shiny shoes. Damius smirked.

"I want to see all of them," Gauthos barked. He was a Vordanian, like the copilot. His skin was a darker pink that contrasted sharply with his jet-black hair. Damius had seen him before but couldn't remember where. Likely during their first excursion here.

"They are all the same," Damius said.

"I am not paying you 10,000 titanium strips without seeing all the merchandise. Be glad I don't want a demonstration."

Koda moved the cases one by one off their transport and opened them, showing the buyer the contents. Gauthos waved one of his men over to follow behind Koda.

"Looks good, boss," the man said over his shoulder, then closed the last box and returned to the buyer's side.

Gauthos nodded and held out a canvas pouch with a long, braided wood-like strap.

Damius raised his hand and stopped him. "Open it first."

"You don't trust me?" the buyer asked.

"Not on my life."

The buyer laughed and opened the pouch. "Nothing but your titanium slips."

Damius reached forward.

An older woman's screeching voice carried over the dirty alley toward them. "Stop loitering in my doorway. I do not care what the Sanctuary security says. All you street workers are a disgrace. Get out of here now. Go on."

"Looks like Maudie is at it again." Gauthos snickered.

The men turned to see an old woman with a broom poking a younger woman out of her doorway and down the alley. "You can sell your body all you want, but you will not be displaying your wares on my property." She poked again, and the younger woman stepped closer, her back toward him. "I run a respectable boarding house, and we do not allow your kind here." Maudie shoved the younger woman one more time, and she stumbled, bringing her within arm's distance of Damius and Gauthos. "Here. I'm sure one of these men would be happy to accommodate you." The old woman glared, hand on her hip and the other gripping her broom. "In fact, all of you get the hell out of here before I call the Sanctuary security and they can deal with your lot."

"I am not a sex worker," the younger one argued.

Damius snapped his gaze toward the source of that voice. A voice that usually heated his blood, but now brought icy tentacles around his lungs.

Gauthos grabbed Annwyn by the arm and jerked her toward him. "I think I'll take this one with me. You're so big you'd probably rip her in two."

Annwyn twisted in his arms.

"What is this? A security com?" He pointed a finger at her com button with the emissary insignia etched into it.

Annwyn pushed at his chest and twisted, then froze and stared directly at Damius. "Damius? What are you doing? Where is your team?" she asked, scanning behind him.

"You know her? You're not Smit," Gauthos growled. He raised a weapon from under his coat and fired at Damius and Koda.

Wren came charging out from the shadows toward the buyer's man, knocking him to the ground as his shot went out. It hit the old lady.

The buyer grabbed his case and jerked Annwyn, wrestling her toward his transport. Once there, he hit her over the head and shoved her body inside. Jumping in, he lifted his chin.

"Rot in the darkness, Oya," he screamed, and ordered his driver to get them out of there.

Chapter Twenty-two

"I'm fine. Go, go after her," Koda urged, before collapsing and pressing a hand to his side.

"Call in Noden." Damius turned and whistled for Wren. "And get Nicheo out here to clean up," he yelled over his shoulder. as he knelt and checked on the older woman. She'd been grazed, but the shock must have scared her so much she'd gone unconscious.

Naiba. That Hunee would be the death of him yet. What was she thinking?

Damius and Wren ran toward the small transport they'd arrived in. In unison, they leapt aboard, and Damius steered it to follow Annwyn and her kidnapper.

Wren howled low and deep while he stared straight out the front of their craft. Gauthos flew up over the tops of the market covers and around the back of a local storage warehouse. Where was he going? Damius powered up the shuttle weapons system and pulled the lever to edge the shuttle faster. He had to get Gauthos's communication system knocked out so he couldn't alert anyone else.

Within several ticks, Damius grinned as the buyer's shuttle slowed to dive under some hovercraft shuttling tourists from one sector of the city toward the departure zones. He jerked left and went wide, swinging around and coming up facing the port side. *Wait. Wait.*

"Target acquired."

Damius punched the firing button, and a short blast shot from the front of his shuttle, directly hitting the communication booster attached to the top of Gauthos's shuttle. What a stupid place to have those. His heart pounding, he gripped the lever tighter, maneuvering between the fleeing shuttle and the town center. He couldn't let Gauthos take Annwyn there. The Circle would know, and the whole planet's political issues would blow up.

Gauthos swung right and headed straight for the jungles lining the roads outside of town. A quick check confirmed it was the same road they took when he'd first arrived on Chalar. Damius followed the front shuttle as it dropped to fly around twenty feet above the ground along the dirt road. Pedestrians dove into the ditches on the sides to get out of the way as both shuttles skimmed above their heads.

A loud pop echoed in his ears, and smoke filled the cabin.

Wren howled loudly. *Danger.*

Damius searched the controls and found one of his engines hit. But how? He sucked in a breath when he noted another blast shooting from under Gauthos's shuttle and aimed their way.

Wren, prepare to jump.

Flames crept along the back of his shuttle when the second blast hit and rolled them over.

He grabbed for Wren, and they both jumped to the ground, tucking and rolling into the plant-covered ditch. Damius jumped up, scanned for Gauthos, and growled when he saw his shuttle dive into the woods away from the town center. His breath rushed out as Wren growled with him.

Let's go, boy. You're lead on this. Damius picked up his pace into a fast run when Wren shot into the twenty-foot-high wall of dense plant life. *Don't go too fast. We need to locate and recoup before action. Remember.*

Wren grunted. Together they ran through the tall sprouts with smaller limbs that whipped lightly at their bodies. Damius followed behind Wren, jumping over fallen debris and ducking under low-hanging branches. The soft moss-covered ground silenced their footsteps.

A small stream appeared before them, and Wren splashed through without stopping. Damius pressed on, ignoring the burning in his legs. His lungs filled with the humid air, expelling with puffs of breath as they pushed farther into the darkness. The tall greenery blocked the bright light of the sky, splashing small spots along the ground where it poked through the limbs above.

The humming of a small shuttle engine grew louder as they continued running. Wren slowed to a light jog then down to small steps. His paws padded the overgrown ground beneath their feet. He stopped and Damius joined him. Dropping down into a crouch position, they both scooted between the bushes toward the sound of the shuttle.

The engine stopped, and Damius and Wren fell to their stomachs and shifted the leaves to peer between them. The damaged shuttle sat in a small clearing with the side opening facing toward them. Annwyn sat staring at the ground. Her hands and feet were both bound. Rage ricocheted through Damius. His hands tightened into fists, and his vision tunneled onto Annwyn. He jerked to rush toward her but froze when Wren rolled onto him, pressing him into the ground. He locked his legs and forced his breaths to even.

Gauthos's swearing caused Damius to jerk his gaze away from Annwyn. Apparently, the man only now realized his communications were knocked out with the way he was hollering and ripping wires from the communications center of his shuttle.

Damius grinned. *I'm good. You go right, and I'll go left.*

Wren nudged his nose against Damius's neck and shifted to trot quietly toward the right side of the scene before them.

Damius crouched and moved left, keeping his gaze on Gauthos. *Don't look at her. Focus. Focus.* He waited until Gauthos stepped out of the shuttle, then pushed off into a fast run and jumped. He grabbed the man by the chest and knocked him to the ground. They rolled as Damius allowed the fury of seeing Annwyn tied up unleash itself into the punches he aimed at Gauthos's face. Wren jumped in and clamped his jaws on the man's leg, causing him to scream in agony. One more chop to his chin, and Gauthos fell limp.

"Is he dead?" Annwyn whispered.

"No, but he will wish he was. You can never allow yourself to be taken," Damius said, then rose and rushed toward her. He loosened her bindings and wrapped his arms around her.

Without thought, he clasped her tight against him and took her lips with his, kissing her.

Her fists pounded against his chest. She shoved away from him when he released her. "What in blades are you talking about?" She waved toward the now unconscious Gauthos. "You actually believe I allowed myself to be taken?"

"Of course not. But you put yourself in a situation where it might happen. You must avoid doing that ever." He paced a short distance away. He had to put space between them or he'd grab her again. His chest ached at the idea of never seeing her again. He released a pent-up breath. "Annwyn—"

"No," she interrupted. "Stop right there." She pointed a finger at him. "I had no idea where you were. I had no idea where the team was." She waved her hands in front of her. "I had no idea what was going on because you didn't tell me anything. Just like before." She wrapped her arms around her middle. "I thought we were beyond that."

"We are," he said. They were. "I didn't have time to get you a message. Surely you understand that?"

"I understand, but it still makes me angry."

He grabbed her hand and wrapped it in his, needing the contact to slow his heart. "I gave you and only you access to my quarters. Not even my team has access."

Her jaw dropped for a tick before she closed her mouth. "You did?"

Damius wrapped her in his embrace. "Mandis," he whispered.

She wrapped her arms around him and mumbled into his chest. "We need to get that man tied up. Then we need to sit down and talk. I'm not leaving here until you tell me everything that has happened since we separated."

"Yes, of course," he whispered in her ear." Mandis, I need you." He clamped his lips on hers and kissed her deeply. Heat poured into his body.

Wren howled softly through his teeth, which were still locked onto Gauthos's leg.

Chapter Twenty-three

Damius pounded his fist on Astole's desk for the second time in as many ticks.

"Per the Directorate's writings, you must yield your interrogation facilities to an officer of Larunda Force when needed," Damius growled.

"That may be true, but the writings do not say when I must let you use my facilities or what I can ask in return." Astole tented his fingers together and looked directly at Damius and then at Annwyn standing to the side and a little behind Damius. "How do I know you don't want to use my interrogation room for a tumble with her." Astole waved his hand in the direction of Annwyn and smiled.

Damius's face flushed, and he stepped in front of Annwyn. Wren circled from behind to stand in front of her too. "I need your interrogation room now. You will either provide it for me, or I will go to the station admiral and inform her, once again, your refusal to abide by The Directorate writings." He had never met a more insolent officer. How Astole had risen to this level was beyond him.

"Balder!" Astole yelled into his communicator. "Bring up the prisoner that Major Elkwood wishes to interrogate. Place him in room two."

"Now, since you are going to be busy in my interrogation room, I will visit suspect Gront in the Emissary's quarters."

"Excuse me!" Annwyn chimed in, stepping in front of Damius to face Astole.

Annwyn's sudden anger was like a punch to his gut. He knew he should keep his shields up around her, but it was growing increasingly difficult with their connection. He still was reeling from almost losing her in the market. What had she been thinking?

"As his 'guardian,' you can be there at the interview, of course. Why don't we get started in your quarters?" Astole stepped from behind his desk as Balder entered the room.

"Interrogation room two is ready for you."

"The security center is yours, Major."

Damius couldn't take it any longer—he pushed Annwyn aside and grabbed Astole by the collar, lifting him up off the ground.

"If you behave in any way that could be deemed inappropriate, I can guarantee you will live to regret it."

"Are you threatening me, Major Elkwood?"

"Most definitely."

Wren brushed against his leg.

"Annwyn, do you wish to be present while he interviews Gront?"

"Yes," she said.

Damius detected the slight quiver in her voice. He couldn't let her go with Astole alone. He sat Astole back on his feet and tapped his communicator. "Lt. Nicheo, will you please meet

Emissary Silk at her quarters to be present while Major Astole interviews Gront."

Damius nodded. "Lt. Nicheo will meet you for the questioning."

"I do not approve of him joining us."

"I don't care. Like it or not, I outrank you in every single way that matters. So, though you may be the major of this space station's security, I am Larunda Force, and you will answer to me." Damius moved to walk out of the room, then turned back toward Astole. "Do we understand each other, Major?"

Damius let the silence stretch out. Finally, Astole looked away.

"Tell your man not to interfere."

"Oh, he will be completely professional, as I expect of you as well."

Damius released his pent-up breath when he shut the door behind him and Wren. *Not the smartest thing I have done.*

He moved away from the door and toward the second interrogation room. *Why does Astole want him in that room? Was he being paranoid to think there is a reason?*

Annwyn touched his arm to pull his attention back to the present. "Astole wants to go now, while you are doing this. I wish I could be two places at once."

"Astole is up to something. I don't trust him. Go watch out for Gront's best interest. If he pushes things too far, have Nicheo get you counsel."

"I will. Be careful."

As Astole and Annwyn walked out of the security office, Balder waited until the door closed behind them. He pointed to his ear and then the ceiling, then pointed to his eyes, and dropped his hand to point at his chest.

So, the place was wired and had a camera. Not surprising. "Lt. Balder, could you please move the prisoner into a different interrogation room?"

"Yes, sir, I believe four will do well for your purposes."

"Thank you, Balder."

He waited a few ticks before he went into the interrogation room with his tablet. It was set up like the other interrogation rooms he'd used in the past. The walls in this one were a leafy green in contrast to the usual grey. A rectangular table was in the center, and Gauthos sat there. Damius set up his camera on the ledge behind him. There was a two-way mirror. Annwyn was to be on the other side of that mirror, able to communicate with him through either their link or traditional coms. He finished setting up his recorder then took one more tick to pull up the files on his tablet before bothering to look at Gauthos.

"I should've known you were an off-worlder."

"And why is that?" Damius asked as he sat down across from the buyer.

"You were too damn meticulous."

Damius laughed. "Man, I don't know. I think I would worry if my mercury switch supplier wasn't a little meticulous."

"How's the pretty little Hunee? I hate I didn't get time to taste that morsel. The people you work for, do they know you have?"

Damius had to get control of the interrogation, but his instincts were to defend Annwyn at all costs. Wren lay down on his feet, grounding him.

Play him, don't let him play you.

"She is a member of my team."

"Yeah. You keep telling yourself that, off-worlder. You suck at this lying thing. How did you ever get to be a major in Larunda Force?"

How the hell did Gauthos know more about him than he did about Gauthos?

"Oh, I know a lot, Elkwood." Gauthos leaned across the table, his eyes boring holes into Damius.

"Well, obviously not enough or you wouldn't have offered me a case full of titanium slips."

"I'm not going to tell you anything."

"Well, why don't I do some guessing? You are the buyer. Now, you do seem to have a place of operations on Chalar, but you travel. And not surprisingly, your travel dates correspond to a few moon cycles before a bomb."

"Is that so? Well, I guess that means I'm not responsible."

"We both know you didn't plant the bombs, but you delivered them to whoever did."

"Is that so?" Gauthos leaned back in his chair, crossing his arms.

"Yes." Damius breathed in and expanded his energy out through the room. When he was bullied in his first solar phase in school, his mother taught him how to 'stand tall' as she called it. It was difficult for him with the heritage of his mother. He simply felt what those around him felt, and it overwhelmed him as a child. He would frequently go sit in the corner away from everyone. That was why the bully came after him. He was different.

While his father told him to stop isolating himself, his mother taught him to 'stand tall'. He would fill the available space with his energy, pushing negative things away and shielding himself from others.

The hair on the back of Damius's neck stood up, and he knew that he had turned the table on Gauthos. "So, unless you want to rot on the prison colony for the rest of your life, I suggest you start talking about your buyers."

"And you think they would let me live if I told you?" Gauthos laughed, then leaned back in his chair. "I am the buyer. I am the seller, but to the end of my life, I am Chalaran."

Wren flew from his feet under the table and knocked the man onto his back. Wren was on Gauthos's chest, growling when Damius came around the table and waved him off. White foam was dripping from Gauthos's mouth, and his body shook with a seizure.

Naiba. Damius hit his com button and called for a medic. The foam and now blood dripped from Gauthos's mouth as his body suddenly stopped his violent shaking.

Damius stood, backing away as the medic team rushed in to the body of Gauthos. He kicked the table and threw the chair, causing Dr. Buehl to raise an eyebrow at him.

"What happened?" she asked, pulling equip and drugs from her bag. She plunged two needles into Gauthos's hearts.

"One moment we were sitting here talking, then he was foaming at the mouth and seizing."

Dr. Buehl slipped on a glove and placed two fingers into Gauthos's mouth. When she pulled them out, there were the remains of a capsule in between her fingers.

"His soul is gone, by his own hand," Dr. Buehl announced.

❦ ❦ ❦

Nicheo met Astole and Annwyn at her quarters. He didn't speak, only inclined his head and called her Emissary Silk. The shuttle ride back to the station had been decidedly quiet. No one on the team spoke to her. They blamed her for everything going wrong.

No, it wasn't her fault. It was Damius and his team's fault for not communicating with her and leaving her out of the loop. She tried to tell herself she didn't care if they liked her, but it was a lie.

This was the third time Astole asked Gront about what he did the star rise of Cress's death.

Gront's breathing was steady, and his eyes never wavered from Astole. Nicheo sat next to Astole at their refreshment table, and she next to Gront.

"How, again, did the blood get on your hands?"

"Blades! He has told you multiple times how he got blood on himself and his clothes. How many more times does he need to relay it to you?"

"Until I no longer ask the question."

"That's it. We're done." Annwyn rose from the table, walked to the door, and opened it. "If you want to 'interview' Gront anymore, you will need to get permission from the space station admiral."

"You cannot dismiss me, Emissary Silk," Astole said as he rose, as did Nicheo.

"Major Astole, please report to security. We have an issue with a prisoner." The announcement rang through the station.

Astole pressed the communicator in his ear. "Why am I being paged throughout the station?" He kept silent while he listened. "I'll be right there," he said, then glared at her with a red face and deep scowl.

"One of my men has advised Gauthos is dead," Astole announced as he rushed for the door. "Seems Damius has gone and gotten the prisoner killed. Luckily I was here with you."

Nicheo and Annwyn shared a look as Astole ran out. After the portal doors closed, Annwyn frowned.

"Convenient, don't you think," said Nicheo. It was the first time he had spoken to her since Astole's arrival. "Let's find Balder and meet in the command center. The Major is going to need us."

Annwyn nodded.

By the time Annwyn made her way to the command center, she had slowed her breathing and heartbeat. How the blades did Gauthos die? Did Damius kill him?

She walked through the door to the command center, and all the men faced her. "Sorry, I came as fast as I could." She took her seat, her legs bouncing underneath the table.

"I just got here, had to be cleared by medical in case I had any of the substance on me," Damius announced.

"Substance?" Annwyn asked.

"Yeah, our Gauthos had a suicide pill on him," he replied.

"I searched him myself," Mirbeck said.

"As did Balder. I remember him searching him again on the plane," Nicheo mentioned.

"He knew who I was. Something isn't right here. But the important thing is we found the bomb supplier," Damius stated.

Mirbeck looked at his tablet. "Communication from Cudala coming in from the planet, Major."

"Put it on the screen."

Mirbeck flicked the screen on his tablet, and Cudala appeared where they could all see her.

"Major, I have a channel that Tercora set up for me. I'll be able to contact you, but do not try to contact me. I have to shut it down when I'm not using it."

Raised voices sounded in the background.

"Tercora may have to fight Raine for control of the Circle. Things are heating up down here, and the Circle is splitting in two."

"Are you safe?"

"For now. I don't think I'm in danger. I'll be back in touch tomorrow rising. Raine is not doing well and even if it comes down to a battle between the two, I have confidence in Tercora."

"Keep us updated. We can be there on the next shuttle."

"Make sure to bring Annwyn with you," Cudala said before signing off.

Chapter Twenty-four

"**W**hat do you mean?" Annwyn frowned when the screen disappeared. Why was her presence needed? She glanced at Damius, and shrugged at his raised brow.

"Nicheo," Damius said. "Get your report filed on what occurred during Astole's questioning. Balder will write up a report, and I'll add to it, once he's done on Gauthos's situation. Clear?"

"What about my report?" Annwyn asked.

"I wish to discuss what happened first." He stepped away from the table and toward the door. "Have all the reports ready and submitted this star setting. I'll review, and we'll meet back here at the rising. Clear?"

"Clear," everyone except Annwyn responded.

Damius motioned to her. "Please join me in my quarters. I have something to show you, then we can discuss what occurred with Astole and Gront."

Should she join him there? He'd saved her from Gauthos, but then the guy died...by a suicide pill? Would he tell her everything? She had to know. She jerked her head in a nod and followed Damius out and down the hallway. He shortened his strides, so she kept up next to him. She tapped her fingers against her thighs as they walked in silence. Wren loped between them.

Once in the lift, she leaned back against the side and peered up. He stared straight ahead with his lips clamped tightly together. Wren nuzzled her leg, and she stopped her tapping to stroke his head.

I almost lost you, and I wasn't prepared for the emotions that incident on planet caused.

Annwyn blinked. He hadn't said that aloud. Warmth filled her body, and she caught her breath in a short gasp. *Being prepared for any unplanned emotions is part of the training I received,* she mentally responded.

He cut her a quick glance before returning to stare at the portal. I hadn't realized you'd hear me. Wren must be our conductor.

Or it could simply be your gift inherited by your mother. Does your father know?

Damius frowned. *No, and he never will if I can help it.*

Why?

I'll explain it to you, one star setting. Right now, we need to talk about everything that's happened. You're still upset about the events on planet-side.

I am. "But that doesn't mean I can't be objective in the case."

"I know," he said.

The lift doors whooshed open, and they turned together toward his quarters. When they arrived, he waved toward the portal doorway. "Open it," he said.

Annwyn used her code and bit her lip when the doors swooshed open immediately. If only she'd known. Damius made a motion for her to precede him. She did.

Once the doors closed, Annwyn spun around and launched herself into his arms. Damius lifted her, and with one hand holding her against his chest, he used the other to pull her head to his, kissing her hard. Heat speared through her and pooled in her belly. She dug her hands into his hair and kissed him back fervently.

I need you. His mind whispered into hers.

Yes. Their mental connection kicked her pulse into a rapid beat. She wrapped her legs around his waist and held on. *Again, now.*

♆ ♆ ♆

Damius carried her to the portodesk, swiping it clean with one hand before he set her down.

When he'd seen the other man touching her, he wanted to rip him from limb to limb. He couldn't stand the thought of how close he came to losing her today.

His hands tangled in her hair, and he pulled her neck to one side, bending down to whisper in her ear.

"I need you." He had to say the words, not simply think them. They needed to be voiced and given life as his hands worked to free Annwyn of her clothes. As he pulled them off, his hands traced down her body, touching every inch.

Her skin was silk under his. He cupped her breasts and lowered his head down to them. Her nails dug into his back as he reached down to undo his pants. They fell to the floor, and he kicked them away. He pulled his shirt over his head as her hand reached down to touch him.

He hand slapped on the table surface, and Annwyn's smugness at his reaction was easy to read.

I'm going to win.

This isn't a game...but if it was, you would lose.

Damius dropped to his knees, stopping Annwyn's protests as his tongue found her most sensitive spots. He raised her hips with his hands, and she moaned in response.

Told you so.

She reached the first of the many climaxes he was determined to give her.

Mandis. He rose, using his hands to tilt her body as he entered her. Slowly, he moved, ignoring her protest to increase his pace.

"In time," he whispered as he slid all the way inside of her and paused. "Patience."

His barriers began to break and crack, weakening before the fall, and soon her emotions would rush over him, swallowing what little control he had left.

He looked down into her grey eyes then pulled her body in contact with his. Her skin sent short electrical jolts through his, causing his blood to pulsate inside his veins. He kissed her again, their tongues doing battle as he finally increased his pace.

She broke the kiss, panting for air and saying his name over and over as they moved together.

Her nails felt like flames across his back as she reached the apex right before him. She collapsed against him, and he rotated his hips, slamming into her as hard as he could, wanting nothing to be between them. He buried his face in her silky hair as his climax washed over him. He rocked back and forth, hiding his face and the tear that ran down his check.

He couldn't lose her. She was a part of him now.

Annwyn stroked a light finger down his arm and clasped his hand with hers. So small, yet so strong. He'd used the trick he learned to block their mental reading of each other as soon as he caught his breath.

"Will you teach me how to do that?" she asked.

"Of course. But understand I have a lifetime of practice with mine, so it will not be so easy at first." When she stiffened, he squeezed her hand. "I will never intrude without permission, Mandis. You need not fear my reading your thoughts."

Her body relaxed, their faces so close, he only needed to bend a bit to kiss her again. No. Now was not the time. Maybe after he answered her questions, he could take her again. Better yet, she could take him. Lust filled his body and he shivered.

Annwyn shifted away and scowled. "No. You're going to answer some questions before we go further with anything."

Damius nodded, picking her up to carry her into the bedroom. "Nothing says we can't be comfortable while we talk." He laid her down on the bed.

"Good." Annwyn wrapped the sheet around her and sat up. She grinned at his scowl and pointed at her covered body. "I don't want you distracted from our words."

He sat and shifted back to lean against the wall, then nodded.

"So, this Gauthos buys bombs and distributes them to other planets?"

"We haven't confirmed if his position is to supply different planetary groups or a single rebel group operating around the galaxy."

"But you know he is the supplier?"

"Yes. Noden discovered the buyer Gauthos worked for supplied the mercury bombs." He pulled the sheet around his waist.

"Who?"

Damius shrugged. "At this point, we don't know. We stopped him, which means no more bombs will be sold nor delivered to anyone."

"But the bombs you secured are the only ones left? How many other deliveries did this man make? We can't be sure there aren't more bombs out there waiting to be planted."

"We can. Noden's clean-up men found the ledger showing how many bombs were sold. So, all the mercury switches and bombs are accounted for."

"Good. At least we know that there will be no more mercury bombs." Annwyn leaned forward. "But Gauthos was only the middle man. Who was he selling the bombs to?"

"Unfortunately, not for us to determine. We'll submit our reports and move on to where Larunda Force sends us."

"What? So, this is it?"

"We've stopped the supplier of the bombs. No more explosions will occur. We've done as ordered. Once we finalize the reports, this case will be closed."

Annwyn gasped. "Closed?"

"Yes," Damius said and crossed his arms. "Closed."

She glared at him." And what kind of security investigation team does Larunda have that stops only one arm of the investigation without pushing further to find the origins?"

Damius rolled his shoulders and left the bed. He stood and stared at her. "This security investigation team. If you truly wish to join me, this is part of the way it works. We follow Larunda Force orders. We were tasked with figuring out where the bombs were made and to stop more. That was our directive. We did that."

Annwyn dismissed his nudity and focused on his face." I want to be part of your team. But I can't believe…" She recalled Moiran's words of warning. "I still think there is more we need to investigate. However, if that is what procedure dictates, who am I to argue?"

Damius studied her, and she turned away from him to avoid his gaze.

Scooting out of the bed, she strode to the bio chamber. "Shall we get washed?"

Damius grabbed her arm before she could go farther. "I'm not saying I believe the investigation is complete. I am only saying this portion of it is. The bombings are over. We'll close that case, then report to The Directorate and show them the information we have."

Annwyn faced him and searched his face. He told the truth. "So, you agree there's more to this?"

Damius nodded. "How much more, I don't know. But I am determined to discover all. I have those I report to. I need more to give them to continue this. Once I do, you can be sure my team will be leading the investigation."

Annwyn smiled. "As long as I'm on your team, I'll be fine."

"Do we need to wash right now? I'm not yet sleepy, and I want you again."

Annwyn twirled and beckoned him toward the bed. "Again, then."

Chapter
Twenty-five

Annwyn scratched Wren's head before she slipped out of Damius's quarters. Her thoughts were doing gymnastics about the case as she'd lain beside him earlier. *Who killed Officer Cress? Who was behind the bombings?* She spun puzzle pieces in her mind of people and places. Damius was not involved, nor any of the team. That, she was certain, but what about the Lead Emissary and Astole?

Astole… What drives him?

Her skin crawled whenever she was near him. She needed to dig deeper into his actions, and that thought had nagged at her until she kissed Damius goodbye and went back to her quarters. She'd start with a general background, then pull his com records, or at least what her access gave her.

She tapped in her code, and the portal door to her quarters swooshed open. The low light and greenery immediately calmed her as she stepped inside.

"I assume you are sleeping with him," Gront said from the table.

Her skin burned with embarrassment. *I am a grown Hunee. I can sleep with whoever I want.* "That is none of your business."

"So, you are."

"Yes."

"He can't be trusted. I thought we decided on that."

"We did, but on Chalar, I decided differently."

"I see." Gront tossed the tablet he was reviewing on the table and rose. "Don't blame me when you get hurt. I am going to bed, if my lady says it is okay."

Annwyn frowned at his behavior. They'd always been open and honest with each other regardless of his position. However, this was close to overstepping his boundaries. She sighed and waved her hand toward Gront's quarters. Now was not the time for a fight with him over his misplaced ideas. Maybe there was something in the Lead Emissary's files she'd missed.

She and Damius would have to be more circumspect with their lovemaking if they didn't want the entire team to know. She cut up some of the fruit Gront had left out for rising feast and started to look over the files. The grumbling of her stomach reminded her it'd been some time since she'd last ate. Add in her recent activity and food was foremost on her mind. She smiled as she licked the juice of the mollypear off her fingers.

She and Damius had explored each other's bodies more thoroughly, and she knew more of what he liked. Though their lovemaking wasn't the game she usually played, she still liked knowing what made her partner aroused.

She rose to wash, letting her mind drift over the investigation. *Nothing*. Nothing was making sense.

What am I missing?

She ran water over her hands then scrubbed them to get the fruit sap out from underneath her fingernails. Sometimes she wished she had a bio basin like the one in her lab. It was important to keep things clean.

Clean. Wait.

She dried her hands hurriedly and rushed to her workstation. She pulled up the reports related to Officer Cress's murder. With the surge in the bombings case, she'd forgotten to take a second look at the lab's findings concerning the murder weapon.

She pulled up the report. The weapon was completely clean. No bio evidence whatsoever on the knife. How was that even possible? Someone would have to have access to the proper equipment and the weapon to remove any trace of bio tags.

Astole.

He was the only one who would have access to both. She blew out a breath and bounced on her toes. Time to learn everything she could about him.

Two hours later, she was well versed in the life of Astole. There was nothing spectacular, nothing more than ordinary, other than he liked luxury items. She needed access to his credit logs to see how he afforded such purchases since the last she'd known, even someone in his position couldn't afford some of the items listed in his personal inventory.

The com records were the only thing left, and she only had access to a few. She scanned the records. *Hmm.* The last com he'd received was from the Sanctuary. Why would they contact him? She frowned. She scrolled farther back. Who else did he communicate with that would be unusual?

"Blades!" Annwyn pushed her chair back from her workstation. "No, he wouldn't... He couldn't." Her hands shook as she read the screen again while a slow burn built in her stomach. "I should've known," she whispered as tears ran down her face.

She stood, wiped her tears, straightened her clothes, then tucked a stray strand of hair behind her ear. Enough was enough. She would not be used.

She looked toward Gront's closed door and whispered, "I'm sorry," as she exited her quarters. As she headed toward Astole's office, she tapped her fingers together. The communicate logs verified repetitive contact between her father and Astole. Of all the people to choose as a guard, her father picked the most disreputable officer on station to bribe into watching her. No wonder Astole afforded such luxuries. That was about to end. Obviously, Astole didn't realize she'd trained with the best competitors on her planet. A lazy princess, she was not.

Ⱳ Ⱳ Ⱳ

Damius stared at the empty chairs in the squad room, then scanned the faces of his team. "Annwyn should be here soon." He pulled up their reports and reviewed them while his team fidgeted in their seats.

Wren nudged his leg under the portodesk.

After a few ticks, he glanced up. "What is it?"

Nicheo cleared his throat." Annwyn sent a message earlier stating she would not make the meeting, Major."

"Message?" He searched his com history. He'd received no message. "I don't see it here."

Mardem leaned his head toward the side, then back before staring at the ceiling. "I don't recall receiving one either." He glared at Nicheo. "How come only you got a message?"

Nicheo's face darkened, and he stared down at his tablet and shrugged.

Damius clenched his jaw and fists. *Naiba*. What now? Where is she? "Send the message to me so I may review it." He sat forward and read the short message she'd sent to Nicheo only. That didn't make sense. Only a short time before, she'd clawed his back with her nails, begging for release. Yet, she sent a message to Nicheo and not him?

He unclenched his hands and rubbed the back of his neck when an itch climbed up his spine. No. He read the message again. Something here didn't sound right.

"It's a hurried message. Like she was in a rush sending it." He looked at Nicheo. "Don't you think so?"

Nicheo cleared his throat. "I've only received a few messages from her. I don't think I could tell."

Mardem reached forward and grabbed Nicheo's tablet. "She's had me review her reports for clarity in the past. I'll be able to know if something doesn't sound right." He dropped his gaze to the tablet and pursed his lips. He shot a quick frown toward Nicheo before turning toward Damius. "You're right, Major. This doesn't sound like her normal messages." He tossed Nicheo the tablet. "She is very deliberate. This is not."

Nicheo caught it and growled." Careful with this."

Damius raised his hand for silence and read the message aloud. His squad nodded." There doesn't seem to be a code in there, but it doesn't sound like something she'd say."

Wren growled and rose, then paced between the squad and the portal door. Damius watched him. *Exactly. But we need more information before running off, boy.*

Wren trod away and dropped down with a huff.

ⵣ ⵣ ⵣ

Astole yanked Annwyn toward the shuttle.

"Hey, that hurts," Annwyn snapped. Dear Larunda. Even a first-level player wouldn't have made this mistake. She should have been more prepared. Her father would laugh at her mistake in thinking she could use her royal status to control the situation.

"It's going to do more than hurt, *Emissary*, if you don't cooperate. I don't have the time, nor the inclination to keep you unharmed. I'm sure your father will pay the ransom to bring you home even if you are a little roughed up, or worse." Astole ran his hand down her body.

Her hand connected with his face.

Astole pulled her roughly against his body and pressed a laser against her side. He kissed her temple then leaned and whispered in her ear, "We're going to slowly walk to my shuttle. Do not try to attract any of the guards or workers. You will cooperate, or I will kill you."

"If you kill me, you won't be able to ransom me to my father." She glanced around the docking bay. "Besides, how are you going to justify shooting me here?"

"For all they know, you're my prisoner. If you run, I shoot."

"Damius and his men will find me."

Astole laughed. "His men are still mad that you ruined their covert op on the ground and almost got several people killed. So, I don't think they will look too hard."

"You must know who I am on Haevis. If my father founds out what you've done—"

"Your father's money is the honey on the fruit I've enjoyed."

The fight drained out of Annwyn as a burn built in her belly. Annwyn nodded and looked at the ground. Damius would find her, with or without his team. The question was would he forgive her for confronting Astole alone, and would she still be alive? Please let the communication Astole forced her to send alert them.

She allowed Astole to pull her into the shuttle. Once seated and out of public view, he slapped restraints on her wrists.

"Fast. I'm not paying you to follow the speeding laws," Astole snapped at the pilot.

Annwyn looked out the shuttle's window, trying to get her bearings once they reached the planet's sky. She'd only been to the surface twice. As they rounded a bend, she knew their destination. *Sanctuary.*

"We're about to arrive. Make sure it is your people meeting us at the gate."

The shuttle came to a stop at one of the platforms past the welcome area. Astole pushed her out of the shuttle.

Annwyn stumbled, landing on her knees. *How did I get myself into this mess?*

"We'll have enough time for you to be on your knees later, Emissary."

Two guards walked up to them.

"Madame Raine awaits your arrival. She will see you now," one guard announced.

"Great, this trash needs to be secured."

"I will place her in the holding area."

"Fine. I need a secure line," Astole barked as he followed one of the guards.

The other guard linked a chain lead to Annwyn's bound hands and yanked for her to follow.

Annwyn ran to keep up with the much taller Chalaran. She tried to focus on where she was being taken. The long hall dead-ended, and they took a right. They stopped at the fourth door on the left, and the guard produced keys.

She opened the door, unhooked Annwyn's restraints, and shoved her inside. Annwyn hardly registered someone sitting on a bench at the other side of the room before she spun around to face the guard. The guard looked up and down the hallway, stepped inside the room, almost shutting the door, and moved Annwyn to the side.

"Annwyn!" Cudala gasped as she rushed to her.

"Ma'am, I can't stay. Is there anything you need?" the guard asked softly.

"My bag and equipment, please, Parstia. We need to be able to warn Tercora."

"Agreed, ma'am. On my next security pass, I should be able to get it to you. I believe they are going to the residences. It will not be long before the uprising is in full swing."

"We will need a way out."

"She"—the guard pointed toward Annwyn— "has complicated things. I will see what I can do. In her name." The guard bowed and saluted Cudala.

"In her name." Cudala bowed back.

The guard slammed the door shut, and the locking pings echoed.

Cudala turned toward Annwyn. "What are you doing here?"

"Astole kidnapped me. He's hoping my father will pay a ransom."

Although barren, the room did not encourage long stays. One cloth-covered bench against the far wall stood next to a similarly covered chair. The lighting was dim, yet not enough to inhibit sight.

Annwyn sucked in her breath. "The guard's name is Parstia? Who don't you know here?"

"I knew that slime ball Astole was no good," Cudala said and returned to sit on the bench.

Annwyn turned around. "My father or Astole?"

Chapter
Twenty-six

Cudala chuckled, then paused, studying her. "How did Astole mange to get his hands on you?"

"I confronted him on the station," Annwyn said.

"By yourself?"

"Yes." She shifted her gaze away from Cudala's frown.

"You are brave and stupid. I'm surprised by the stupid."

"I was filled with rage when I saw he had communicated with my father."

"He what?" Cudala jumped up, causing the dim light to enhance the sparkling pinkish tinge of her skin.

"On the star rising of Cress's murder, and later that setting."

"Your father…"

A beep silenced Cudala. Annwyn spun toward the door as it slipped open only far enough that a bag could be slipped inside and dropped before it closed again. Cudala grabbed her bag and returned to her seat. After pulling out her mini-tablet, she punched the buttons while Annwyn watched in silence.

After a moment, Cudala paused and lifted her gaze. "You really think your father—"

"Yes," Annwyn interrupted. "King Silk, Leader of the Hunee, and currently representing Haevis with The Directorate contacted Astole, and right afterwards, my guard was killed, and my servant taken into custody."

"You truly believe your father hired Astole to kill Cress, and Astole agreed?" Cudala whispered and shook her head. "I don't know about your father. But Astole couldn't be that much of an idiot to risk his career like that."

"Oh, he could if he was offered enough to do so. The only life my father respects is his own, and he is too used to flaunting his power to gain what he believes is his. If he's hired Astole, then they're both at fault. If you can get me into Astole's banking records, I bet we can prove the connection. From Astole's detailed planning with my father, I had a feeling he'd done this before. My father isn't or wasn't his only client."

"I'm set to connect. We must make this quick, so we're not caught. I'll grab the financial and communication records. You review them as fast as you can. Once you find what we need, I'll send a message to the team."

"How did you end up here?"

"Raine's people stormed the inner circle, and we ran. I held them at bay while Tercora escaped." Cudala tapped a few more keys, then went back off grid. "Let's see what we can find."

Cudala and Annwyn scanned the documents, looking for a connection.

"Wait, go back." Annwyn ran her finger down the screen. "There. That's my uncle's company."

"The moon cycle Cress was killed," Cudala whispered.

Annwyn closed her eyes and lowered her head into her hands.

"There are other payments from various sources. Looks like our boy Astole was working on a nice slush fund of his own." She smirked. "Guess he thought he wasn't getting paid enough?" She returned to her mini. "Let me pull up the communication records."

Annwyn breathed in, holding her breath, then breathed out. She had to control her emotions. She slumped on the chair next to Cudala. Just because her father was a corrupt swamp dweller, it didn't make her one. How could he do this to their people? If The Directorate representatives found out... No, she wouldn't dwell on that now. Blades.

"The communications have been wiped." Cudala sighed.

"Can Nicheo access the original records on the station?"

"Yes, but we need to contact them first." Cudala tapped her shoulder. "You okay?"

"No."

The door unlocked, and they jumped. Cudala grabbed the mini and shoved it under the bench's drapes, then tucked her communicator in her waistband.

Parstia opened the door and rushed over to Annwyn to put restraints on her wrists again. As she attached the lead, she stepped toward Cudala and leaned close, grabbing her hand and pressing a lock card pass into it.

"Get out of here after we leave. Our Lady is in the new arrivals area. She needs you," she whispered.

Parstia pulled Annwyn toward the door.

"Where are we going?" Annwyn stared at Cudala, who stepped forward only to stop short when another guard appeared.

"Astole wants her brought to the meeting chambers," the guard said.

The meeting chambers? Annwyn scanned the halls as they pushed her forward. The composition of their surroundings was made from the same wooden substance as the main center. Likely as thick and strong as the brown wood from her home planet. *Can't break through* those. She frowned and studied the direction they headed. Not very complicated. She could find her way back to Cudala easily. But then...she's escaping to meet Tercora. *Blades. Damius will never forgive me for this.* Once again, he was forced to come to her rescue.

The guards stopped in front of an elaborately decorated set of portal doors. Each side was trimmed with rune marks of the Inner Sanctum she'd seen earlier. Would Madame Raine be present as well? Then it hit her. The white powdery substance on the plants of the Circle's gardens on her first visit. Raine's skin rash. How could she have missed it when she scanned Gront's book *Ancient Metals*? Not only did she have the symptoms of mercury poisoning, it had been going on for some time. She gasped. Dear Larunda. There must have been a mercury deposit on the Circle grounds. Why else would her symptoms develop so rapidly?

She stiffened when the guards opened the door, removed her shackles, and shoved her inside. She tripped over the floor covering designed to replicate a scene from the Ceremonial Plateau.

When she caught her balance, she found Astole standing near a large window with a braided wood frame. He approached her with pursed lips and ran his gaze from her head to her feet. She inwardly shuddered, and her stomach clenched. She froze and glared at him, stiffening her back. *He will not see my fear.*

"I have decided you must keep that overbearing Damius away from here with a second message to him. I don't want him to suspect you've come to the surface." He tossed a small communication dime bar, and she caught it deftly.

Tipping her head to the side, she raised her brows. "And if I refuse?"

He slapped her across her face with such force, she wheeled backward and fell. She placed a hand across her cheek to ease the sting and bit her lip to keep from crying out. She rose and glared at him once more.

"You will record a message advising Damius and his team that you have gone into one of your Hunee meditation turns and will be unavailable to work the investigation for at least seven moons."

"Or you will beat me? Do I look broken?" Her fists clenched at her sides.

"Oh no, my little green one. If you do not record your message now, I will take you to my rooms and attempt to convince you otherwise."

Bile climbed up her throat, threatening to spew. She pressed her lips tightly together and bit the inside of her cheek.

"I plan to take you there either way. It's your choice if it is to be now...or later."

Blades. "I'll record it."

"Smart choice." He waved toward one of the plush blue benches placed in the center of the room. "Sit there and do it now. No tricks or clues. I'll be listening closely."

I doubt you'd know a clue if it slapped you in the face. Which is exactly what I'm going to do very soon. Annwyn sat and recorded her message, then returned the recorder. *No one can win against a trained Hunee when clues are to be hidden, fool.*

Astole handed the dime bar to the guard with Parstia.

"Send that immediately," he ordered, then turned toward Parstia and pointed to the portal.

"Get out there and be sure we're not bothered at all.

Parstia frowned at Astole before turning and leaving.

Annwyn held her breath when the brute faced her, grinning. "Maybe it's time we get to know each other a bit more?"

A sudden explosion threw Annwyn to the ground. Debris flew on and around her. She covered her face and crawled under the bench. Another explosion rocked the room, causing the floor to shift as though it prepared to collapse. Astole's scream pierced the air.

᰸᰸᰸

"When was the last time you saw her?" Damius said into his com.

"I have not seen her since the setting," Gront responded.

"I see. So, basically you are telling me you have no idea when she left? She left you no message at all?"

"None."

Nicheo spoke up. "Major, Annwyn wrote 'Convenient, don't you think?' I said that about Astole after he interviewed Gront."

"Don't leave your quarters, Gront. Let us know if she decides to show back up. Elkwood out." Damius disconnected his communication and turned toward Nicheo.

"Where is Astole this rising? I figured he would be all over me about Gauthos's suicide." Damius said, then ran his gaze over the team. "Mirbeck, track him down. Nicheo, get Balder up here."

"Astole's com isn't on the ship." Mirbeck tapped on the screen. "A private shuttle left with Astole shortly after rising on a private shuttle to the planet. He had another passenger with him," Mirbeck informed them. "It is his time off according to the station's duty roster."

"Bring up the security footage of the area. I want to know who was with him," Damius said.

"Balder is on his way," Nicheo announced.

"Tell him to meet us at Astole's quarters. We're going through them, and I want him there."

"Here's the footage sir," Mirbeck said as tapped on his screen turning it so they all could see.

They watched as Astole entered the shuttle bay area, yanking a woman with him.

Damius's posture stiffened. There was only one female Hunee on station. Annwyn.

ꙮ ꙮ ꙮ

Balder arrived at Astole's quarters the same time as Damius and his team. He punched a code on the sensor and the doors whooshed open.

Damius turned to Balder. "You understand what's going on here?"

Balder frowned and nodded. "Unfortunately, I do. It's a sad moon cycle when a fellow security officer goes bad. You're sure your information is good?"

Damius opened his mouth to respond when Balder held up a hand. "No one has the right to go against Larunda Legacy Force. If what you find creates problems with the Penduli representative on The Directorate, we must follow the writing and maintain exact processes." His shoulders dropped. "I hope you understand my position."

Damius jerked his head in a quick nod. "I do, and we will adhere to the LLS's regulations and run this strictly by the writings. I can promise you that." He waved his head toward the opening. "Which is one of the reasons I contacted you for entry. You first."

"Thanks," he said then entered Astole's quarters.

Clothing and papers were strewn over every flat surface with dirty feast ware mixed among the rest.

"He wasn't very particular about his surroundings, was he?" Nicheo mumbled as he passed them to collect the papers.

Mirbeck shoved clothing around and opened containers and doors. He turned toward Damius. "Nothing here. I'm checking his sleeping area."

"What are you expecting to find, exactly? I know whatever it is will end his career if it has any connection to the bombings."

"Here we go," Nicheo announced, sitting at the black portodesk in the corner. Damius and Balder joined him. "I've got access to his records, but there's some files locked in his security slot. I need his security clearance to access that information." He looked at Balder, who nodded and handed him a dime bar.

"That will allow access to all his files." Balder shrugged. "Any files kept through Penduli Station are marked with a back entrance for our reviews...if needed. There are protocols required and writings to file if we do enter a back entrance. Which means, I'll be working late after star setting to get them submitted."

"Sorry," Nicheo said with a grin and began punching keys.

A bright green ribbon hanging on the side wall caught Damius's eye. He stared, and every muscle bunched with fury. A long lock of black hair was adhered to the cloth, and it wound against a small piece of braided wood. What the naiba is this? He did a quick scan and noted Nicheo's nose buried in electronic searching. Balder had cleared a spot at the table where he currently typed away on his mini. Ever so nonchalantly, Damius leaned toward the wall and inhaled. His body jerked when Annwyn's scent hit him.

Wren howled and paced in a circle in the middle of the room for a moment before grabbing a piece of Astole's clothing between his teeth. His growling muffled between tears and rips of the fabric.

Damius stared at his companion. *Exactly, boy. Rip it apart like I'm going to do to this male when I find him.*

Balder coughed, then spoke. "Um, should we stop him?"

Damius grinned. "I'm not. But if you wish to, I must warn you it will be at your own risk. He is one very angry wolf at this time."

"I see," he said, then turned back toward his mini.

Mirbeck rushed out of the side private sleeping area. "Major, you're not going to believe what I've found." He stopped in the center of the room and held out a small fabric-wrapped package. He unwrapped it, revealing Cress's com badge.

Balder jumped up. "What on Penduli is he doing with that?"

"He's got liquid borosite stored in his bathing chamber along with lunar fiber. The exact things he would need to erase all biological evidence from a weapon."

Damius planted his fists on his hips. "So, he kills Cress and frames Gront. Why?"

"Because he was hired to do so. He's been selling shuttle pass-thrus for the last three solar phases. Looks like he was setting up for life after the station until this star rise. It appears he's decided to quit his job early," Nicheo announced from his chair.

"And only Larunda knows who he's sold those pass-thrus to and why." Balder stomped over and covered the badge before taking it, then hit his communicator. "Send recover team A to Officer Astole's quarters."

Damius lifted a brow.

"They're the most discreet team I have here." Balder turned toward the door when a team of three security officers arrived. Handing over the wrapped badge, he spoke to them quietly.

They nodded in unison and spanned out in the quarters with boxes.

Balder faced Damius. "We'll be taking samples, and everything needed to evidence. I'll forward the reports to you for review as you'll need to determine if anything is connected to the bombing case, I assume?"

"Yes." Damius placed a hand on Balder's shoulder." Thank you. I appreciate it, and when this mess is all over, The Directorate will know how helpful you've been to us, as well."

Balder's face flushed a dark maroon. "I appreciate it."

"Give over what you've found to Balder's team. We're headed to Annwyn's quarters next." Damius turned to leave, then spun around to face Balder again. "I will advise you if we discover anything in her quarters that may be relevant to Astole."

Balder nodded.

Damius spun around and left. Nicheo and Mirbeck followed on his heels while Wren ran ahead, leaving a trail of Astole's ripped clothing behind him.

When they arrived at Annwyn's, he halted and raised a hand. "Let me speak with Gront first, and then we'll search. Clear?"

"Clear, Major," they responded in unison and stepped to the side of the door.

Damius punched the key panel, and the doors whooshed open.

Gront rushed over to greet him. "How may I assist you, Major Elkwood?"

Damius studied the deep lines recently made along Gront's face. Hunee dehydration. "You have no idea where she is, do you?"

Gront's head dropped, and he refused to meet Damius's gaze.

"We have footage of her leaving the station with Astole." He entered the main room. "We need to search her belongings to see if we can find any connections between them."

Gront stepped back and crossed his arms, still staring at the floor. "I have no say in the matter," he said.

"No, you don't," Damius responded.

"She has no connections to Astole. She hated him."

"I don't think she went willingly." Damius said then called over his shoulder to Mirbeck and Nicheo.

Gront's head jerked up when they stepped in. He stiffened and pointed at the men. "They will not be allowed to search my...Annwyn's belongings."

Damius held his hands in front of him. "Liquidate, Gront. Mirbeck will stay out here and look around and will search your sleeping area with you present. I will search Annwyn's alone. Nicheo is going to go through her reports and files."

Gront stepped forward and stopped when Mirbeck placed a hand on his arm. "Sorry, buddy. You've got no say in this matter. Remember your position, and don't make things worse."

Gront jerked his arm away and raised his voice. "My position? How dare you."

Mirbeck released his arm. "Gront, the more you help us, the more we can help you."

"My loyalty lies only with Annwyn," he shouted before rushing into his sleeping quarters.

Mirbeck shrugged at Damius, who frowned.

"Let him be, and let's get this done," Damius said.

The buzzing of Annwyn's portal caused Damius to spin around. He punched in the clearance code, and the doors slid open to reveal Emissary Leader Moiran. Damius bowed his head. Moiran motioned for him to exit into the hallway. Damius joined him, and when the doors slid close, Moiran spoke.

"I understand from Lt. Balder we have a situation on our hands involving Officer Astole."

"We do."

"There is a possibility that Astole allowed planetists to purchase and deliver bombs which explains the explosions. Is that correct?"

"That is the prevailing thought so far. We have shut down the bombing supplier and builders. I've submitted my report to The Directorate."

"I am aware of that. I am also here to advise you I added to Emissary Silk's duties an investigation of serious consequence concerning communication between your father and others regarding new contact. After what is going on now, I believe you should be aware that she spent many moons researching and clearing your father of any involvement."

Damius stiffened. His father? "I hadn't realized any investigation was being done involving my father."

"Of course not, as it also included you. However, my contacts and Emissary Silk's research have cleared your father and yourself of being involved."

"I suppose I should be thankful?" Damius snapped. He glanced at the closed portal. What if his team found the report? Naiba.

"I suggest you do. In addition, your team will not find the dime bar I gave her about your family. She completed her investigation and returned it to me."

"Major." Mirbeck's voice came over his com badge. "We got a message from Cudala. There's an uprising, and we need to get her off planet."

Moiran nodded and whispered, "Go on and get your team back together. Balder is more than qualified to handle things on station. He has arranged for one of the station's speed shuttles to take you to the Sanctuary directly."

Damius nodded, spun around, and returned to his team. "She said nothing about Annwyn?"

Mirbeck coughed. Nicheo grunted. Wren snorted and flopped on the floor.

"What is it?" Damius demanded.

Nicheo tipped his head at Mirbeck who growled.

"She stated Nicheo needs to look into communication between Astole and Annwyn's uncle who's been sending payments to Astole for at least sixty moons," Mirbeck said.

Damius searched Nicheo's face while his stomach clenched, and an itch climbed its way up his spine. "Well?"

Nicheo cleared his throat. "I've downloaded everything I can on this dime bar." He held the bar up one tick before sliding it in his pocket. "I can take my time and read it all while we're heading down to the planet. Balder sent word the shuttle is ready to go."

"Let's go, then," he said.

When they finally boarded the shuttle, Damius's head pounded. *She can't be involved. Does she know her uncle is?*

"When we get there, we're going to need to get both Cudala and Annwyn safely back to the station. That is not negotiable."

"Major," Nicheo said, facing his mini where he'd been reviewing the information on the dime bar. "This confirms payments received from Annwyn's uncle to Astole. It appears he was purchasing several pass-thrus, as well as bribery funds for planetist leaders on Penduli." He swore.

"Spit it out, Nicheo."

"I'm seeing Annwyn's signature trace here as well."

"Which means she also knows about the payments and relationship between Astole and her uncle."

"Yes, Major."

Mirbeck swore this time. "So, she was aware of Astole's actions and said nothing?" He leaned forward. "I hope whatever else is on that dime bar doesn't make this worse for her, or we may have to consider having to take her into custody after we rescue her."

Chapter
Twenty-seven

"**W**hat have I done?" Madame Raine's voice echoed through the meeting chamber. The bench Annwyn took refuge under pinned her to the floor.

"Madame Raine, please, you have to stop this madness," Parstia begged.

"I wanted to secure our future. I didn't want another planet contact to change our way of life again." Raine started to pace. "I helped the planets because I thought their objectives aligned with ours. I was wrong. My soul. I provided the mercury for the switches… I am responsible for the loss of souls. I have poisoned people with my deeds."

"We need to leave." Parstia grabbed her arm, but Raine pulled it away from her.

"No, no, I need to die." Raine pulled a dagger from her robes and raised it in the air above her chest. "Tell Tercora to rebuild the Sanctuary. She truly is the Madame now."

Annwyn screamed as Raine plunged the dagger toward her chest. The platform shifted, causing Raine to lose her balance and fall to the ground.

Parista scrambled toward Raine and threw the dagger out of her grasp. "You will not die by your own hands. That is the coward's way. You will face what you have done and atone for it. I will not let you escape the fate you have created."

Parista threw Raine over her shoulder.

"I'm taking her to the receiving area where Tercora headed. We'll be safe there!" Parista took off running as Annwyn pushed the bench off her legs and rose to follow her.

"Oh, no you don't." Astole scrambled out of the debris and grabbed her by the hair, pulling her back. Blood was running down his arm where shrapnel was embedded. "" I'm not done with you yet."

ꙮ ꙮ ꙮ

Silence except for the punch of keys filled the shuttle. *Had his own lust blinded him to her actions? Is she involved in all of this? She's from Haevis which thrives on cunning games.* Without words, he knew every time his team found another damning piece of evidence against Annwyn. His stomach clenched as if someone had punched him. *Heart or mind. Which should he follow?* Wren moaned at his feet.

How could she have played us both? Is your connection with me so strong, it made you blind to her true motives? Damius mentally asked Wren.

Wren sat up in front of him and rested his head on his knee.

The conflict of emotions both inside himself and his team made his insides feel like he fell out of an airbus that spun without warning. *Dear*

Larunda. Was everyone on this ship in crisis? He could feel anxiety radiate from the cockpit, making his stomach turn even more.

Damius laid his head back against the seat and closed his eyes. He needed to control his emotions. He started his breathing exercises.

Annwyn filled his thoughts. *Is she okay?*

He focused on her, replaying their time together in his mind. Surely, she didn't fake her reactions. He felt her body spasm around him in the throes of passion.

She is a Hunee.

Mirbeck's thoughts drifted over to him. Was Mirbeck right? The Hunee were known for their separation of logic and emotion. Everything was like a game to her. Was he another round to win?

Wren growled at him, and he opened his eyes.

I can't trust you. You are a love-sick puppy when it comes to Annwyn.

Wren harrumphed at him and laid back down.

The shuttle banked hard to the right.

"Buckle in," the captain said over the com. "We are in for a rough ride. We need to avoid the fires at the Sanctuary."

Nicheo and Mirbeck stowed their gear and buckled into their seats.

A look passed between them, and Mirbeck whispered, "You're the second. You tell him."

The shuttle shook and came to a sudden stop outside the tri-level receiving arena.

"Major Elkwood, I won't be able to get you any closer. You'll have to take a glider to the top of the Sanctum. I've been called back to transport more fire suppressers."

The copilot rushed back to open the shuttle doors. He put a hand on Damius's arm before he could exit, and a wave of worried tension grazed across his skin where the copilot touched.

"Please, keep an eye out for a guard at the Sanctuary named Parista. She is my sister," the copilot said.

Damius nodded and exited the shuttle. He walked toward the receiving arena entrance, Nicheo and Mirbeck following.

"Major Elkwood, Larunda Force, I need access to a glider to the inner sanctum," Damius said to the Circle guard.

"No one…"

"Stop. Your Sanctuary is on fire. Your leader is in trouble, and you will either allow me access to the hyperdrive with a glider controller or I will have you arrested, restrained, and then I will figure the thing out myself." Damius stood, hands behind his back, and flanked by Wren, Nicheo, and Mirbeck.

The guard's shoulders dropped. "The next glider will arrive momentarily. A controller is already on board."

"I understand additional fire suppressers are on the way. You will need to get them over to the housing areas to begin evacuating your sisters." Damius ran up the ramp, followed by his team.

The door to the glider slid open as they approached, and Wren was the first one inside.

The guard caught up with them as they settled into their seats. "I've had the controller set a direct route, but it will still go through the stations. The ride may be a little rough. Our systems are separate, but we do have some debris falling."

"Thank you," Damius said as she punched the side panels closing the doors. Within ticks, they were on their way.

Mirbeck punched Nicheo's arm and angled his head toward Damius.

"Will you just tell me," Damius growled.

"Major, we don't mean to overstep…" Nicheo started.

"But why the salahi did you have to sleep with the crazy treason lady? I mean really, Major, you wait what—years—to scratch that itch, and you pick her? The Hunee?" Mirbeck ranted.

"Shut up." Nicheo pushed Mirbeck back against the wall. "You are not helping."

"Well, it isn't my fault our leader and his pup are love-sick daalzhins."

"Enough!" Damius yelled, and Wren howled next to him.

"Sir, what Mirbeck is trying to say…"

"Oh, I think I get what Mirbeck is saying, no trying to it."

"Major, she talked to her father right after Cress was murdered."

Damius went silent. *Naiba, she did.*

"There isn't a call log because of both of their statuses, but we can't deny the implications that she is involved," Nicheo said.

"Yeah, the implication that you are a daalzhin," Mirbeck whispered.

Damius could no longer control the energy surging through his body. He lunged and pushed Mirbeck back against the clear glider wall, rocking it.

"I am still your leader, *Sergeant Mirbeck*, and you will treat me as such." Damius kept him pinned to the wall as he took a deep breath.

Wren growled at the pair.

"If she needs to be arrested, I will arrest her, but until we have solid evidence and not coincidences, I'm done talking about it." He released Mirbeck and took a step back, looking at both him and Nicheo. "Do I make myself clear?" *What have I done? I never should've trusted her.*

"Yes, sir," they said in unison.

"Good. Do we have any intel on the layout of the inner Sanctuary?"

"I'll see what I can find," Nicheo said as he pulled his tablet out from his bag.

"Mirbeck, see if you can get into the com system and contact Cudala or Tercora. I'd feel better if we knew for sure where they were."

Damius walked forward and looked through the glider windows. Fires burned all around, and debris from leaves and wood floated and bounced above the hyperdrive. A loud screech blasted the interior as a large sacred tree branch sailed by the hyperdrive, scraping a path toward the back, narrowly missing their section of the hyperdrive.

Suddenly, the glider stopped.

"Hyperdrive has deactivated. Hold on. We're going to drop!" Nicheo yelled.

Everyone scrambled to grab a side bar, seat, or anything they could wrap their arms around. Damius curled one arm around Wren and jerked him close to his chest as the glider dipped, then dropped, then shifted front end down first and fell. Within ticks, it crashed down with a loud bang. Damius shook his head to clear it when the safety measures clicked on.

"Attention passengers. The hyperdrive has disengaged and is currently being repaired. Please remain seated." A monotone voice rang through the glider.

Naiba.

A pop followed by a short boom caused the glider to shake as though it were ready to break open. Damius gritted his teeth and held on to Wren who began howling and tugging away from him. *Hold still, boy.* Wren growled low and then stopped. Then there was silence. Damius scanned Wren, but he appeared fine. He crouched and froze when he discovered smoke entering through a small space between the glider doors.

"Major." Nicheo rushed the doors and tried prying them apart. More smoke entered, and he coughed, dropping to the floor.

"Stay low, men. We got this," Damius said.

"I'm afraid I disagree, Major," Mirbeck retorted. "Look." He pointed toward the back.

Damius whipped around to see small flames licking their way up the back end of the glider.

He scanned the ceiling. Smoke billowed around and above the glider, filling the hyperdrive.

Wren whined from his position on the floor.

Another boom shook the glider with such force, Damius slammed against one of the leaf-decorated benches and hit his head. Blackness descended.

Chapter
Twenty-eight

"**S**tupid, stupid woman. If she'd listened to me, we could be in the next galaxy ready to live the life of comfort. But, no, she had to have second thoughts," Astole complained while dragging Annwyn beside him. He'd wrapped the entire length of her dark hair around his left arm while holding a blade in his right.

Her vision blurred when they turned the corner and met yet another wall of smoke. Both she and Astole coughed, and the floor rolled, throwing them against a wall. Her head hit the wall with enough force to blast spots across her vision.

Her lungs ached from inhaling smoke, and her leg screamed from the burn she'd received earlier. She continued working on the stiff fabric tied around her wrists, the chafing scratching at her skin. She tripped when Astole pushed away from the wall and tugged her along beside him when he turned another corner. She'd lost track of their location long ago and struggled to focus her vision.

"We're almost there. Keep up," he screamed at her over the now blazing ceiling.

"You'll never get away with this," she yelled. Her hoarse voice barely reached above the popping of wood splintering behind them. "The fire is out of control. You'll likely die here."

Astole jerked her closer and pricked her neck with the blade. "I'm not dying here, and neither are you. Keep those pretty lips of yours closed." He reached behind her and tapped the key pad next to a door. The door slid open with a screech, and he jerked her through the opening. When it closed, he paused, taking in big gulps of air.

Annwyn realized the room was clear of smoke and did the same, shaking her head to clear it as she filled her lungs with clean air. "I'm only slowing you down. You should leave me behind and get away as fast as you can," she suggested.

Astole laughed. "After everything I've done to get to this point? Raine promised to go with me. I'm going to have to hide for several phases to let everything cool down, and you think I'm going to do it alone?" He tugged her close and licked the side of her face. "I want someone to play with while I wait."

Annwyn's stomach churned while she tried to pull away from him. Blades, she'd had enough. Fury clawed its way through her. "If you think a few solar phases will give you your freedom, you're lying to yourself. Making a deal with my father insured you will never be able to hide. He won't go down alone, and more likely, he'll use you as bartering to free himself from punishment. You and I both know how far his reach goes. Do you think your plan will work?"

"You fool. You think the planetists are only on Chalar? They're on every planet of Larunda. Chalar was only one group, and the youngest...more foolish with their plans. I tried to help them. Get them pass-thrus. What did I care they wanted to stop new contact? I only wanted payment, and I got it. You're my bonus."

"And here I thought I was getting the bonus." Noden's deep voice boomed from behind Astole.

Astole whipped around, loosening his grip on Annwyn enough for her to shove away from him and roll across the floor. She crouched in the corner, preparing to fight. Her muscles tensed as she ripped the bindings from her wrists. She glared at Astole's back and prepared to pounce.

Astole fell to the floor facedown with a loud thud. Annwyn froze and stared at the prone body before her. Her gaze travelled up toward Noden's smiling face. He rubbed his hands together. She dropped and felt for a pulse. Nothing.

Standing, she planted her fists on her hips. "You've killed him."

"I have."

"I wanted to do it."

Noden shrugged. "We don't have the time, and the time was right." He moved toward her. "Raine has ordered the burning of the Sanctuary, starting with the Ceremonial Plateau. It's spreading fast, we need to get out of here." He turned, heading for another portal door, and spoke over his shoulder. "I have a shuttle close by. Let's go."

Annwyn grabbed his arm, and he stopped to face her. "Cudala is still here. I think she's down at the receiving arena. We need to get her."

"You're willing to risk your life for a Larunda Force officer?"

"She's also a friend. I can't…*won't* leave without her."

"What about the rest of her team?"

Annwyn gasped. "What do you mean?"

"They landed a short time ago. Apparently to rescue Cudala and you. Most of the Sanctuary will be in ashes soon, and I don't have time to play babysitter." He grabbed her arm and tugged.

She pulled away. "No. Stop that. Why do you males always believe in grabbing and pulling without talking first?" *Blades*. "We need to find Cudala and the team."

"I need to find Cudala and the team," he stated. "You need to let me get you out of here, so I can finish my job."

"I'm going with you."

"Is Damius aware of your stubbornness?"

Her heartbeat thudded, and she grinned. "He is."

"Fine," Noden said, then spun around, heading toward the portal.

Annwyn chased after him through the portal and down another smoke-filled hall. She ripped a piece of cloth from her top and wrapped it around her mouth. Together they ran and jumped fallen debris, turned corners only to retract and go down another corridor. Soon, Noden stopped and tapped the entry pad of a room. Nothing happened. He tugged out a gyrolever from his belt, popped it open, jammed it between the portal doors, then wrenched them open.

Annwyn ran in first, ducking low under the smoke floating at the ceiling. She scanned the room and found Cudala lying on the floor facedown. She rushed over to her and blew out a quick breath when she discovered Cudala lived. Patting down her body, she realized Cudala's arm lay at an odd angle. She gasped. Continuing to poke and prod, she found a large bruising circle forming over Cudala's left temple.

She lifted her gaze toward Noden. "She's unconscious and has broken her arm."

"I can see that." Noden ripped strips of fabric from a nearby bench and wrapped them around a braided wood piece which might have been part of the room's viroframed artwork.

She helped as he secured the wrapping around the broken bone and stood when he rose with Cudala in his arms.

"Let's get her out of here."

Together, they continued through the burning halls. How far had it spread? Images of Damius formed in her mind as she blindly followed Noden. What if he got caught in the Circle's blazing storm? What if he died trying to rescue her and Cudala? If he'd only had to worry about Cudala, he might not have gotten too close. But now the Circle burned, Cudala was injured, she was injured, and Damius was missing. She blinked away the moisture gathering in her eyes.

Noden passed through a small portal, and she jogged along behind him, then stopped when they reached a small, cleared ledge. She grinned as Cudala came to and began swearing before turning around and scanning the area.

Annwyn gasped. They were near a kilometer from the top of the Circle's Sanctuary. She peered up and clapped her hand to her mouth.

Multicolored flames shot out from the Ceremonial Plateau. Debris floated down from the burning plants and flora, their leaves curled from the heat, petals blackened from the fires. Her shoulders dropped, and she turned to walk near the edge. Tears dripped down her face when she caught sight of smoke spiraling out of every level of the Sanctuary. Alarms, screams, and the hissing of burning wood pelted her. She bit her fist to keep from screaming with them.

"Silk let's go," Noden ordered, revving up the shuttle.

Annwyn nodded, her gaze still searching below. A glider entered the hyperdrive and suddenly stopped several kilometers inside. A loud popping sound reached her, and she watched in horror as the glider fell from the center of the drive to the bottom. Smoke curled near the top.

"Noden," she called. "Look." She pointed below her.

Noden joined her. "The hyperdrive stopped in that section. The heat from these fires must have warped the solar panels feeding that section. If we don't get it back working, the other sections will stop." He pointed to the hyperdrive sections leading toward the receiving arena where other gliders were heading in the same direction. "Local fire suppressors fill those gliders. They need to get inside."

"If we can't get that section working, the remaining gliders will stop, and the fire will destroy everything," Annwyn said.

"Agreed," Noden said.

"We must do something."

"Tercora was to meet me at the receiving arena. She is our priority as the Circle's new leader and representative with The Directorate," Cudala stated. "Noden, your shuttle is now needed to get her to safety."

"I thought you'd say something like that." Noden frowned and stared at the scene below.

"I'm going down there. All the gliders but that one."—she pointed at the glider surrounded by smoke—" looks safe. I think I saw someone in there, and they'll die of smoke inhalation if we can't get them out. You go with Cudala and get Tercora. I'll get down to that glider and get whoever is in there out safely."

"You better hurry. I'll get over to the main switch which will set replacements for the panels damaged after I help Cudala. You'll have less than an hour to get them out before the hyperdrive kicks back in. Since the coms are down, there's no way for me to know if you succeeded or not. I'm turning the switch on to save the Sanctuary. Understand that." Noden ran back toward his shuttle and called out over his shoulder.

Annwyn scanned the side of the Circle's tower where several long, thick vines hung and wrapped their way around and down toward the exterior of the receiving arena. They appeared undamaged from the flames.

She turned and faced Noden while backing up to the edge. "Get Cudala and Tercora, then get to the switch. I'm going this way."

Noden jumped out of the shuttle and ran over to her. "You can't be serious. It's faster in the shuttle, and you need to save time. If I flip that switch and you or anyone is in that glider section, you'll get plastered to the walls. The space expansion alone will kill you."

"We don't have time for this, Noden," Cudala called out. "Get over here and pilot this shuttle, or I'm leaving you here."

"These vines are like those on Haevis. I used to play on them while growing up. I can do this."

An explosion above them boomed, and they simultaneously raised their heads. A large pillar of stone tipped over the ledge and fell directly above them.

Annwyn shoved Noden. "Go now!" She spun around and jumped, then grabbed the first vine she reached.

Chapter
Twenty-nine

Shunning her foot covering on the downward jump, Annwyn swung her lower body toward the side. As she slid down the vine, she somersaulted and landed deftly on another wider vine. The life force of the plant hummed into her feet and up her legs. She ducked and weaved to avoid other hanging vines, following the side of the large tree of the Circle. When the vine dipped, she slid down on it, keeping her footing as she ran and dove for another hanging vine.

The vine held her weight when she twisted and released her hands to land on a small limb below her. Grabbing vine after vine, she swung, dipped, and worked her way toward the ground, then landed with a thump on the moss-covered back patio of the receiving arena. She rushed around the corner and pushed open the maintenance door, slipping inside the hyperdrive chamber.

Without thought, she broke into a fast run toward the smoke-filled glider, bending low to see as the smoke rose. By the time she reached the glider, the entire chamber had filled with smoke. Multiple pairs of hands beating against the clear walls of the glider were barely visible. *Dear Larunda. There's more than one person in there.* She felt blindly with her hands along the smooth surface until she located the portal doors. With her fingers, she traced the seam for any type of trigger which would open them.

A low howl reached her ears and she froze. *Damius? Is that you in there with Wren?*

Mandis, we cannot escape, and the glider is filling fast. All electrodes have shut down.

Weapons?

No. We tried once, and it ricocheted. Nicheo's arm is bleeding, but it's a scratch. We're searching for any kind of gyrolever or something to use as one to break open the doors.

These gliders have escape hatches. Let me find it.

I don't think there's time. There's a fire near the front, and if it spreads in here...Mandis. I can't have you so close if it happens.

Blades, Damius. I know I haven't given you much reason to trust me. But I'm not going to run away and let you die.

Mandis.

Quiet. I need to concentrate.

Annwyn found a piece of the glider poking out closer to the front. She grabbed it and pulled herself atop the glider. Heat scalded her leg as she shimmied over the top and searched for the escape hatch comp pad. Her lungs burned from the smoke and her eyes watered. She blinked several times and pressed her face low to the surface. *There.* She scooted closer until the button pad sat right below her nose. Peering close, she ran her fingers along the edges. Something sharp and flat is what she needed to lift the panel. Flattening her palms on the heated surface, she searched around her, until her fingers touched a small piece of bent metal.

Grabbing it, she slipped it under the edge of the panel display door and wedged open the box. She winced at the fused wires. Again? She blew out a breath and stretched her fingers, ignoring the small cuts created by the sharp item. She had to do this and do it right, or she'd lose him. She swallowed past the lump in her throat and tugged out the clump of wires. One by one, she used the sliver of metal the strip them. When she cleared the melted thermoform coverings, she began reconnecting them.

The fire has entered the glider, Mandis. Please go as I cannot keep the barriers up during my last breaths, and I do not wish for you to carry that memory with you.

I will not leave you, Damius. I will not let your team perish in there. I will not allow anyone to die such a death. Trust me, please.

As you wish.

Wrapping the now exposed wires together, Annwyn blinked and paused a moment to turn her head to the side and cough. Her lungs ached from the scratching of unclean air filtering into her. She swiped her face with her top and refocused. She tucked the reconnected wires back into the panel compartment. Replacing the panel, she stared at it. Blades. She didn't have the override code.

Damius? Damius can you hear me?

A low howl came from below her, quickly followed by a whine.

Wren, if you can hear me, you must wake him. I need the override code, now.

A series of numbers flashed in her mind. She punched them into the panel. Her head jerked back when a pop and flash blinded her. Scrambling for the handle, she tugged with all her might. *Please let it open.* A whoosh loud enough to make her eardrums ring as a cloud of smoke burst out of the opening she'd created.

She leaned over and yelled into the smoke, "Escape hatch is open up here. Come on!"

She leaned back and waited. *Wren, do whatever you have to do to get these guys out. I've got an opening near the front at the ceiling.*

A loud growl followed by an even louder yelp sounded like a song from the willows at home.

She grinned when Damius's head poked up through the hatch, but he dropped back into the smoky interior.

Nicheo's face showed up next, and his arms followed. She helped pull him up. Once free, he spun around and reached down to grab another set of arms. Annwyn shot a glance toward the exit, which was practically invisible. She snagged the rope looped in Nicheo's belt and began tying it off in sections.

Mirbeck joined her coughing and hacking loudly. He searched her face, grinned, then checked the rope she'd worked on. Nodding, he circled his finger in the air, and she turned, allowing him to attach it to her vest. She turned back and did the same for him as Nicheo pulled out a whining wolf. She motioned for him, and he rushed to her licking her face.

Not now. Let me attach this to you.

Wren shook his massive head and nipped at her hands.

I'm not losing you in this smoke.

"He can see in the dark. He'll be fine." Damius's raspy voice spoke near her ear.

Annwyn bit her lip to keep from crying out in joy at hearing Damius's voice and she reached to squeeze his arm confirming she'd heard him.

Mirbeck attached the rope to Nicheo, and Damius grabbed the remaining length in front of her to place in her hands.

"Get me attached so we can get out of here," Damius ordered.

A long, grinding whine peeled through the air and echoed down the hyperdrive.

"We have to go now. Run!"

As though they were one, all five dropped to the ground and began running after the large grey wolf ahead of them.

Annwyn's lungs burned as she pushed on, keeping pace between Damius and Mirbeck. At one point, Nicheo tripped, but they all reached for him at once, jerked him upright, and kept running.

"Hug right the opening is coming up. We have to get through it and close it before the hyperdrive begins," she yelled as they continued running.

Another high-pitched whine reached them, and a small wind blew in her face and began to clear the air. The hyperdrive was powering up.

No. Not yet.

Within ticks, the air cleared, and the exit portal doors loomed beside them. After rushing through them with Wren ahead, they turned together and pulled the doors closed. As the seal clicked, debris flew past their vision and the next glider arrived. The doors opened, and the front man paused, staring at them.

Damius stepped forward. "The hyperdrive is fixed. The gliders can take you to all exterior points of entry. The smoke is billowing out of every crevice, but the main fires are near the top. It began at the Ceremonial Plateau." He gestured toward the large vines hanging all around the area. "The ones with orange plumes naturally carry liquid inside them. If you must do so, slice a few open, and it will help the suppression work."

"Yes, sir." The man stepped back, and the glider doors closed.

A scream pierced the air, and in unison, everyone turned toward the sound. Annwyn gasped. Damius swore and Wren howled. Two kilometers above them, a guard and Cudala wrestled with Madame Raine near a high ledge that protruded out of the side of the tree.

"What in naiba is going on?" Damius roared and ran toward the recently arrived glider.

Annwyn grabbed his arm. "No, you won't get there in time, and the suppressors need those gliders to put out the fire."

❦ ❦ ❦

Damius glared at her, when suddenly the image of her swinging along the vines popped in his head. He raised a brow, and she smiled in response. "To the vines. We'll climb our way up there." He stopped and glanced at Wren. *You stay here.*

Wren whined at his back when he started moving.

The team rushed over and leapt for the nearest low-hanging vine. One by one, they pulled themselves up until they reached a thick limb. Damius jumped onto the limb and climbed with the team right behind him. At the end, he reached out and jerked another vine toward him.

"Everyone grab on," he ordered. They did, and he pushed away from the limb. The vine carried them over to another thick vine that rose straight up. "Let's go."

As rapidly as he could, Damius rose along the streaked green vine twisted like a thick rope with ease. Damius grinned. They'd make it in no time this way. He scanned the sky above him and noted no feet hanging over the ledge where the women wrestled. Good sign.

He called over his shoulder, "Nicheo, you and Mirbeck get the guard. Cudala and I will handle Raine."

And me? Or have you not forgiven me yet?

"Change of plans," he hollered as they continued climbing. "Nicheo and Annwyn get the guard. Mirbeck, you watch our backs. There's those liquid-filled stems with the orange plumes hanging above the ledge. You can cut some if we need dousing."

"Got it," Mirbeck responded.

Thank you.

When this is over, Mandis...we'll talk.

They reached the plateau and climbed on. Raine screamed and ran away from them toward the other side of the ledge. Damius rushed after her, and as she jumped, he grabbed her arm. Her weight and the momentum of her path carried him with her toward the edge.

Annwyn flew over to grab his legs, calling for help. A howl burst from behind right before Wren's jaws clamped on his belt like a vise.

A boom echoed out, and the ledge tilted. Nicheo and Mirbeck rushed over and grabbed hold of his arms. Together, they pulled him back, along with Madame Raine. A burst of fire shot out from the opening behind them, followed by a short blast of falling rocks.

We must get out of here.

Damius held the now unconscious Madame Raine and lowered her to the ground, then pulled his blade from its sheath and began cutting the vines above the opening. Liquid poured forth like a waterfall and doused the fire.

He spun around and faced his team. "Go back down the way we came." He lifted Raine into his arms. "Wren will lead me out."

"You can't go back in there alone, Major," Cudala said.

"I won't be alone," he said with a quick glance at Annwyn. "Wren got up here unscathed. He will lead me back down just as safely. You have your orders. We meet back in the receiving arena."

His team faced him with black soot marks streaking their clothing and faces. Annwyn stood tall and nodded.

"Yes, Major." She ran toward the edge, then leaped and grasped the vine which carried them up.

"That one's acting like a team member now," Mirbeck muttered as each ran and followed Annwyn.

Damius took a deep breath and faced Wren. *Let's go, boy, we need to get out of here.*

Chapter Thirty

Damius followed Wren's paw prints. He ignored the flames and smoke dancing in front of them and focused only on Wren. Their connection buzzed, and they moved as one. Wren soared over a fallen tree limb and waited while Damius struggled over with Raine. They took off again at full speed, but then Wren howled.

Stop!

The platform was gone in front of them. What were they going to do now? He felt the vibrations before he heard the engines. A shuttle appeared in front of him, the door sliding open, and Tercora beckoned him forward.

"Hurry! More of the limbs are falling."

Wren ran and jumped the distance to the shuttle. Damius slung Raine over his shoulder and took off running.

"For Larunda," Damius yelled as he soared over the distance to the shuttle.

He landed with a thud. Tercora slammed the door to the shuttle closed.

"Get us out of here, Noden," she yelled.

Damius lowered Raine to the floor, and Tercora pulled her into her arms, cradling Raine.

"I...I—" Raine coughed.

"You're safe now," Tercora said.

"Madame Tercora, I ask for the Circle's forgiveness," Raine whispered, her eyes half opened.

"Madame Raine..."

"No!" With an energy Damius did not think she had, Raine raised herself up in Tercora's arms. "You are the leader. You must rebuild what I have destroyed. In her name..." Raine's body went limp.

"In her name," Tercora whispered. "I am the First. I am the Madame of Sanctuary. In her name…"

Damius lost his footing and fell onto the floor as Noden banked the shuttle sharply to the left.

"Oh yeah." Noden always was an adrenaline junky.

"I'm sorry," Damius said to Tercora.

"Don't be. She is at peace now. I will never understand why she did what she did, but I am not sorry her pain is over."

"You will rebuild."

"Of course. Sanctuary was before, Sanctuary is after, Sanctuary is forever. Nothing will prevent that, not new contact, not Larunda Legacy, nothing. Raine's past and her present misled her."

"Landing in thirty ticks. You might want to brace for impact. Not sure how much this old girl has left in her."

"At least we are already on the floor," Tercora said. "Where is Cudala? She pushed me back on the shuttle and took off after Raine."

"My team should be at the receiving center waiting for us, Cudala included."

"Good. I have not known her long, but she has a part of my heart with her."

"I understand," Damius said right before the shuttle impacted with the ground.

Seeing Annwyn move along the vines, working as one with his team… He knew without words that she was not involved with any of her father's dealings.

"Good to see you again, Bo," Noden said as he offered Damius a hand up.

"You going to learn to fly one day?"

"Where is your sense of adventure?"

⚌ ⚌ ⚌

Annwyn was doubled over with her hands on her knees, trying to breathe. Mirbeck limped over to her and shoved a liquid tube in her face.

"Drink," Mirbeck grumbled.

She took the tube from him and drank, then handed it back.

"Finish it. Your legs are short. You have to take two steps for every one of ours."

Annwyn stared at him, not knowing what to say.

"Kidding is Mirbeck's way of saying he accepts you," Cudala said as she sat on a bench in the reception area. "I punched him before I realized it."

Annwyn tipped the tube back and drained it.

"Thanks for getting us out of the glider." Nicheo sat down next to Cudala and pointed to the burns on Annwyn's legs. "Are those from crawling on top to open the hatch for us?"

Annwyn nodded.

"We'll get a medical on you as soon as we get back to the station. The fire team seems to have things under control now, and the sisters are safe."

"Has anyone seen Noden? Tercora was with him," Cudala said.

"Has the party started?" Noden's voice boomed through the reception area as he ushered in Tercora.

Cudala moved toward her lover. They held hands, their foreheads touching.

"It's good to see her, so..." Mirbeck started.

"At peace," Annwyn finished.

"Yeah. I hassle her a lot for it, but she is the best of us."

Mirbeck and Nicheo rose and nodded toward Damius as he approached. "Major."

Damius put a hand on each of their shoulders before he moved to sit next to Annwyn. *We make a good team.*

She would never get used to Damius's voice in her mind, but it was comforting in a way she didn't expect.

We do. All of us. Annwyn looked around at the team.

True.

"Coms are back up, sir. Balder has asked if we want a shuttle back to the station," Nicheo announced.

"Yes. Do we know where Astole is?"

"Astole is where I left his dead body," Noden answered. "If you are through with me, I've got a reputation to uphold."

"Do you need transportation?"

"Bo, I got it covered. My man should be outside in a few." He bowed to Damius and then to Annwyn. "You're spunky. He needs that."

"I'll be sending you paperwork."

"Good luck with that, Bo. I was never here." Noden winked. "Balder will know how to reach me if you need me." He chuckled before walking away.

"He is very unique," Annwyn said.

"That is possibly the nicest thing anyone has ever said about him."

❦ ❦ ❦

Annwyn winced as the medical applied the burn salve to her legs. All she wanted was to be alone with Damius, but the entire team was scattered throughout the med unit.

The medical pulled a piece of equipment over to her stretcher. She placed the injured leg inside a biotope.

"Please, remain still while the regenerator heals your leg. It will make the process faster." The medical pressed a few buttons, and there was a whirl and swirl of lights inside the tube. "Dr. Buehl will check on you when it is done."

Damius was talking to a medical behind Mirbeck. Cudala's arm was in a bone repair unit, and Nicheo's shoulder burn was being cleaned for regeneration.

"Sergeant Mirbeck, there is no need to use archaic methods on your leg wound. We can simply clean it and regenerate it," Dr. Buehl said.

"No regeneration. Clean it and sew me up."

"He thinks the ladies will think he is tough if he has scars," Cudala shouted from her bed.

"I refuse to provide you subpar treatment," Dr. Buehl argued.

"Then give me the needle, and I'll sew it up myself."

"Sergeant, let the doctor do her job," Damius said as he approached Mirbeck's bed.

"I want the..."

Damius used an injection unit on Mirbeck's neck before he could finish.

"I think you'll find him more cooperative now, Doc," Damius said as he handed the injection device to Dr. Buehl.

"As much as I would like to, I can't do a non-life threatening medical procedure on him without permission."

"I give you permission. Dr. Buehl, he is on my team, a member of Larunda Force. Therefore, he is my charge if he cannot answer for himself, such as he is now."

Annwyn stifled a giggle.

"Very well. Thank you for your assistance, Major."

Damius walked over and took Annwyn's hand. "There is a team headed to your uncle's house to take him into custody. The unlocked communication records revealed all your father did was ask Astole to keep an eye on you and Gront. Your uncle's communications were more in-depth."

"He is taking the fall for my father."

"The evidence says he is guilty."

"Of course it does." She sighed. "Astole told me there were other planetist groups out there."

"Yes, our team is assigned point."

Annwyn tried to ignore the sinking feeling in her stomach.

"Dr. Nonyx has decided to return to teaching full-time. Given the nature of our investigation, we will need an alchemist, if you are interested?"

"Yes," Annwyn replied without hesitation.

It's the quickest way I can get you on the team. You'll be a consultant to Larunda Force and under my supervision.

I like the idea of being under you.

Damius coughed suddenly.

"Major Elkwood, are you okay?" Dr. Buehl asked." Let's get a full set of rays on your lungs."

"No, no, I'm fine."

"I insist. That is a horrible cough, can't be too careful."

🦌 🦌 🦌

The team spent the night together in the medical unit. Damius still blamed Annwyn for the torture he went through with the lung treatments. At star rise, they all went their separate ways. There were reports to fill out, and bags to pack, but they had a few days of atmospheric quietude coming their way. Annwyn left to advise Gront of their next assignment.

Damius still wasn't sure of how Gront was going to fit into the mix, but Annwyn had been insistent that he stay with her, and given her father's behavior, Damius couldn't disagree.

His quarter's portal door buzzed, and he hit the side panel button to open it. The light from the hallway highlighted Annwyn's hair, making her look like one of Larunda's stars.

"You are beautiful."

"Are you going to invite me inside?"

Damius's face heated, and he stepped aside. The door closed behind Annwyn.

"I have lunch," he offered.

"It can wait." Annwyn stretched up on her toes, wrapping her hands around the back of his neck. "I've waited too long for you."

He kissed Annwyn deeply and lifted her up in his arms. "We made it."

"You trusted me."

"And you followed my orders."

"Don't let it go to your head."

Damius kissed her again as he carried her to the bedroom. "You need to know something before we...again."

Damius held Annwyn in his arms and looked into her grey eyes. "I know on your world that making love is a game in some sense. It is not for me. It never has been and never will be. And with you, it is more than I have ever experienced. You set my senses on fire. Your emotions wash over and through me. When we join, there is no you and me. There is only us."

"This isn't a game for me."

"I can't promise I can control what happens, Mandis."

"Then don't. Maybe I want to just feel for once."

Mandis. He tore her clothing, leaving shreds on the floor. Too much talk and time had elapsed for him to be gentle. She made quick work of his as well. His hand wrapped in her curly black hair, tugging her head back so that he could kiss her once again, then bite her neck at the juncture of her shoulder where his mark from before was fading.

He laid her down on the bed, then started at her feet, kissing the arch, then slid his tongue up around her ankle. His hands traveled up her legs and between then, her green skin covered in goose bumps. The scent of her arousal filled him as he licked up her body. His fingers explored her depths, preparing her for later. He felt her clench down on his fingers as he moved his mouth up her breasts. When he reached her mouth, he kissed her then flipped her on top of him.

As they joined, he felt the barriers break away, and he understood her fears, her ambitions, her pain. In the one part of his mind that was not joined with hers, his most private place, he made a note to have a discussion with her father about the pain he'd caused her.

Soon, that thought fell away as shivers traveled up her body then down his. Like a gentle breeze, the mere touch of her fingernail on his arm made him forget everything. Her nails dug into his arms as their bodies rocked against each other. His reached his hand between them, touching her.

"Mandis," they cried in unison as they reached completion together.

֍ ֍ ֍

Annwyn and Gront stood next to their bags as they waited for the rest of the team to arrive. Her body was still buzzing from her morning lovemaking with Damius.

Almost there.

She heard Damius's thought a few ticks before Wren bounded into the loading bay. He put his paws on her shoulders and licked her.

"Good boy, Wren." She smiled as she tugged his ears.

He butted his nose on hers and she giggled.

"Why do you let him do that, Princess?" Gront groaned beside her.

"Because I like it."

Damius and the rest of his team came rushing into the loading bay with a plethora of equipment.

"Sorry, our orders got delayed," Damius said as he handed a dime bar to the pilot.

"What's our first stop?" Annwyn asked.

"We report for the Larunda Base for debriefing with Lead Emissary Moiran, and then we head to Haevis. The Directorate scheduled a gathering there in twenty moons, and we're arriving early to help prep the Isha Station security team."

"Haevis," Annwyn whispered. She'd promised herself she would never return home.

"Yeah, looks like we are going to get to meet your old man," Mirbeck teased.

"That's King Silk, you bakayarou," Cudala said as she slapped Mirbeck.

"At least you'll get that first awkward meeting of her father out of the way," Nicheo teased.

"And we'll all be there to stand up for you," Mirbeck added, looking right at Annwyn. "Larunda Force is a family, after all."

Mirbeck, for all his bravado, was more aware than people gave him credit for. Annwyn nodded to him.

"Family," she said.

She belonged. For the first time in her life, she had a group of people who liked her for who she was, not who her father was. She looked at Damius.

Family.

Mandis, together we can face anything, including your father.

Damius took her hand as they walked on the ship.

ACKNOWLEDGEMENTS

Have you ever had a moment when you know that magical events are happening around you? In the fall of 2015, we became writing camp partners. We got together once or twice a week to encourage each other to write. By the next year, one of us suggested we write together. Something clicked in that crazy moment, and Penduli Station was the spark that was given life by our family, friends and village.

Lindsey Loucks had the daunting task of taking our manuscript and trying to tell us, oh so politely, that we had issues. Thank you, Lindsey, for your patience and diligence. Penduli Station is better because of you, but all mistakes remain forever ours.

Thanks to Jana Oliver for the fastest turn-around ever, Jana – you are both a marvel and an inspiration.

Clarissa of http://yocladesigns.com/ is a cover artist that captures your attention and translates your words into images. She is the spark behind the visual images of our brand.

Jerrie Fillion is not just Sherrie's twin sister; she is also the woman who slaved away at formatting this book. Thanks for removing Tyra's double spaces, so we didn't have to.

This book is a testament to the power of networking and the support of romance writers. We met because of Georgia Romance Writers (GRW) and became writing camp partners because of GRW's annual conference, Moonlight and Magnolias (M&M). Now, not only are we co-authors, we are co-chairs of the conference for 2018 and 2019. The women and men who attend GRW and M&M inspire us and help to feed our writers' souls. Without these amazing groups, we would not have met and Damius and

Annwyn would not be fighting over who Wren likes best.

In honor of Kathryn Ann Fernquist Hinds - We say her name.

Special acknowledgements from Sherrie:

The Village - I am forever grateful for your constant support and encouragement.
Leonard Nimoy - Your character and then you became my idols and began my love of Science Fiction and Nature. Whenever I hear Sci-Fi, your face comes to mind.

Dad - Thank you for being the delegated handyman/dog sitter around the house so I could focus on this book.

Heather & Orlando - Thank you for loving each other the way you do, and I am so very proud of you both.

Branden & Steph - Thank you for loving each other in your own special ways and make me proud to call you mine.

Bennett - Thank you so much for keeping me company so I didn't have to write alone. I couldn't have asked for a better dog, even though I had to become your Emotional Support Human. You'll always be close to my heart.

Ellie - Thank you for keeping Bennett on his paws and keeping my spot on the bed warm.

To Tyra - It's hard to believe we've known each other for such a short time. Thank you for teaching me how to co-author so well, with your patience, constant kindness and permission to wear my pajamas to your house. I'm so very glad we met and became such good friends.

Special acknowledgements from Tyra:

I am one of the lucky ones. My husband is a never-ending source of encouragement and love. He gives me space to write, to be my own person and pursue my own dreams so much so that my dreams have become our dreams and his dreams have become mine. Thank you for all you do, my love, especially the laundry.

To my family, thanks for supporting me in my journey wherever it leads. Sherrie has Jerrie and I have Miriam and Genia. Two better sisters would be hard to find.

To my socially engaging fur babies - Clover, Bandit and Shadow - for being my constant companions in their search for body heat, pets, and love.

Jennifer, Brian, Shaun, Liam, Wil, Rachel, and many more - thanks for your friendship and love. To my students, thanks for always pushing me to continue to grow, learn and do.

To Sherrie - who knew what we were starting when we decided to meet for writers' camp in 2015? Thanks for putting up with my 'comments' in the manuscript, my devil's advocate with the characters, and with my constant need for coffee. You helped me find my writing rhythm.

You make me a better writer and a better person. Thank you for helping make this dream come true.

To Jana – you remain my touchstone of sanity even while enjoying the expat life in Portugal. Thanks for still being here even when you are there.

Lastly, to my mom and dad—without your influence in my life, I would never be who or where I am. You continue to be my heroes, and I miss you both every single day.

Join us on our path through Larunda Legacy.
www.facebook.com/Larunda-Legacy
www.larundalegacy.com